Devoted

Caylin's Story

Book Two

By

S.J. West

List of Watcher Books in the Watcher Series

The Watchers Trilogy

Cursed

Blessed

Forgiven

The Watcher Chronicles

Broken

Kindred

Oblivion

Ascension

Caylin's Story

Timeless

Devoted

The Redemption Series

Malcolm

Anna

Lucifer

Redemption

Other Books by S.J. West

The Harvest of Light Trilogy

Harvester

Hope

Dawn

The Vankara Saga

Vankara

Dragon Alliance

War of Atonement (2015)

Devoted

CHAPTER ONE

Heaven. Not exactly somewhere I thought I would be going at my age. And, to be totally honest, the reality of it isn't what I expected either. I feel…like I don't belong in this place. A little voice inside my soul is telling me I should leave, that it's not my time to be here yet. I do my best to ignore it and just hope we find the help my mother seems to think is here for us as quickly as possible.

I stand beside my mom on a sidewalk in what looks like any ordinary little neighborhood in America. Yet, the cars parked on the streets and the colorful clapboard houses with white picket fences surrounding them look like something you would see in a movie set in the 1950's. I hear bluesy jazz music of that era come from one of the houses down the street and see a young black woman dressed in a white sundress with a black and red rose pattern waving at us and smiling for all she's worth.

"Who's that woman?" I ask my mom.

When I don't get an answer right away, I look over at my mother to see she has tears streaming down her cheeks.

“Are you ok?” I ask, worried by her reaction.

My mom wipes at the wet trails with her free hand and nods.

“Yes,” she says, tightening her hold on my hand. “Come on. I want you to meet Utha Mae.”

“That’s her?” I ask, having grown up hearing stories about Mae’s namesake, and someone I knew my own mom thought of more as her mother than my Grandma Cora.

“Yes,” my mom says. “That’s her.”

We walk down the quiet street hand in hand towards Utha Mae.

She isn’t exactly the way I imagined her either. All of the pictures my mom has of my Aunt Tara’s grandmother were taken when she was old. The woman we’re walking towards now looks like she’s in her late twenties. But, I can tell it’s Utha Mae because of the way her eyes sparkle with happiness as she watches us approach. They hold the same love and understanding I saw in her pictures.

“Hey, baby,” Utha Mae says to my mother when we’re only a couple of yards away. Her gaze shifts to me, and I see her smile become even brighter. “Well now, I haven’t seen *you* since you were up here waiting to go to your mama.”

My mom lets go of my hand and walks up to Utha Mae, hugging the other woman tightly around the waist and resting her head against her shoulder, like it's something she's done a hundred times before.

“I didn’t think I would see you again until it was my time to be here,” my mother says with a small sniffle from crying.

“Me neither, baby. Me neither. But, God works in His mysterious ways I guess ‘cause he told me I needed to help you out a little bit.”

My mom pulls away slightly to look at Utha Mae.

“In the dream,” my mom says, “you said you had something for Caylin that would help her.”

Utha Mae nods. “Yes, baby. I didn’t know what they were when I first found them a little while back, but God came to me and explained she would need them one day. I guess that day’s come.” Utha Mae looks over my mom’s shoulder at me and smiles. “But, right now I would really like to hug your little girl again before we get into all that.”

My mom turns to me and holds her hand out for me to take.

I walk up and take her hand as I meet the woman who raised my mother to be the person she is today.

"Caylin," my mom says, "I want you to meet Utha Mae."

"Oh," Utha Mae says wrapping her arms around my shoulders, "we've met. She probably just doesn't remember."

As soon as Utha Mae hugs me, I feel a familiar peace settle over my heart.

"I think I kind of do actually," I tell her, not having visual memories, per se, but emotional ones.

Utha Mae leans back away from me and smiles.

"Love has no barriers," she tells me, her eyes filled with that emotion as she looks at me. "I think you probably remember that I loved you even before you were born."

"So, I was here with you before I was sent to Earth?" I ask, a little confused by the concept.

Utha Mae nods as she looks at me in wonder. "You were one of the brightest souls I've ever seen, child. And look at you now," Utha Mae says standing back from me slightly to look me up and down, “all grown up into a beautiful young woman. Maybe God’ll let me meet your children before they’re sent to you.”

“I probably won’t have any kids for a while,” I tell her, “at least not until after college.”

“Well, I know they’ll be gorgeous, especially with that handsome angel you’re in love with.”

“You’ve seen Aiden?”

“I get to see a few things up here,” Utha Mae says with a wink. “And yes, I’ve seen your man, and I know he loves you very much which is all I’ve ever wanted for any of my babies, true love.”

“Utha Mae,” my mom says regaining her attention, “how can you help us with the princes?”

“Well, you two come on in, and I’ll show you. Maybe you’ll know what to do with what I found because it just looked like junk to me.”

Utha Mae walks up the two remaining steps to the front porch and opens the screen door. My mom and I follow her into a quaint living room decorated simply with basic furnishings. The music I heard when we first arrived is emanating from an old-fashioned turntable record player in the room sitting on a cabinet against the far wall. Utha Mae walks over to the cabinet and kneels down to open the double doors at the front. She pulls out a cherry wood lacquered box about the size of a shoebox. Inlaid in the wood are strange symbols written in silver. Oddly enough, I know what the symbols say.

Utha Mae stands and walks over to my mother handing her the box.

"I found them one morning lying on my front lawn. They shined so bright it was like they were diamonds," she tells my mom. "I didn't know what they were for, so I put them in this box I had. Then when I closed the lid the symbols appeared, and I couldn't open the box anymore. God said you would know what to do with them, baby."

My mother takes the box from Utha Mae and studies the symbols. She looks over to me and hands me the box.

"Can you read what it says?" She asks me, almost like it's a test of some sort.

I take the box from my mom because I *can* read the message.

"Yes," I tell her, staring at the box in my hands. "It says 'Caylin'. But, I don't understand how I'm able to read it. What kind of writing is this?"

"It's angelic writing," my mom tells me. "And you can read it because it's something you inherited from your grandfather. Why don't you see if it will let you open it?"

I'm a little hesitant to open the box and wonder if this is how Pandora felt when she was given her own magical box to peer into. I take in a deep breath and swing the lid open back on its hinges to discover what help lies within its depths.

Lying inside the box is a multitude of small, oddly shaped pieces of silver.

"They were just sitting out on the lawn one morning," Utha Mae tells us. "And nothing up here just appears for no good reason. So, I gathered them all up because I knew He would want me to do something with them one day. I hope you know what they're for and how they can help you because He didn't tell me."

I look over at my mom. "Do you know what they are?"

"I think so," my mom says, staring at the pieces of silver. "Did you hear me ask Jess about the crowns earlier?"

I nod. "Yes. But, I didn't know what you were talking about."

"When she and the other vessels closed the Tear, they used their archangel crowns to put the princes into a type of stasis. The crowns siphoned some of the princes' powers which helped provide enough energy to close the Tear. The crowns flew into the Tear and no one knew where they went, until now."

"So, you think this is what's left of the crowns?" I ask. "Do you think we can use them to put the princes into stasis again?"

"I have to assume so," my mom says. "I don't see any other reason for God to give them to us. We'll just have to figure out how to use them."

"There's something else that God told me when He came to visit," Utha Mae tells us with a troubled frown. "He said when the princes were exiled from Heaven, they stole something that was very important."

"Did he say what it was they stole?" I ask.

Utha Mae shakes her head. "No, child. He didn't tell me that much. But, He did bring me a gift that day."

"What kind of gift?" My mom asks.

Utha Mae smiles and turns slightly towards the back of the house. “Why don’t the two of you come with me, and I’ll show you.”

We walk to the far side of the house and through the kitchen to a partially screened in porch.

Out in the backyard, I see a handsome young black man swinging a brown haired, brown-eyed girl, no older than seven, with porcelain white skin on a tire swing. Her laugh is like the sound of pure joy and her smile easily brings my own smile to my face. I instantly feel a well of emotions come to the surface as I watch her and have to wipe at the unexpected tears spilling from my eyes. I hear my mother sniff beside me and know the girl is having the same effect on her as well.

“Who is she?” My mother asks Utha Mae.

“She says her name will be Anna,” Utha Mae tells us, smiling proudly as she watches the little girl play. “And apparently she’s going to stop the princes from whatever shenanigans they have up their sleeves.”

“Does she know what they plan or what they stole?” I ask.

Utha Mae shakes her head. “No, child, she doesn’t. But, she seems awfully ready to stop them. She’s the spunkiest little thing I’ve ever seen.”

“Why is she here with you?” I ask.

Utha Mae smiles. “I think it’s God’s gift to me. He lets me spend a little time with your babies before they have to go to Earth.”

“But,” my mom says, “from what He told us, she won’t be born for a long time.”

“Time here doesn’t move the same as it does on Earth, baby,” Utha Mae tells my mom. “She could leave at any moment but still go who knows how many years in your future. I got the feeling when He left her that He wanted the two of you to see her.”

I look back at the little girl and feel my heart swell with love and pride, even though I don’t know her at all. Perhaps God wanted us to see her so we knew who we were fighting for. We would need to set the stage for the work she would be born to do. And now, after seeing her, I feel even more determined to find a way to stop the princes in my own timeline so that her job is made easier when the time comes.

The little girl seems to notice us and asks the man to stop pushing her. She scrambles off the swing and runs up to the steps leading to the porch.

"Hi," she says to us, smiling for all she's worth, "I'm Anna."

As I look at her, I can already see the beginnings of the beautiful woman I saw in the vision of the future.

"Hello, Anna," my mom says. "It's nice to meet you."

"Don't worry about anything," Anna tells us with a small shake of her head. "You'll figure out how to stop the princes. I know you will. And when I'm born, I'll get back what they stole from God. I promise."

"I'm sure you will," my mother says smiling at the little girl's rambunctiousness.

"And, Lilly," the girl says in all seriousness displaying a maturity beyond her young years, "don't be sad about Malcolm. I'll take good care of him. I promise you that with all my heart."

My mother simply nods, too choked up on emotion to say anything in reply.

"Caylin," Anna says as she turns her gaze to me. "God told me to tell you something."

"Tell me what?" I ask.

"Blood binds."

I feel my forehead crinkle in confusion.

"What's that supposed to mean exactly?"

Anna shrugs. "Sorry, I have no idea. He just said it was something you would need to remember."

Anna smiles at us before turning back towards the man and waves before saying, "Bye!"

She runs back to the man who is beaming with pride and love as he lifts her up and places her on the swing again.

"My husband is flat out in love with that child," Utha Mae tells us with a small laugh. "He's going to hate it when she has to leave. But, like all you girls, she was made to do a job and seems ready to go do it, bless her heart."

I grip the box I hold tightly.

"We should get back," I tell my mom. "The sooner we figure out what needs to be done the better. I don't want to let Anna down."

My mother turns to Utha Mae and gives her another hug.

"You know, I've met your little ones already," Utha Mae says to my mom.

My mother pulls back and looks at Utha Mae in confusion at first then seems to realize the implications of what she said and starts to laugh.

"Well, I guess Brand will be happy," my mom says, but I can tell she's happy too. "But, did you say little *ones*?"

"I most certainly did," Utha Mae says.

My mother giggles. "So now I have to come up with two names. I'm running out of ones that mean something to me."

Utha Mae winks. "You'll figure it out. I have faith in you, always have."

Utha Mae walks over to me and gives me a kiss on the cheek and a hug.

"And you take care of yourself, child. Don't let them little devils scare you any either. You've got God on your side, always remember that."

I nod. "Yes, ma'am. I won't let them win."

I look over to my mom.

"Ready to go back?" she asks.

I look down at the box. "Yes. I have a feeling we have a lot of work to do."

As I phase back to my room, I have to wonder what it is God wants us to do with the remnants of the archangel crowns. How are we supposed to use them? And what exactly did the princes steal from Heaven that God wants to get back so desperately?

CHAPTER TWO

When we phase back to my room, my mother turns to me.

"I'm going to go wake your father," she tells me. "I think we need to tell the others what we learned and brought back. Maybe one of us can figure out what we're supposed to do with the crown pieces."

"Ok, I'll go wake Aiden."

My mother phases and I follow her lead and phase to the living room where Aiden is sleeping.

My parents offered him a bedroom upstairs, but, for whatever reason, he said he wanted to sleep on the couch down here.

I stand there in the semi-dark beside the couch looking down at him. The only light coming into the room is from the moonbeams shining through the wall of windows where the river rock fireplace is. Aiden is sleeping on his stomach hugging the pillow I gave him from my bed underneath his head with both arms. His hair is tousled and partially covering the side of his face that is exposed. He isn't wearing a shirt leaving his torso bare, but he is wearing a pair of loose fitting gray pajama bottoms that hug his hips. I stand there for a few seconds just watching the gentle rise and fall of his back from his breathing and realize one simple fact.

He's beautiful.

"I know you're there," Aiden says, a slow grin lifting the corners of his mouth. He opens his eyes and in one smooth motion, turns to lie on his back, raising one arm over his head and resting the other across his abdomen as he looks up at me.

I feel the walls of my heart tighten as our eyes meet and instantly find my gaze drawn to his lips. The memory of our first kiss is fresh and the feel of his lips against mine lingering.

"Are you ok?" Aiden asks, becoming worried over my continued silence. I see his eyes drop to the box in my hands, and he instantly sits up. "Where did that come from?"

"Heaven," I tell him, sitting down on the edge of the couch beside him. "My mom and I just came back from there."

I tell Aiden about meeting Utha Mae and how she came to be in possession of the crown pieces. But, I don't tell him about meeting Anna. For some reason, I feel like her identity should remain secret, like I shouldn't talk about her to anyone. I'm not sure why I feel this way, but I know it's the right thing to do.

“What was it like up there for you?” Aiden asks.

“I felt like I didn’t belong,” I admit with a small shake of my head. “It was almost like something there was telling me to leave.”

Aiden absently places his hand on my right thigh in what he must think is a gesture meant to bring me comfort, but it’s just the opposite. The warmth emanating from his hand seeps through the thin material of my pajama bottoms, causing unfamiliar yearnings to stir inside me.

“You don’t belong there yet,” he tells me, squeezing my thigh with the tips of his fingers in a reassuring up and down motion. “I plan to make sure you have a long, long life here on Earth filled with as much happiness as one person can have in one lifetime.”

I can’t help but smile because I know he will succeed in his quest. How can he not when a large part of my happiness stems from my loving him?

“Well,” I say, leaning in closer to him until our faces are inches apart. I notice his lips separate of their own accord as his breathing becomes noticeably more labored. “You’re doing a better than average job so far, Aiden.”

He doesn't pull away as I lean in even closer and tentatively touch his lips with mine. As I press my lips more firmly against his, I realize that our relationship is slowly evolving into one where a kiss is expected instead of denied. My heart smiles at the thought, and I deepen the kiss tasting the sweetness of his mouth like sugar against my tongue.

Aiden moans softly as we kiss before pulling away. The action seems reluctant because he immediately leans in again and kisses my swollen lips lightly.

"You're becoming really good at that," he murmurs with a small smile as he seems to force himself to pull away and look at me.

"Really? Because I think I need more practice," I tell him, matching his smile and hoping he takes the hint.

Aiden chuckles and his expression becomes a little shy. If the light was on in the room, I have a feeling I would catch him blushing.

"Practice does make perfect," he agrees while nodding his head. "And I will forever be at your disposal for more lessons."

The living room light suddenly comes on like an unwanted intruder, breaking the intimate moment. I hear my father clear his throat loudly and walk into the kitchen noisily starting to prepare a fresh pot of coffee.

I stand up and Aiden swings his legs off the couch to stand beside me. He leans over, grabs a gray V-neck t-shirt from the back of the couch, and slips it on over his head. I have to admit I'm a bit disappointed in the action, but know there isn't anything I can do about it, especially with my dad banging around in the kitchen giving every indication that he wants me to know he's close by.

Still holding my box with both hands, Aiden and I walk to the kitchen area together.

My dad is already dressed for the day in a pair of jeans and a white Henley. He's just pouring the water in the coffee maker's reservoir when we walk in.

The clock on the microwave display above the stove indicates it's 3:30 in the morning.

"Your mom went to get Jess and Mason," my dad tells me as Aiden and I sit next to one another on a pair of stools at the kitchen island's bar.

I sit my box on the counter in front of me.

"So can you read what the symbols say?" Aiden asks me, looking at the intricate designs inlaid in silver around the sides of the box.

I nod. "Yes, my mom said I could read it because it's a trait passed down from my grandfather. Why? Can't you read it? It's supposed to be angelic writing."

"It's archangel script," he tells me. "We regular angels aren't allowed to read it. What does it say?"

"It just says Caylin."

"Just," Aiden says with a small smile, like I've made the understatement of the century.

My mom phases in with Jess at her side.

"Where's Mason?" I ask them.

"He went to get Malcolm," Jess tells me, walking the few steps to me to give me a hug. "You doing ok, kiddo?"

I nod. "Yes, I'm fine."

Jess leans away from me and sighs heavily. "I wish…I wish I could spare you from having to go through all this. If there was any way I could take your place, I would do it in a heartbeat and not think twice about it."

"I'll do what needs to be done, Jess," I tell her, feeling a new sense of purpose for my life. "God will never give me anything I can't handle. And I have all of you to help me. Our family is much stronger than the princes could ever think of becoming. We'll win."

"Sometimes winning comes at a high price," Jess warns me, and I see a sadness enter her eyes.

I know Jess lost at least two people she cared about because of her fight against the princes to seal the Tear. One was Faison's childhood sweetheart, John Austin. Apparently, he had been the first casualty of the battle. Then there was Isaiah, a Watcher I had only met once. He had been in charge of the Memphis Watcher headquarters at one time. Aiden took over Isaiah's job after he was killed in an incident to save Chandler's life. None of it was told to me in any great detail, but I knew both deaths had affected Jess deeply.

"I'm not scared, Jess," I say, placing my hand on top of the box. "Especially now that we have something that's meant to help us."

Mason and Uncle Malcolm phase into the kitchen.

It's obvious Mason just woke Uncle Malcolm up because his hair is still all mussed up like he didn't even bother to run his finger through it before coming over. He's only wearing a pair of black silk pajama bottoms and a matching robe hanging open at the front.

"What's going on, dearest?" Uncle Malcolm asks my mom. "What's happened?"

My mom goes on to explain about her dream and how it lead her to take me to Heaven to meet Utha Mae. I notice she doesn't say anything about meeting Anna and make a mental note to ask her why later. For the story that needs to be told, Anna doesn't play an important role. But, I wonder if my mom feels the same need to keep her out of the discussion just like I did when speaking with Aiden earlier. It's almost like our meeting with her was something only meant for us.

Once my mother is through with her tale, all eyes turn to me and the box.

"Can we see the pieces?" Jess asks me.

I place both my hands on the box and lift the lid back on its hinges. Everyone stares at the oddly shaped pieces of silver. Some pieces look melded together and others look like they have edges as sharp as a knife's. None of them are the same size, and it really just looks like a mishmash of metal to me.

"And how is that supposed to help us exactly?" Uncle Malcolm asks in exasperation. "What are we supposed to do, throw the pieces at Lucifer's minions and hope they stick?"

Jess' brow creases with thought after hearing Uncle Malcolm's suggestion.

"Actually," she says, "that might not be a bad idea."

"I was joking, Jess."

"I know," she tells Uncle Malcolm. "But what if we *could* throw the silver at them and make it stick?"

"What are you thinking?" Mason asks her, crossing his arms over his chest as he waits for his wife to explain her thoughts.

"Can this silver be melted down?" Jess asks.

"It would take fire hotter than anything here on Earth," my father answers.

"Well, what about Leah's fire?" I ask. "It's different, right?"

"It could be hot enough," my dad says hesitantly. "It's worth testing at any rate."

"If we can melt this silver," Jess says, "maybe we can coat Zack's daggers with it and do exactly what Malcolm suggested, throw it at them."

"But Zack's blades don't last very long," Mason points out. "They disintegrate into sand after a few seconds unless they're in a living target."

"It won't matter," Uncle Malcolm says. "If we can encase the blades before they breakdown, then they should still remain in the shape of the dagger plus, hopefully, keep the traits of Zack's power inside them."

"But they'll be dull blades, won't they?" I ask.

"Not necessarily," Mason says turning to Uncle Malcolm. "A skilled weapon smith with our strength might be able to sharpen the blades with a little muscle."

"Brutus?" Uncle Malcolm asks, but I can tell the question is just a formality.

Mason nods.

"If anyone can help us, it's him," Uncle Malcolm agrees. "He might even know whether or not Leah's fire will be hot enough to melt the silver before we involve her in things. I'll go see what he's doing."

Uncle Malcolm phases.

"And where is Brutus exactly?" I ask, looking at Uncle Malcolm's phase trail but only seeing sand and ocean.

"Greece," Aiden answers. "After the Tear was closed, he bought an island out in the Mediterranean so he could make his weapons without being bothered by too many people. His swords are highly sought after commodities by sword collectors."

"He's that good?" I ask.

"The best," Aiden answers unequivocally. "If anyone can help us with making the daggers, it's him."

Only a few minutes pass before Uncle Malcolm phases back with Brutus in tow.

I guess I shouldn't be surprised by his appearance. I'm sure Uncle Malcolm didn't give him any time to get ready to come see us. The first thing I notice about Brutus are his bulging muscles. His biceps look as thick as logs. And his torso looks like it was chiseled out of granite. He's shirtless and a bit sooty and sweaty. I immediately assume he was probably in the middle of working on a project when Uncle Malcolm found him and drug him back here. He has long wavy brown hair pulled back into a ponytail at the nape of his neck. His muscles are astonishingly well defined, but it's his eyes that capture my attention the most. They are ice blue and piercing as he looks at me. I almost feel like he's able to see into my soul.

"Brutus," Uncle Malcolm says, "I want you to meet my niece, Caylin."

Brutus wipes his right hand on the thigh of his tight fitting jeans before walking up to me and holding it out.

I shake his hand with a firm grip so he knows he doesn't have to treat me gently like an ordinary human.

Brutus seems surprised by my strength but doesn't comment on it, just smiles at me.

"It's a pleasure to finally meet you, Caylin," he tells me. His voice is deep like one of those voices you hear in a movie trailer or one a boxing ring announcer would have.

"Thank you for coming, Brutus."

Brutus looks into the box still sitting open in front of me.

"Do you mind if I examine the pieces?" He asks me.

I shake my head. "No, that's what you're here for. We need your help."

Brutus grins at me and then turns his full attention to the remnants of the archangel crowns inside the box. He picks one of the pieces up and examines it.

"Hmm," I hear Jess say as if disappointed.

I look over at her as she stands beside my mom on the other side of the kitchen island.

"What's wrong?" I ask.

"When we first found the crowns," Jess tells me, "only the person who the crown belonged with was able to lift them. Since Brutus can handle the pieces, it makes me wonder if they still hold the same powers that they once did."

"Well, I don't know anything about that," Brutus says, holding up one of the pieces with two fingers and examining it in the light. "But, I can tell you I think Uriel's vessel should be able to melt them."

"What about the rest of our plan?" Uncle Malcolm asks.

Brutus gently puts the crown piece back into the box with great reverence and turns to face Uncle Malcolm.

"If you're asking me if I think it will work, I have no way of knowing. It's not exactly as if this sort of thing has ever been done before. But, if Zadkiel's vessel's daggers can survive being dropped into molten silver, I don't think I'll have a problem making them as sharp as you need them. I should be able to mold them into proper weapons."

"And the daggers will put the princes back into stasis like the crowns did?" My mom asks.

"Theoretically they should, I think," Jess says, not sounding completely sure. "But for how long, I don't know. I have a feeling a lot of the crowns' powers were drained when the Tear was sealed. I don't think they have enough juice to keep them in stasis forever."

"Well, we already know they won't stay like that forever, don't we?" I ask. "We saw my descendant in the future fighting one of the princes."

"True," Jess admits. "We at least know Amon comes out during that time."

"I think we should just trust that God wouldn't give us something useless," I say. "They won't be freed until the time comes for them to be."

"Speaking of the future," Uncle Malcolm says to Mason, "I've already spoken with Andre about taking over when it's my time to step down. He's willing to stay for as long as it takes to make sure Lilly and Caylin's descendent does whatever it is she's born to do."

I look away from Uncle Malcolm because I feel sure he'll know something is wrong if he looks into my eyes. It's not my job to tell him the truth about his future, only my mom can do that. And I have a feeling she won't tell him anything for a very long time.

"And after we place them in stasis," Aiden says, "what do we do with them?"

"Let me worry about that," Mason says. "Though, I might need your help, Caylin."

"My help?"

Mason winks at me. "We'll talk about it after the reception when we meet with the other Watchers. Don't worry about it right now."

"Oh God," Jess says, slapping the palm of her right hand against her forehead, "I completely forgot about the wedding. On top of everything else, we have to deal with that."

Mason walks over to Jess and takes one of her hands into his. She looks over at him.

"When have we ever been given something we can't handle?" He asks her quietly. "This won't be any different. We've been given the pieces we need to succeed. Now all we have to do is put them into play."

"I know," Jess tells him. "And you know I don't think this will be the last thing we'll have to do."

Mason gives her a tight-lipped grin and nods as if he's already accepted their fate.

I have no clue what they're talking about, but I get the feeling Jess thinks God has at least one more mission for her after she helps me.

"Do we know where the other princes are right now?" My dad asks.

"We have people assigned to monitor their movements," Uncle Malcolm says.

"Who was supposed to be watching Levi?" I ask. "Because they didn't follow him very well."

"That was Jered," Mason tells me. "He said Levi gave him the slip that day, and he wasn't able to locate him again."

I see Uncle Malcolm raise a dubious eyebrow at the news.

"And was Jered telling you the truth?" Uncle Malcolm asks.

Mason nods. "Yes, I would have known if he was lying."

"I can understand how that happened," Aiden says in this Jered's defense. "Baal almost did the same thing to me the day he attacked Caylin. I'm just lucky I found his phase trail in time to follow it."

"I get the feeling you don't trust this Jered," I say to Uncle Malcolm. "Why?"

"Because he used to be a lackey for Lucifer," Uncle Malcolm grumbles. "Anyone idiot enough to follow the biggest fool of all time isn't to be trusted in my opinion."

"Malcolm," Mason says, a warning in his voice, "we've discussed this. Jered deserves a chance at redemption just like anyone else who wants it."

"I know you think he does," Uncle Malcolm says, "but I haven't quite joined that bandwagon of thinking yet."

“I guess I’m a little confused,” I confess. “Who is he exactly?”

“Right before Mason and I got married,” Jess tells me, “a group of Watchers working with Lucifer attacked us at Mama Lynn’s. After the Tear was sealed, we gave the ones we captured the chance to redeem themselves. The ones who didn’t pass Mason’s lie detector were….disposed of by Zack. Jered was the only one who truly seemed to want to change his ways and find forgiveness. As long as some people,” Jess says looking pointedly at Uncle Malcolm, “will give him a chance to prove himself.”

Uncle Malcolm shrugs. “I never said I wouldn’t give him a chance. But it’s going to take more than what he’s done so far to prove to me that he’s really changed.”

“He’s trying, Malcolm,” Mason says. “We need to give him our support not our ridicule.”

Everyone falls quiet, and I feel like we’re all ignoring the giant pink elephant in the room.

“So, do any of you know what the princes stole from Heaven?” I ask.

No one says anything, and I notice Uncle Malcolm and Mason aren't meeting my eyes. I know that can't be a good sign.

"No idea at all?" I ask again, not understanding how the angels in the room don't know about a theft that's so important.

"It wasn't something we were told about," Mason says. "I had no idea they took anything until your mother just mentioned it. But, God obviously wants it back, whatever *it* is. And, apparently, the responsibility of doing that will fall to your descendant. I'm not sure if we'll ever be told what was taken."

"It's highly doubtful," Uncle Malcolm grumbles. "Unless we just happen to run across the answer on our own. I don't see our father telling us what it is considering the fact he hasn't even mentioned it in all these years."

Silence reigns supreme again in the room, and I think we've pretty much said what needs to be said for now.

"Well, since we're all awake," my dad says breaking the quiet. "Anyone want some breakfast?"

"I could really go for some chocolate croissants," my mom says looking straight at Uncle Malcolm.

"Chocolate croissants?" Uncle Malcolm asks somewhat confused by the request. "But you and Tara only want them when one of you is pregnant."

My mom smiles at my uncle. My dad, smiling for all he's worth, comes up behind her and wraps his arms around her waist almost protectively.

"I guess you could say I got my first birthday presents early," my mom says. "We're having twins."

Uncle Malcolm shakes his head.

"And here I thought only Abby and Sebastian were breeding enough children for their own soccer team." My Uncle Malcolm grins and tells my dad, "Congratulations, Brand. For an old man, I guess you still have it in you."

I phase over to Uncle Malcolm and hit him lightly on the arm.

"What was that for?" Uncle Malcolm asks me, rubbing the spot like it actually hurt.

"If Aunt Tara was here, she would tell you to stop being rude to my dad," I tell him. "So, I'm saying it in her place."

Uncle Malcolm rolls his eyes at me. "You need better role-models in your life."

I wrap an arm around the one I hit on Uncle Malcolm. "I have the best influences in my life. Aunt Tara is just a little more violent than the rest of you."

Jess, Mason, Brutus, and Aiden congratulate my parents on their latest bundles of joy on the way.

I see Aiden look over at me and smile shyly.

I don't have to be a mind reader to know what he's thinking about. But, having a child of our own is in my distant future as far as I'm concerned. I guess Uncle Malcolm's baby doll booby trap did teach me one thing. I'm not ready to become a mother. There's so much I want to do before I devote myself to the proper care and raising of a child.

And I want to do all of it with Aiden by my side.

CHAPTER THREE

After breakfast, Jess and Mason leave to pick their kids up from Mama Lynn's house. Brutus returns to his island and promises to see us again at the reception. Uncle Malcolm leaves to go talk to Andre Greco about what we learned in Heaven and what we plan to do with the crown pieces. From what Uncle Malcolm said earlier, Andre would become Uncle Malcolm's second in command when he took over as the leader of the Watchers. I still feel an enormous amount of guilt over not being able to tell Uncle Malcolm about his future, but Anna's words to us make me feel slightly better.

"*I'll take good care of him.*" She promised my mom.

I pray she keeps her word once she's born into our world. I know she won't remember meeting us in Heaven, but I hope she will come to understand how special Uncle Malcolm is. I know it can take some people time to warm up to him and understand his personality. I just hope Anna is someone who can see past the façade he shows to others and cares enough to find the real man underneath.

"We have a few hours before we need to get ready for the wedding," I tell Aiden while he and I load the dirty dishes from breakfast into the dishwasher. “Would you like to sit with me in my studio while I work on my mom’s birthday present?”

Aiden grins. “Of course I would. There’s nowhere else I want to be but with you.”

“You sure you won’t get tired of me?” I tease.

“Is there any chance of you getting tired of *me*?” Aiden asks in return.

“Not a chance in this world,” I tell him with absolute certainty, handing him the last glass to place in the dishwasher. “Not even if I lived the next thousand years.”

Aiden’s grin grows wider. “Good because I plan to be in your life for as long as we both shall live.”

I giggle and dry my hands on a towel hanging on the refrigerator door handle.

“We’re going to my studio,” I tell my parents who are sitting at the dining room table discussing something.

“Ok, sweetie,” my mom says almost absently, giving me the impression she and my father are talking about something important.

Aiden grabs my coat from the rack by the door and helps me into it before grabbing his own black leather jacket. Thankfully, we both changed clothes while breakfast was being made so we weren't heading out in our pajamas.

Aiden casually takes my hand as we walk to my studio in the boathouse.

"I meant to apologize to you," Aiden says to me as we walk side by side.

I look over at him.

"Apologize for what?" I ask, trying to rack my brain to figure out what on Earth he would need to apologize to me about.

"For letting them catch me and use me against you."

I walk in front of Aiden to stop him by placing a gentle hand on his chest.

"Why do you think you need to apologize about that, Aiden? They had you out numbered five to one," I say, feeling the heat of my anger about that particular point resurface and relishing in the fact that I tore Levi's heart out for it. A part of me hopes he felt some pain from the act.

"But I should have been more careful," Aiden says, like the incident was all his fault. "If I'd been thinking straight, they wouldn't have been able to ambush me so easily."

"What had you distracted?"

Aiden sighs heavily and looks down at our entwined hands.

"Do I have to admit to it?"

"Uh, yeah. After asking that, I have to know now."

"I…didn't like you dancing with Hunter. I felt a little …jealous."

"Oh," I say, hating myself for feeling somewhat pleased by Aiden's admission. "Well, if it's any consolation, I didn't really want to dance with him. I wanted to dance the last dance with you."

Aiden looks back up at me.

"I didn't have any right to feel jealous," he says. "I don't own you."

"No, you don't own me," I tell him, finding it impossible not to smile at him. "But you did lay full claim to my heart the first time we saw each other."

Aiden raises his free hand and lifts the half heart pendant hanging around my neck off my chest.

"Would you mind if I took you somewhere for just a few minutes? I've been wanting to give you something for a while now but there never seemed to be a good time."

“Take me,” I say, tightening my hold on his hand.

Aiden phases us and I find myself standing in a large bedroom with a four-poster bed and matching suit of furniture. The room is dark because it’s still only a little after five in the morning. Aiden tugs on my hand and walks over to one of the nightstands beside the bed. I feel my heart lurch excitedly inside my chest as I wonder why he’s taking me so close to the bed.

Aiden bends down and switches on the lamp sitting on the nightstand. The light glints off something dangling just past the edge of the lampshade, and I instantly recognize what it is, the other half of the heart to my pendant.

He lets go of my hand and pulls the chain the pendant is hanging from off the top post on the lamp.

“I’ve kept the other half of the necklace here in Memphis with me,” Aiden says, unlatching the hook of the chain and sliding the pendant off into the palm of one of his hands. “It made me feel a little closer to you to keep it nearby.”

“Beside your bed?” I ask, wondering if Aiden thought of me often while he lay there at night looking at the pendant.

Aiden grins as he looks up from the pendant in his hand to meet my eyes.

"Yes, beside my bed. Are you bothered by that?"

I slowly shake my head. "No. I used to sleep with my sketchpad of you underneath my pillow every night. So, I understand the need to have something you felt connected us close by."

"Can I see your necklace?"

I touch the pendant, which has been next to my heart since I turned fifteen.

"I haven't taken it off since you left it on my windowsill," I confide to him, reaching for the clasp at the back of my neck. I slip the necklace off and suddenly feel naked without it against my skin. I hand it to Aiden.

He takes it and slides his half of the pendant onto the chain. It's only when he lifts my half of the pendant to his that I see his has an opaque protruding part in the middle. He places mine on top of the part that juts out from the side of his, and I hear a distinct click as the two pieces are joined together. When Aiden lifts the pendant up for me to look at, I see a solitary white flame in the center of the heart where the two pieces meet.

"This is how my heart felt when I first saw you," Aiden says, "like it was suddenly on fire."

Aiden takes a step closer to me with the ends of the chain in each hand. I lift my hair from the back of my neck as he leans in to put the necklace back on me.

After Aiden fastens the clasp, I feel his fingers caress the sides of my neck gently before he pulls his hands away and back to his sides.

"And now that we're finally together," Aiden says, "my heart feels whole again."

I reach out with both my hands and grab the front of the black sweater he's wearing. In one quick movement, I pull him to me.

Aiden smiles.

"Was there something that you wanted, Caylin?" He asks teasingly as he grins happily.

I smile back. "Why yes, Aiden, there is something that I want from you. How *ever* did you know?"

"Oh," he says with a small shrug, "just a wild guess really."

I loosen my grip on his sweater and slide my hands up his chest until they find their way behind his neck beneath his wavy black hair.

Aiden watches me but doesn't say anything or make a move to lower his head near mine. I lean into him and have to raise myself up on the tips of my toes slightly to bring our faces closer together. Aiden rests his hands on the sides of my hips, and I feel him squeeze them slightly with his fingers.

"I'm going to kiss you now," I warn him.

"I kind of already assumed you would be," he whispers with my favorite lop-sided grin appearing on his face.

I close my eyes and press my lips to his. My heart suddenly feels swollen inside my chest from the love I feel for the man in my arms. I press my body even more firmly against his and deepen the kiss, feeling his lips part easily and his tongue respond to my own.

I'm instantly aware when Aiden's hands slide up underneath my shirt and begin to caress the small of my bare back. When I sigh in response to his touch, his hands find their way back to my hips as we continue to kiss. After a while, I finally force myself to pull my mouth away from his and rest my head against his chest to catch my breath. I hear the hammering of his heart and can't help but smile at the irrefutable evidence that I have the same effect on him that he does on me.

"I think you're getting a little too good at that," Aiden says breathlessly.

I raise my head and look up at him. "Is that even possible? To be too good at kissing?"

"In your case, I would have to say yes," he tells me, caressing the left side of my face with the tips of his fingers. "And I think we should go back now."

"Why?"

"Because it's not right for you to be here in my bedroom kissing me," he says simply, and I suddenly find myself standing right outside the door to my studio.

I feel a little disappointed at being whisked away from Aiden's bedroom so suddenly. The bed looked comfortable enough to have a make out session on which was something I was hoping for, but Aiden obviously wasn't having the same thoughts as me.

As if sensing my disappointment, he leans down and kisses me tenderly on the lips, making me feel completely cherished and loved with the simple act.

"Don't frown," he begs as his kisses venture across my cheek and down one side of my neck, evoking an involuntary gasp from the pleasure of feeling his lips against the sensitive flesh for the first time.

"I'm not frowning," I sigh, as Aiden's lips kiss the sweet spot where my neck and shoulder meet which causes my heart to race into my throat.

Aiden lifts his head and looks down at me.

"Yes, you are," he tells me. "I don't like to see you frown."

"Then why did you bring us back here so quickly?"

"Because I'm not strong enough to have you in my bedroom alone kissing me like that, Caylin."

I'm not stupid. I know what he's talking about. I felt his physical desire for me first hand when I used Jess' bracelet to better understand every emotion he felt where I'm concerned. And, to be honest, I'm not ready to make love to Aiden yet. I'm still just getting used to kissing him, and I want to explore that aspect of our relationship more fully before venturing further. Yet, I wonder if he will get to a point where kissing isn't enough for him…

I take hold of one of Aiden's hands.

“Come on. I want to show you what I'm making my mom.”

I open the door to the studio and turn on the light.

A long time ago, my dad paid someone to put in a central air and heating system in the boathouse to make sure it stayed a comfortable temperature for me no matter what the season. The warmth of the inside welcomes us, and we both take off our coats and hang them on the coat rack by the door.

I walk over to the easel holding the canvas I've been working on and slip off the sheet hiding it from view to show Aiden. He looks at it and smiles.

“A family portrait,” he says looking at my efforts. “It's beautiful. Your mom will love it.”

Aiden takes a seat on the other side of the table from where the easel I'm working on stands.

He watches me as I paint and strangely enough, I don't mind it at all. I enjoy his nearness and find it amazing that someone who can excite me with just a glance in my direction can also bring me so much peace in a quiet moment like this.

I sigh in complete and utter contentment.

"You sound happy," Aiden says.

I look over at him. He has one of his arms on the table bent at the elbow with his head leaned against the palm of his hand watching me with an easy, happy grin on his face.

"Of course I'm happy," I tell him. "You're with me."

Aiden's grin grows wider and his eyes glance down at the table before meeting mine again.

"I've lived a very long time," Aiden tells me, his grin fading as his thoughts seem to be running through his life thus far. "But right now is the happiest I've ever been. I'd pretty much given up on having a life like Jess and Mason and your mom and dad. I never thought that was in the cards for me until I saw you for the first time. Now, all I can think about is our future and all the happy memories I want us to make together."

I put down my paintbrush and phase over to Aiden.

"Can I make a happy memory right now?" I ask him as he turns towards me on the stool he's sitting on, his legs spread just far enough apart for me to take a step forward and stand between them.

"And just what type of memory would you like to make, beautiful?" He asks in a husky voice, looking me up and down.

"Oh, I think you might know," I tell him, resting my hands on his shoulders.

Aiden grins but unfortunately, the memory I want to make has to wait because there's an unexpected knock on the door.

I quickly step away from between Aiden's legs and clear my throat before I say, "Come in."

"Or don't," Aiden grumbles under his breath, turning on the stool with his arms crossed in front of him looking as frustrated as I feel by the intrusion.

The door opens just enough for a man I've never seen before to poke his head inside the room and look between the two of us.

"I hope I'm not interrupting anything," he says in a crisp British accent, much like my father's.

Aiden uncrosses his arms and stands up. The frustration on his face is quickly replaced by confusion as he walks the short distance to the door. The other man walks inside, and they shake hands like they're old friends.

The man is of average build with short brown hair and penetrating brown eyes. His face is handsome and clean-shaven but looks slightly worried.

"What on Earth are you doing here at this time of day, Jered?" Aiden says to the man.

"Not so early for me," he replies with an easy grin. "It's lunchtime in England. But, Mason called me a little while ago and said you were here and already up and about. I hope I'm not barging in unwanted."

"No, it's fine," Aiden reassures him. "Jered, have you met Caylin yet?"

Jered looks over at me. "No, I haven't had the pleasure."

"Caylin," Aiden says, "this is Jered. The Watcher Mason and Jess mentioned to you earlier."

I walk up to Jered and hold out my hand for him to shake.

"It's nice to meet you, Jered," I say.

Jered shakes my hand with both of his and the earnest expression on his face tells me he truly is pleased to finally meet me.

“I wasn’t sure I would ever be able to make your acquaintance,” he tells me just before letting my hand go.

“Why?” I ask, thinking this an odd thing to say.

“Malcolm doesn’t trust me, and those he doesn’t trust are kept away from you and your family.”

I knew the reason Uncle Malcolm didn't trust Jered, so I decided on a course of action.

“Do you mean me or anyone in my family harm?” I ask him point blank.

Jered doesn't seem surprised by my question and firmly shakes his head.

“I give you my word that such a thought has never even entered my mind since I decided to change my ways.”

He was telling the truth. If he had been lying, I would have known.

“Did you intentionally let Levi escape you yesterday?” I ask, needing to know the answer to this question even more so to truly judge his trustworthiness.

“No,” Jered says, his eyes lower to the floor at my feet as if he's too ashamed to meet my questioning gaze as he answers. “I did not let him escape on purpose.”

Jered looks over at Aiden.

“I came here to apologize to the both of you for letting him get away from me,” Jered says, seeming to need Aiden's forgiveness more than mine. “I should have notified someone that I lost his trail, but I didn't want to look like a fool. It was my pride that allowed them to capture you. I hope you can forgive me for being such an idiot.”

“There's nothing to forgive, Jered,” Aiden says, placing a hand on the other man's shoulder. “You did the best you could. That's all any of us can ask from one another.”

“I feel like I should have done more.”

“Well, at least now we know for sure that they figured out the importance of the anklets. That was something we'd been wondering about for a while. Now we know they understand what they do.”

“I suppose that's one way to think about it,” Jered admits. “I just wish the information hadn't come at such a high price.”

“I'm fine now,” Aiden says, trying to reassure the man. “This isn't something you need to feel guilt over. It could have happened to any one of us.”

“Let me keep my guilt for a while,” Jered says, “maybe it'll make me more cautious the next time around.”

Aiden sighs.

“Don't keep it for long,” he tells Jered. “Otherwise it'll start to eat you up and that's no good for anybody.”

Jered nods and holds his hand out to Aiden again.

As the two of them shake hands, Jered says, “I won't let either of you two down again. You have my word on that.”

And I know Jered means what he says because my internal lie detector would go off if he didn't.

“I'll let the two of you go back to what you were doing,” Jered says with a small smile, as if he might suspect I was about to make out with my boyfriend before he knocked on the door. “I'll see you both at the wedding later.”

“See you then,” Aiden tells him.

Jered phases and Aiden and I are alone again.

He sits back down on his stool and assumes the same position he was in before Jered interrupted us.

"Now," Aiden says, "what happy memory were we about to make before we got interrupted."

I giggle and walk back to Aiden, standing between his legs again and resting my arms over his shoulders.

"Let me show you," I tell him before lowering my lips to his and making a memory we would never forget.

CHAPTER FOUR

I stare at myself in the full-length mirror in my room and wonder what the heck I was thinking when I agreed to be one of Faison's bridesmaids. I look like I was tarred and stuck into a bag of pink tulle only to escape looking like a deranged ballerina.

I turn my back to my reflection and immediately go to my closet to pick out another dress to take to Leah's house. I plan to take the nightmare bridesmaid dress off right after the wedding pictures are taken. Jess' idea of changing clothes was absolute genius, and I plan to take full advantage of her suggestion, especially since Faison gave us her blessing to do it.

I walk down stairs with my change of clothes over one of my arms only to hear the cackle of my little brother as I enter his line of vision.

"You look like a pink puffball," he says through his hysterical laughter.

I narrow my eyes at him.

"Don't make me hurt you," I warn in all seriousness.

Will rolls his eyes at me as if he thinks I'm making an empty threat.

“You always say that but you know you can’t hurt me,” he says full of confidence. “You love me too much.”

I know he’s right, but I can’t let him think he can tease me to no end either.

“What happened with Katie Ann yesterday?” I ask instead, effectively changing the subject.

Will grins.

“She melted like butter in my hands after she read the poem I wrote for her,” Will says. “We’re official now.”

I can’t help but smile because Will looks so pleased with himself over his conquest of Katie Ann's heart.

“Congratulations,” I tell him, not feeling like teasing him about his first love.

I seriously doubt it will be his last, but for right now, it’s new and exciting for him. I can understand the feeling, and I wouldn’t belittle his moment in the sun of Katie Ann's adoration for anything in the world.

“KK!”

I look up the stairs and see my mom, dad, and Mae walk down all dressed up to go to the wedding. Mae looks angelic in her little pink flower girl dress. I feel somewhat jealous and wish my dress looked more like hers with its simple, classic lines.

"That's some dress you've got on," my dad says to me, but I can tell he's holding back a laugh with a smile.

"Which is why I'm taking extra clothes," I tell him, patting the dress across my arm with my free hand.

My dad chuckles. "Good idea."

I see his gaze drop to my necklace.

"It looks a lot better whole," he comments.

I raise my hand up to the pendant and smile. "Yes, it does."

"Aiden has good taste," my dad tells me, and I know from the look in his eyes he doesn't just mean Aiden's taste in jewelry.

"I'll meet you all at the church," I tell my family. "I'm going to phase over to Mama Lynn's house first and leave my clothes there to change into later."

My mom leans in close to me and kisses me on the cheek.

"Be careful," she says.

I nod. "I will. It'll only take a second. I'll see you there."

I phase to Mama Lynn's front door and knock.

It's immediately opened by Leah who looks like my mirror image. She busts out in laughter.

“We look ridiculous,” she declares.

“I'm fully aware,” I tell her as she steps back from the doorway to give me space to walk into the house.

I lay my dress on the back of the couch in the living room and turn around to face Leah.

She isn’t laughing anymore or even smiling.

“We never should have left you with Hunter,” Leah says frowning. “Joshua and I are so sorry, Caylin.”

I shake my head.

“Don't apologize for something you had no control over,” I tell her. “Aiden and I are fine.”

“But if we had only stayed with you...”

“Who knows what might have happened,” I finish for her. “It could have turned out worse. You both might have gotten hurt, or they could have used you against me too. I had the element of surprise on my side. Levi didn’t expect me to be so strong.”

“I heard about what you did to him,” Leah says, her frown deepening. “Are you ok with what happened?”

“If you're asking me if I feel any guilt about it, no, I don't. He deserved worse if you want to know what I honestly think.”

“Good,” Leah says, her worry for me disappearing. “You shouldn't feel any guilt over it. And I agree, he deserved worse.”

“Come on, Faison,” I hear Jess say in exasperation as she walks down the stairs from the second floor. “You're going to be late for your own wedding if you don't get a move on.”

Jess descends the staircase in a pink puff of organza but somehow she still manages to look beautiful.

She smiles when she sees me.

“Hey, kiddo. How are you doing?”

“I'm wonderful actually,” I admit.

How could I not be with the morning I just had with Aiden?

After Jered left, we kissed for a long time and then I finally tore myself away from him long enough to finish my painting for my mom. I wanted to make sure I got through with it because I had no way of knowing what might happen in the next few days, and her birthday was only five days away. I felt sure the time in between would be taken up with the plan we had to put the Princes of Hell into stasis.

My attention is grabbed by Faison as she descends the staircase in a billow of white silk. Mama Lynn trails behind her with the long train draped over her arms.

"Oh, you girls look so cute," Faison says, crinkling her nose at us like we're the most adorable things she's ever seen in her life.

Her smile is so bright and filled with such happiness I almost feel guilty for feeling stupid in the dress she's making me wear.

"Well, you look gorgeous!" I tell her, truly meaning it.

Faison smiles shyly, as if she isn't used to such praise. "Thanks."

"Zack's going to have a heart attack when he sees you," Leah declares.

"Thanks, little sis," Faison says.

"Caylin, can you just phase us all to the church?" Jess asks me. "We're running late because someone was fussing over her hair."

"I wanted to make sure it looked perfect," Faison says to Jess in her own self-defense.

“It was perfect an hour ago,” Jess tells her sister. “Zack would think you were perfect even if you were completely bald with buck teeth and a wandering eye!”

Faison tries not to laugh but fails miserably and begins to laugh so hard she's on the verge of tears.

“Don't make me laugh again!” She tells Jess pointing a strident finger at her. “I'll ruin my make-up if you do!”

“You need to laugh,” Jess tells her in all seriousness. “It's your wedding day. It's supposed to be the happiest day of your life.”

“And we're going to make sure it is,” Mama Lynn declares as she gathers up the rest of Faison's train in the back. “Now let's go to the church. We don't need to keep your man waiting at the altar forever.”

I grab Leah's hand and walk over to the other three women. Everyone touches me and I phase us to the very front of the church where we’re all supposed to line up. When I do, I instantly see Aiden and openly gawk at his perfection.

He’s on the other side of the little foyer speaking with Chandler, Joshua, and Mr. George, Mama Lynn’s husband. Aiden is wearing a dark gray frock suit, matching the antebellum theme of the wedding. Underneath the coat, he has on a silk vest that matches the pink of my dress, a white shirt and grey silk cravat around the raised collar. He's left his hair loose and curly, just the way I like it.

When Aiden sees me, I expect him to at least chuckle at my attire, but all he does is smile at me, somehow making me feel like the most beautiful woman in the world even though I know I don't look the part. He excuses himself from the others and walks over to me.

"Why do you look so good?" I ask him, wondering how he can look so handsome in antebellum style clothing.

"Because I picked a good body to come to Earth in?" He asks jokingly.

I roll my eyes at him. "Well that's obvious, but how can you look so good dressed up in these clothes? I look like I got attacked by a bag of cotton candy!"

Aiden shakes his head at me as though I'm being ridiculous and leans down to kiss me on the cheek.

"You look beautiful," he tells me.

"And how can you say that truthfully?" I ask, knowing his words weren't a lie.

"Because you always look beautiful to me," he says in a low voice. "No matter what god awful outfit you're wearing."

I giggle somewhat relieved that at least he acknowledges the dress is hideous.

As I look Aiden up and down, I tell him, "I have to say I like you in that suit. You really do look good in it."

Aiden grins. "Good enough to dance with later?"

"Good enough for more than that later," I whisper, past the point of being overly shy in telling him what I want.

Aiden seems to get the gist of my meaning because I see a small hint of a blush appear across his cheeks as he grins at me.

"Ok boys and girls," Jess says, interrupting our moment. "Time to get this show on the road so we can get out of these clothes."

We pick up our bouquets from a table near the entrance of the church and line up in our designated order. Jess handles keeping Mae and Max in line and giving them last minute instructions on what they are supposed to do once we enter the sanctuary. I stand beside Aiden and take a deep breath.

"Are you nervous?" Aiden asks me.

“I don’t like crowds or people watching me,” I confess.

Aiden holds a bent arm out to me, and I loop my free arm through it. He pats my hand reassuringly.

“I’ll be right by your side,” he says. “Just look at me if you get nervous.”

I look up at Aiden and know without any doubt that he will always be by my side. He will always do whatever he has to do to protect me. And he will always love me. To be my age and have someone like that in my life is a blessing not many people get to have. I silently promise him that I will not take him, my gift from God, for granted.

As we walk down the aisle together, I see my parents in a pew near the front of the church smiling at me. It makes me think back to the vision of me walking with my father down a church aisle on my own wedding day. I didn’t look much older than I am now in the vision, and it makes me wonder how soon it will be before Aiden and I decide to get married.

As we reach Zack standing with the preacher at the front of the church, Aiden and I have to separate so he can go stand on

Zack's side of the altar. I feel him squeeze my hand on his arm gently before letting me go.

The ceremony goes by quickly and without a hitch. I'm thankful Faison is able to have the wedding of her dreams to Zack and know they will have a happy life together.

After the ceremony, we're forced to take about a million pictures by the rather bossy little woman photographer Mama Lynn hired. I feel like I'm in boot camp, and she's my sergeant giving me orders on where to stand, when to smile and when to get out of the way. I'm thankful when we're given permission to leave and change clothes to go meet all the other guests at the reception.

The reception is set up behind Mama Lynn's house in a large white tent that was erected just for the occasion. Even though it's February, there are a sufficient number of heaters to make the inside of the tent feel toasty warm and comfortable. When Leah and I enter the tent after changing into more comfortable dresses, I immediately see why Mama Lynn had Leah's father, Remy, and Zack making so many origami swans. They're hanging everywhere from white silk ribbons draped from the center pole out to the sides of the tent.

The other thing I notice immediately is the large group of Watchers on one side of the tent chatting it up with one another. Aiden is among the group talking with a Watcher I know but have never personally met before.

“I’ll catch up with you later,” Leah tells me before making a b-line to her honeybun, Joshua, who is speaking with Jonathan, Mason’s son.

I head over to Aiden.

Almost as soon as the Watchers see me approaching them, they stop talking to one another and start staring at me.

Can we say uncomfortable?

I look to Aiden and he smiles at me, making me lose some of my unease at the sudden onslaught of undivided attention from the other Watchers.

The Watcher he was speaking with turns to face me as I approach. He has shoulder length brown hair that is wavy at the ends and dark brown eyes. His smile is an easy one, and I instantly feel at ease in his presence.

Aiden holds out his hand for me to take as I get closer, and I’m thankful for the comfort of his touch as I slip my hand into his.

"Caylin," Aiden says, "I would like to introduce you to Desmond. He's a very old and good friend of mine."

I hold out my free hand to shake hands with Desmond.

"It's nice to meet you," I tell him.

Desmond shakes my hand exactly like Jered did, cupping my hand between both of his.

"The pleasure is all mine, Caylin," he tells me with a slight bow of his head in my direction.

I notice an Irish lilt to Desmond's voice, but it doesn't take me by surprise. I already know he's the Watcher in charge of the United Kingdom headquarters.

"Aiden was just telling me the two of you will be attending Yale together. I have to say I'm a bit jealous of him."

"Why jealous?" I ask.

"I think we all wish we could meet our soul mate," Desmond confesses to me. "Aiden was lucky to find his, and considering his soul mate is you, doubly lucky."

I feel my cheeks grow warm under Desmond's intense gaze.

"Stop flirting with my girlfriend," Aiden tells Desmond good-naturedly.

"Well, can you blame me?" Desmond says with a grin to Aiden. "I hope you realize she's far too beautiful for someone like you. She should really be with someone… oh, I don't know… maybe more like me with ruggedly handsome good looks instead of pretty boy ones."

"You better watch yourself, Desmond," someone behind me says.

I turn around to see a Watcher who rivals Brutus in the department of most muscles. Even though he's wearing a nicely tailored light gray suit, you can still see his bulging muscles because they're pushing against the fabric as if they want to get out. His skin is the color of caramel. He's bald and wearing an easy, open smile on his face as he walks up to us.

"Or have you forgotten Aiden is a War Angel?" The man asks Desmond.

"Was," Aiden corrects the other Watcher, "not anymore, Slade."

Slade stops once he's in front of me and bows to me at the waist.

“It’s a pleasure to finally meet you, Caylin,” he says as he stands back up to his full height.

“It’s nice to meet you too,” I reply, but find it odd that the Watchers I have met lately keep bowing to me like I’m royalty or something.

Slade grins. “We heard what you did to Levi. I have to say I’m impressed and that doesn’t happen very often. None of us knew you had our strength. Is there anything else we should know about you?”

“A girl should never share all her secrets,” I tell him.

Slade laughs. “Isn’t that the truth? Aiden said you beat him at arm wrestling. Mind going up against me one of these days?”

“Sure,” I tell him, “as long as you don’t mind being beat by a girl too. I’m up for it.”

“Cheeky,” he says looking at me sideways, “I like it. Shows spunk. You’re going to need that for what’s to come. Don’t lose it.”

I understand what he’s telling me. I’m going to need to be strong while we attempt to place the princes into stasis. I still don’t know how we’re supposed to do it exactly. They won’t just stand still and let us stab them with the daggers. They're sure to put up a fight.

I just have no way of knowing how far they will go to stop us.

CHAPTER FIVE

Faison and Zack come in soon after and the party is officially allowed to start. They do the prerequisite cutting of the cake, and then we are allowed to eat the buffet lunch that was prepared for us. I can't help but get amused at some of the residents of Cypress Hollow while I stand in the buffet line behind Aiden. The females of the small community seem to be all a twitter about the Watchers at the reception. I can't say I blame them. They do make quite a spectacle when they're all gathered together in one place. But, there's only one Watcher who has my undivided attention.

Aiden's taken off the coat, vest, and cravat of his suit, and unbuttoned the top three buttons of his shirt. As I stand behind him, I find my eyes wandering to just below the waistband of his pants in the back and wonder why I never noticed before now how well-formed Aiden is on that particular area of his body.

"Caylin," I hear Aiden say, forcing me to lift my gaze and look up at his face.

I find him peering at me over his shoulder with a look of amusement.

"Yes?" I ask, only a little embarrassed that Aiden caught me staring at that portion of his body.

"I asked if you wanted some of this chicken," he says grinning for all he's worth. "Unless there's something else that's caught your eye that you would rather have?"

Yep, he said it. And we both know exactly what he means. But, I refuse to blush or feel embarrassed for admiring everything Aiden has to offer me.

"Why yes, Aiden," I tell him, "something else did catch my eye, but I'll settle for the chicken for now."

Aiden's smile falters slightly as he continues to stare at me, and I know I've caught him off guard by my flirting. But, his smile soon returns and is even brighter than before. He turns to me with a spatula in his hand holding a piece of the smothered chicken and sets it on my plate.

"Maybe we can do something about the other thing that caught your eye later," he murmurs so no one around us can overhear.

"Is that a promise?" I ask.

Again, his smile grows even brighter, if that's possible.

"I'll see what I can do," he says and turns away with a faint patch of red dappling his cheeks.

I think that's the second time I've made Aiden blush today. I have to admit I'm quite pleased with myself for accomplishing such a feat. I wouldn't have thought someone with his experiences would blush that easily just from a little innocent flirting.

Aiden and I decide to sit and eat with my family instead of at the wedding party table. I feel like it's important for Aiden to realize he's a part of us now and the best way to do that is to treat him like he's already a member of my family. In my mind, he became a member the first night he came over for dinner, but I'm not sure how everyone else feels about it. Though, from the way my Aunt Tara fawns over him, I have a feeling she's of the same mind as me and wants him to feel comfortable around us.

My dad even seems to have accepted Aiden's permanent place in our family and makes an effort by striking up a conversation about the house Aiden built for us in Colorado. It's a home I want to go back to, but I know it isn't safe just yet. Not until we put the Princes of Hell in stasis at any rate. Everything seems to hinge on doing that, and I feel even more determined to get it done as quickly as possible.

I notice my mother looks a bit reserved during the meal, even sad considering the happy occasion we're supposed to be celebrating. I can only imagine she's thinking about what needs to be done and about Uncle Malcolm. I had hoped Anna's words to her would have relieved her of the guilt she feels concerning Uncle Malcolm's role in the future of our family, but I can tell they haven't.

I'm not the only one who observes her uncharacteristic behavior. I see Uncle Malcolm staring at her with a worried expression on his face. He's sitting on the other side of me, tapping his index finger against the top of the table as he watches my mother closely.

While we're eating a piece of the wedding cake, Uncle Malcolm leans over to me and whispers in my ear, "What's wrong with your mother? Did something happen in Heaven that upset her?"

"No," I whisper back, "nothing bad happened in Heaven. She seemed really happy to see Utha Mae again."

“Oh,” Uncle Malcolm says, “maybe that’s it. Her death hit your mother pretty hard when it happened. It took her a long time to recover from it.”

“Plus she’s pregnant with twins,” I remind him. “I’m sure that’s not helping her emotional state any.”

“True,” Uncle Malcolm says but doesn’t sound convinced as he sits back in his chair and keeps an ever watchful eye on my mother.

“It’s time for the happy couple to dance the first dance!”

Mama Lynn’s announcement draws everyone’s attention, and we watch as Faison and Zack take to the dance floor. A stage has been set up on the far end of the tent, and I recognize the band standing on it as being Chandler’s. Chandler takes to the stage and begins to sing one of his love songs for the happy couple to dance their first dance to as husband and wife.

Jess and Mason soon join them and other couples trickle in to fill the dance floor.

Aiden stands and holds his hand out to me.

“Can I have the pleasure of dancing with you?” He asks me.

I smile and place my hand into his.

"You can have the pleasure of dancing every dance with me today," I tell him as I stand from the table.

Aiden takes me into his arms when we reach the dance floor, and I can't help but sigh my contentment.

"I like it when you do that," he tells me, looking down at me with a faint smile lifting the corners of his mouth.

"Do what?" I ask.

"Sigh like that," he answers. "It's a happy sound, and I like you happy."

"My life is close to perfect," I tell him. "All we have to do is trap the princes. Then, our life is our own."

Aiden smiles fully. "And I like it when you talk like that. You say 'our' a lot."

"Well, of course I say it a lot," I tell him, wondering why he looks so amazed that I do. "I can't imagine doing anything in my life without you being by my side. Can you?"

Aiden shakes his head. "No. I can't imagine my future without you in it."

"Then there you go," I tell him. "This is *our* life now. And I want our life to be as perfect as we can make it for ourselves and for our own family. If that means fighting all seven of the princes at once, then I don't have a problem with that. We'll do what needs to be done."

"You amaze me," Aiden says. "You're so confident about us winning."

"I have no reason not to be confident. My family has always been strong and together we can handle anything that gets in our way. And you're a part of my family now, Aiden. It might not be official yet, but I think everyone understands that you and I will be together forever."

"Forever is a very long time," Aiden murmurs. "Are you sure you're ready to make a commitment like that to me? We've only really been together for a few days."

"I never want to live without you," I tell him. "I wouldn't know how to anymore."

"It's not something you have to worry about, beautiful," Aiden says, lifting a hand to my face and cupping one side of it tenderly, like I'm the most precious thing in the world to him. "I will always be with you."

I lean my face into the palm of his hand and sigh which makes Aiden smile, a smile that lights my heart.

After dancing for a while, I tell Aiden I need something to drink. He takes me back to our table, and I find Remy there now eating a piece of wedding cake and looking happy as a clam while he watches Leah and Joshua dancing and having a good time with one another.

"I'll be right back with your drink," Aiden tells me, leaning over and kissing me on the cheek before he leaves.

"You two look really good together," Remy tells me through a mouthful of cake.

I giggle. "Thanks, Mr. Remy. I think so too."

I look back at the dance floor and smile as I see Leah trying to show Joshua how to fast dance. Poor Joshua, coordinated movement just isn't his thing.

"You know," Remy says, "Leah had the worst crush on the Josh back on our Earth, but he never seemed to have the same feelings for her. I guess some part of Leah knew there was a version of Joshua somewhere out in the universe just for her."

"Do you think they're soul mates?" I ask, looking back at Leah and Joshua.

"Oh, I wouldn't know about things like that. Only God has that kind of insight."

"But you made souls when you were in Heaven, right?" I ask. "Don't you have some sort of 'sixth sense' about connections between souls?"

"No, not really," Remy admits. "But I'm glad to see that you and Leah have become so close. I wondered if you would once you met."

I look back over at Leah's father finding this a curious thing to say.

"Why would you wonder about something like that, Mr. Remy?"

Remy puts his fork down on his plate and looks at me.

"I have a small confession to make to you," he says, clearing his throat nervously. "I, uh, made your soul."

I sit there stunned into silence by this revelation. What exactly do you say to something like that? Thank you?

"Should I have kept that information to myself?" Remy asks worriedly, watching my reaction. "I've been debating on whether or not to tell you for the past few years, but I thought it was time you knew the truth."

"So," I say, letting this new piece of information filter through my brain, "Leah and I…we're like…soul sisters?"

"Which is why I'm glad the two of you hit it off immediately. She needed someone to connect to here, and I hoped that someone would be you."

"Are you like my father too?" I ask, getting a little confused.

"No, not really," Remy says with a shake of his head. "Leah just thinks of me as her dad because I raised her. Seems to me like you have enough father figures in your life. You don't need a third."

"Have you told Leah?" I ask.

"Told Leah what?"

I didn't even notice Leah and Joshua walk over to the table and silently curse myself for being so careless.

Remy looks to his daughter and says, "That I made Caylin's soul too."

Leah stands there just as stunned as I was when first hearing the news. Then, she smiles that gorgeous smile of hers and gives me a big hug.

"I knew there was something special about us!" She says, squeezing me for all she's worth.

"Is everything all right?" I hear Aiden ask as he comes back with drinks for the both of us.

I look at him over Leah's shoulder and smile.

"Never better," I tell him, wiping away the worry on his face with my words.

The reception passes by rather uneventfully. I know that at the end of it we're supposed to have a meeting with all the Watchers. We're supposed to decide what to do about the princes once we place them in stasis. But, I decide not to worry about it and just try to have a good time with my friends and family.

Near the end, when most of the people from Cypress Hollow have left, I notice my mom sitting alone at a table playing with one of the crystal swans Mama Lynn bought as party favors for people to take home. My mom looks sad, and I know there isn't anything I can do to make her feel better.

I see Uncle Malcolm staring at my mom from across the room with a troubled frown on his face. He obviously doesn't like seeing her sad either. He walks over to the band as they're about to change songs and says something to one of the musicians. The man playing lead guitar nods his head at something Uncle Malcolm asks him.

As Uncle Malcolm walks away from the band's stage, one of Chandler's back-up singers belts out the first lyrics to a song I know well.

It's an old song called *Dance with Me* by a group once called Ra Ra Riot, and I know it so well because anytime my mom is having a bad day, Uncle Malcolm will play it and make her dance with him until she laughs.

I see my mom instantly recognize what's about to happen because she closes her eyes and shakes her head as a small, resigned smile appears on her face.

She turns in her seat to face Uncle Malcolm as he dances over to her across the dance floor and holds out his hand for her to take.

She shakes her head at him in exasperation but takes his hand anyway and lets him lead her to the mostly empty dance floor.

"I hope that works," I hear my dad say as he comes to stand beside me, watching Uncle Malcolm twirl my mom around. "But I have a feeling it won't this time."

"Why has she been so upset today?" I ask my dad as we both watch to see if Uncle Malcolm can pull my mom out of her doldrums.

"I was sort of hoping you could answer that question for *me*," my dad admits. "Did something happen in Heaven that the two of you haven't told us about? It seems like she's been upset about something since you came back."

I remain silent because I have a feeling the answer is going to be us meeting Anna. And, I still feel like I shouldn't mention her to anyone, not even my dad. Apparently, my mom didn't say anything to my dad about her either, which is completely out of character for her. As far as I knew, my mom shared everything with my dad. Why did we both feel as though we needed to keep Anna a secret? What was the point?

“Maybe everything that’s happened is just hitting her hard,” I answer instead.

“Perhaps,” my dad replies, not sounding in the least bit convinced.

We continue to watch my mom and Uncle Malcolm, but know his plan isn’t working when my mom burst into tears. Uncle Malcolm looks confused by my mom’s reaction but takes her into his arms and tries to comfort her. He looks over at my dad and pleads with his eyes for help.

My dad sighs heavily and walks over. When he reaches them, Uncle Malcolm lets my mom go so my dad can take his place. The band switches to a slow song and my dad dances with my mom, whispering something in her ear that seems to calm her down. She lays her head against his chest and holds onto him tightly around his waist.

Uncle Malcolm stands off to the side, still looking confused by my mom’s reaction but knowing my dad is the only one who can help her right now. Uncle Malcolm could almost always make my mom laugh, but he knew in moments like this it was my father who my mother needed to bring her peace.

"Is your mom all right?" Aiden asks me, handing me a cup of punch I asked him to get me.

"Yes, she'll be fine," I tell him. "My dad will help her."

I look around the tent and see Mason speaking with some of the Watchers in a small group.

"When are we supposed to have the meeting?" I ask Aiden.

"As soon as everyone from town leaves," he tells me.

I only notice a handful of people from Cypress Hollow left inside the tent.

I drain my cup and turn to Aiden with my hand held out.

"Then dance with me," I tell him, not exactly asking but not exactly ordering either.

Aiden grins and puts his half-full cup of punch down on the table before taking my offered hand.

"As you wish," he says.

We dance until the band announces they need to leave, and I know my meeting with the Watchers is about to begin. I'm a little nervous about it because I'm not sure what will happen or what will be expected of me.

After the band leaves, Mason calls the Watchers together and they all stand in front of us in a staggered formation like soldiers coming to attention before their general. Flanking me on either side are Aiden, Mason, Jess, my mom and dad, and Uncle Malcolm. The vessels stand behind us because we know it's going to take all of us to do what needs to be done. Uncle Malcolm already took Will and Mae home to be watched over by Aunt Tara and Uncle Malik so we could deal with this matter.

"I've spoken with most of you already," Mason says standing in front of his men with his hands behind his back and legs slightly apart, sounding and looking the part of their leader. "And you all know what happened last night between Aiden, Caylin, and Levi."

A blonde Watcher in the front row raises his hand like he's in school requesting permission from his teacher to ask a question.

"Yes, Simon?" Mason says to the man.

"How exactly did she tear Levi's heart out, if you don't mind me asking?"

"Caylin was conceived while Brand was still a Watcher and before God's covenant with us to have children who are born completely human with our wives. Apparently, our father had a special plan for Brand and Lilly's family. Caylin wasn't only born with Lilly's archangel powers which she inherited from her father, Michael, but with our strengths too."

If the Watchers stared at me before, they were practically burning holes in me with their eyes now.

"What *exactly* is it that you want from us?" Slade asks Mason. "How can we help?"

"We have a plan to put the Princes of Hell into stasis," Mason says. "They need to remain in stasis until a girl from Caylin and Aiden's family line is born sometime in the future to take care of them once and for all."

"How far in the future?" Desmond asks.

"We don't know," Mason confesses. "But, from the vision that was shown in the vessels inner realm, it looks like it will be a very long time from now. So, I'm asking for volunteers to help us. Only seven of you will be chosen out of those who volunteer and," Mason looks over at me, "Caylin will be the one who does the choosing."

This was news to me, but I had to assume this is what Mason was talking about the night before. The part of his plan I was to play a role in.

"Now," Mason says, "I want you all to think about this very carefully and with the full knowledge that you may have to stay here on Earth for a very long time waiting for the girl to be born. If you are willing to volunteer for this mission, meet us in the desert in one hour. You all know the place."

As if on some preordained cue, all of the Watchers in front of us phase at the same time.

"Why are we meeting in a desert?" I ask Mason.

Mason turns to me. "It's our tradition. It's the place where we first came to Earth. I wanted to make sure they understood the gravity of the situation. Many of them planned to ask to become human once they fell in love and decided to start a family of their own. We're asking them to give that dream up for who knows how long. And, I can't be sure if some of those who choose to help us will die in the process."

"Why are you making me choose the seven?"

“There are seven princes who will need to be watched over until your descendant is born, and I get the feeling it’s what you’re meant to do,” Mason says. “Don’t ask me why or how I know. It could be our father influencing my thoughts, but I know it’s what needs to be done. You have to be the one who chooses the protectors of your lineage. You’re the only one who can.”

I nod, understanding the gravity of the situation.

I'm just not sure how I’m supposed to know whom to choose…

CHAPTER SIX

Aiden and I go home with my parents to wait out the hour.

When we get there, I go up to my room and change into a comfortable shirt and pair of jeans. After that, I'm not quite sure what to do with myself. I mean, what do you do while you wait to decide the fate of seven men? The burden of such a responsibility weighs heavily on my heart. Knowing that I will be asking the Watchers I choose to give up on their dream of starting families of their own for who knows how long isn't something I want to do. But, the task has been given to me whether I want it or not. I won't shirk it. I'll do what needs to be done. But, it doesn't mean I have to like it.

There's really only one thing that helps me relax.

"Would you pose for me?" I ask Aiden.

He nods as if he understands the turmoil I'm going through and is just relieved he can do something to help me.

"Of course," he says.

We walk hand in hand out to my studio. When we get inside, I have him sit at the worktable he sat at earlier in the day. I put a fresh sketchpad on my easel and grab a pencil.

"Just sit comfortably," I tell him. "I'm not trying to draw a masterpiece, just get my mind off of things."

Aiden leans his arm on the table bent at the elbow just like before and rest his cheek against the palm of his hand.

"Are you worried about what you have to do?" He asks me.

I begin sketching him and simply nod my head, not really feeling in the mood to talk a lot.

"Don't be," he says, "they all know what we're asking, and none of them are being forced to show up. That's why Mason decided to give them a choice."

"What if no one shows up?" I ask, considering this a real possibility.

"I seriously doubt that will happen," Aiden says confidently. "I don't see any of them *not* showing up. They understand what we need to do is important."

"Did Mason tell any of them that the princes stole something from Heaven?"

Aiden shakes his head. "No, he decided to wait before sharing that kind of information. I think he only wants to tell those you choose the whole story about what's really going on."

I continue to sketch Aiden and end up completely losing myself in his portrait. He barely moves as he watches me draw him, and again, I feel comforted just by his presence. As I'm shading the contours of his lips on my sketch of him, I begin to wonder why I'm not kissing those same lips at that very moment.

I look over at Aiden and feel my heart's pace quicken.

One side of Aiden's mouth quirks up into a lop-sided grin and his eyes sparkle with anticipation. I have a sneaking suspicion he knows where my thoughts have wondered off to.

I slowly lay my pencil down and walk around the easel to his side of the table. Aiden doesn't say anything, just watches me as I approach him. When I get closer, he turns to face me and spreads his legs apart knowing what it is I want without me having to say anything. I slide my arms over his shoulders and bury my fingers into his silky mass of curls, not even taking a breath before pressing my lips to his.

Aiden lets out a small moan of pleasure as I tease his mouth open with my tongue. He wraps his arms around my waist bringing our bodies even closer to one another until I'm pressed so hard against him I can feel his muscles move beneath his crisp white shirt.

I feel Aiden's hold around my waist loosen as we continue to kiss, exploring each other's mouths with soft, teasing lips. Aiden's hands begin to rub the small of my back through my shirt for a while before venturing below the hem to slide halfway up my bare back to just below my bra. I sigh from the pleasure, enjoying the feel of his hands against my flesh, but, just like earlier, he slips his hands back out from underneath my shirt and rests them on my hips.

I break our kiss to look down at him.

He opens his eyes and looks up at me like he's confused by why I've stopped kissing him.

"Why do you keep doing that?" I ask him in a whisper.

"Doing what?" He whispers back.

"Touching me then taking your hands away."

"I'm…I'm testing myself," he says, as if the admission is hard for him to make. "I don't want to go so far that I can't pull back."

I cradle the sides of Aiden's face with my hands and look him straight in the eyes to make sure he hears every word I say to him.

“How many times do I have to tell you that you won’t hurt me? I trust you, Aiden.”

“But I don’t trust myself,” he confesses. “If I ever…went too far before you were ready, I would hate myself.”

“I think you’re forgetting something,” I tell him. “I’m stronger than you. If you ever do something I’m not ready for, I can always push you away. I could probably throw you into the next county if I really wanted to. So, please, stop thinking you'll hurt me because I would never let that happen. And, honestly, I don't think you give yourself enough credit. You're stronger than you think, especially where I'm concerned.”

Aiden’s expression turns hopeful, like I’ve just said exactly what he needs to hear.

“Then kiss me, beautiful,” he says with a relaxed grin, “and let’s try this again.”

My lips melt against Aiden’s, and I feel his hands return underneath my shirt to the small of my back. I try not to sigh at the feel of his skin against mine because he seems to take that as his cue to stop touching me, something I desperately don't want him to do. I’m not sure if it’s because the sound of my contentment is more than he can take or if he fears I might become too excited and let him go further than he should. Either way, I try to control my own reaction to his caresses because I want to know what it feels like to have his hands on my body.

Aiden slides his hands over to my sides and begins to rub the sensitive skin there with gentle circular motions of his thumbs. It's a small caress but the effect it has on my body makes me yearn for more from him.

After a while, I reluctantly pull away from Aiden because his words of caution to me also had an effect. I don't want to go too fast, too soon for either of us.

I plant small kisses on both his cheeks which makes him smile. I continue to kiss him across his forehead and finally end our little make out session with a chaste kiss on the lips.

Aiden slips his hands out from under my shirt and straightens it against my hips as if he's trying to make sure everything is in its proper place.

He wraps his arms around my waist again, obviously not wanting to let me go just yet. I cradle his head against my chest and absently play with his curls.

"You're real, right?" Aiden asks me, squeezing me tighter to him as if attempting to answer his own question. "I'm not in some dream where I'll wake up and find myself in a waking nightmare where you don't exist, am I?"

"No, this isn't a dream," I tell him, wishing he felt like he deserved the happiness he's found with me instead of waiting for something bad to happen. "I'm very real, Aiden. And I'm all yours."

This time Aiden is the one who sighs in contentment and I smile.

Aiden's built in Watcher alarm clock goes off, and he tells me he needs to go home to change before the meeting.

"Change?" I ask. "Like change clothes?"

Aiden nods. "For this type of thing, we always put on our formal wear."

I suddenly remember Aunt Tara telling me about the time all the Watchers wore such an outfit.

"So you're about to go change into black leather pants, boots and a feathered cloak without a shirt on, right?" I ask, unable to stop an eager smile from lighting up my face.

"Yes," Aiden says, returning my smile with a knowing one. "Does that turn you on, beautiful?"

I let out a small nervous laugh. "I'd be lying if I said I wasn't looking forward to seeing you in it."

"Do me a favor," he says, losing his smile and turning serious. "Stay by your mother and Malcolm until I come back. I don't think the princes will try to do anything to you if they're nearby. They're cowards for the most part. They like to be the ones who do the outnumbering, not be outnumbered."

I nod. "I will. Go change and come back to me."

Aiden stands from his stool and leans down to kiss me one more time.

"Phase inside first," he urges. "Then I'll go."

"Ok," I say but instead of phasing, I raise up slightly on my toes and kiss him again.

"Don't take too long," I tell him after the kiss.

"I won't," he promises, his eyes sparkling with unadulterated happiness.

I phase into the house and find my Uncle Malcolm there speaking with my dad in the living room.

Uncle Malcolm has already changed into his formal Watcher attire and the image he makes is a little disturbing, at least it is to me. I'm sure to any other normal, red-blooded female in the world Uncle Malcolm's look would lay them out cold or force them to throw caution to the wind and jump him on the spot.

But, for me, his niece, I feel a little embarrassed for finding him attractive. Uncle Malcolm has always shown a lot of chest with his constant array of open shirts. Yet, for some reason, he looks dangerous in his Watcher wear, like a bird of prey about to devour his victim whole. Or, maybe it just seems that way to me because the Watchers who helped Levi were dressed exactly the same way. I'm not sure.

When I walk up to them, I see the same concerned look on both their faces that they had at the reception when my mother broke down into tears.

"How's mom?" I ask them. "Is she feeling any better?"

My dad sighs. "Would you mind going upstairs and speaking with her? She won't tell us anything. It's obvious something is bothering her, but she's refusing to say what exactly."

“I don't like it,” Uncle Malcolm says, his eyebrows drawing together in a frown. “It's not natural for her to be so depressed. She's acting like she did when we lost Utha Mae and Will, like someone is dead. Do you have any idea what's going on with her, Caylin?”

I ignore the question because if I don't I might give something away.

“Let me go see what I can do,” I tell them and immediately phase before Uncle Malcolm can ask me anything else.

I knock on my parents' bedroom door and hear my mother softly say, “Come in.”

When I walk into the bedroom, I find my mom sitting up on the bed hugging a pillow to her body and resting her chin on top of it. She looks over at me when I enter the room and sighs.

“Did they send you up here?” She asks me, not needing to identify who 'they' are.

“Uncle Malcolm and dad are worried about you,” I tell her, closing the door behind me and walking over to the bed to sit beside my mom. “What's wrong?”

My mom shakes her head. “I just...I just can't seem to get Anna out of my head. And the worst thing is I can't even talk about her with your dad. It's like I'm being blocked from even mentioning her to anyone but you. I'm frustrated by that and… not telling your Uncle Malcolm about his future is killing me."

"Then tell him," I say to her. "God said you were the only one who could."

"But that's just me being selfish. He doesn't need to know yet, and I refuse to be the reason he withdraws from us."

"Do you think he would?" I ask, not expecting this answer. "Do you think he would stop coming around us if he knew?"

My mom sighs again. "I don't know. Maybe. He might think it would be easier on him in the long run if he wasn't so connected to our family and able to put some distance between us before we die."

"Then don't tell him," I say resolutely. "He needs us, and we need him. Let him be happy for as long as he can be. If you love him at all, that's what you need to do. You need to sacrifice a little bit of your own happiness to make sure he keeps all of his until you have to tell him the truth. But, you need to snap out of this, Mom. You're making them both miserable."

My mom looks at me and smiles wanly.

"How did you become so wise?"

“I learned from the best,” I tell her. “Now, come on. We have a group of Watchers we need to go meet.”

“Your father and I aren't coming with you.”

I stare at my mom completely convinced I misunderstood her.

“You're not coming? Why?”

“Because this is something you need to do on your own,” she tells me. “This is your decision to make, and I don't want to be any sort of influence on who you choose.”

I understand her reasoning, but it doesn't make it any easier to swallow.

“Aiden will be there with you,” she says. “It's time the two of you start making decisions about your future together. The men you choose will be in your life and the lives of your descendants for a very long time. I have absolutely no doubt that you will make the right choices. Just listen to your heart, Caylin. It'll never steer you wrong.”

“Ok, Mom. I'll do my best.”

My mother places one of her hands on mine, which are clasped in my lap, and squeezes them reassuringly.

“You're strong. And I don't mean your physical strength. You can handle anything that's coming. Remember that, sweetie.”

I nod but don't say anything.

I hope my mother is right because I have a feeling the worst is yet to come.

CHAPTER SEVEN

My mom walks back downstairs with me with a new attitude. I find it weird that I just gave my mother advice that's actually helped her. It's usually the other way around. But, like I told her, I did learn from the best. She is the wisest woman I know, and I feel joy in the knowledge that I have apparently inherited some of her wisdom and her ability to make others see logic.

My mom stops at the foot of the stairs and my dad walks over to her. He runs a hand lovingly down her left arm, taking her hand into his.

“Are you feeling better?” He asks her, concern over her odd behavior evident on his face.

My mother gives him an easy smile, like she's finally come to peace with her decision not to tell Uncle Malcolm about his future and with her need to not mention Anna to anyone, not even my father.

“Yes, I'm better now. I'm sorry I made you worry.” My mom looks over at Uncle Malcolm. “I'm sorry I made you both worry.”

“When have we not worried about you?” Uncle Malcolm asks, not in a joking voice but completely serious.

“Well, don't,” my mother tells them both. “I'm fine now and we have more important things to concern ourselves with.”

There's a knock at the front door.

Reluctantly, my dad lets go of my mother’s hand and goes to answer it.

Aiden stands there dressed in his Watcher formal wear, which is identical in every way to Uncle Malcolm's.

I force myself not to gasp when I see him, but the picture he makes dressed the way he is makes him look like he belongs on a throne in some far off mystical kingdom. With his broad shoulders draped by the black feathered cloak and tight fitting leather pants hugging his hips and legs like a second skin, I find it impossible to take my eyes off him.

“Aiden,” my dad says, “you could have just phased inside the house.”

“I didn't want to presume I had such a privilege,” Aiden tells my dad.

“You have my permission,” my dad tells him. “You're basically a part of this family now.”

“Thank you,” Aiden says with a small, pleased grin on his face as he realizes my father has finally accepted him as a permanent fixture in our lives.

My dad steps away from the door and Aiden walks over the threshold. His eyes meet mine. A smile stretches his lips like he’s amused by something. It's only then I realize my mouth is ajar, and I’m openly gaping at him.

I clear my throat and close my mouth, feeling slightly embarrassed that he caught me ogling him. But, dear Lord, who in their right mind would blame me?

He is magnificent.

Aiden walks over to me. The heels of his knee-high boots click against the wood floor at his approach, and again, I can't help but notice how fluid his movements are.

“Are you ready?” He asks me.

“I don't think it matters if I'm ready or not,” I tell him.

He holds out one of his hands to me, and I instantly grab hold of it, finding comfort in the simple touch.

I sense Uncle Malcolm come up behind me.

"It's time," he says.

I look at my mom and dad.

"You'll do great," my dad says with absolute confidence.

I nod, not feeling as confident as he seems to be in my judgment.

I feel Aiden squeeze my hand and my home slips away as we phase.

I find myself standing on top of a dune in the middle of a desert.

The Watchers stand in front of me all dressed in their black formal wear, making a dark contrast against the white sand. Like a well-trained army, they all fall to one knee in front of me.

"Caylin," Mason says, and I look to the right of me to see Mason and Jess standing there together. "Pick your seven chosen."

I look back out at the Watchers and suddenly realize the choice isn't up to me, not really. Five of the Watchers in the group glow as though the rays of the sun above are shining down on them like a spot light. I breathe a sigh of relief because it looks like God has chosen for me. I glance behind me to look at Uncle Malcolm and see that he’s glowing as well. I had already assumed he would be but needed to make sure. I should have known God wouldn't have changed His mind about Uncle Malcolm's fate, but it was an outcome worth wishing for.

Still holding Aiden's hand, I begin to walk out among the Watchers gathered to let them know who has been selected.

The first Watcher is Desmond, Aiden's friend.

Desmond smiles as I approach him, as if he knew somehow that he would be chosen.

“I guess you need the best on your team,” he says to me with a grin as he stands to his feet. “I would have been disappointed if you hadn't picked me.”

“Then I'm glad to not disappoint you,” I tell him, and feel at ease with my first choice.

With Aiden by my side, I walk by one row of Watchers until I'm standing in front of Brutus.

“Are you willing to help us, Brutus?” I ask him, once against marveling at the girth of the man’s muscles.

Brutus stands.

"I will now and forever be at you and your family's service," Brutus promises me. "I will not fail you."

"I have absolute faith that you won't."

The next Watcher is someone I've meet a few times at my Uncle Malcolm's house, Andre Greco. Jess said he was the prettiest man she had ever met, and I couldn't disagree with her opinion. His eyes are a light blue, like the sky on a sunny winter's day. His lips are a rose petal pink and perfectly bow shaped against a complexion so clear it looks permanently airbrushed.

As I approach Andre, he smiles at me and stands.

"I assumed you would need me," he says, a slight Italian accent bending his words. "I won't let either of you down. You have my word on that."

"I know you won't let us down," I tell him.

I look over to the man kneeling beside Andre, our fourth chosen. He's one I haven't met before in person, but I know who he is. He's in charge of the Chinese Watcher Headquarters in Beijing. I assume he was placed in charge of China because the form he chose to come to Earth in is Chinese.

"Will you help us, Daniel?"

Daniel stands to his feet, and I'm faintly surprised at how tall he is.

"My life is yours to command, Caylin. I am here to serve you in whatever capacity you need me to."

"Thank you," I say, looking between the two men. "Thank you both."

I look to the back of the group of Watchers and see Slade staring at me.

One side of his mouth lifts as Aiden and I make our way to him. I see him smile sardonically because he knows what's coming.

As Aiden and I walk over to him, I hear Aiden whisper, "Are you sure?"

I glance at him before returning my attention to Slade.

"Yes," I tell him, "I'm sure."

"I guess I should have known you would need someone with some pretty big guns to help protect your family," Slade says, standing to his feet and lifting his arms up bent at the elbows as he kisses each of his massive biceps as if they're precious to him.

It's only in this partially unclothed state that I notice the intricate tattoo work covering Slade's left shoulder and arm down to the elbow. It looks like a tribal tattoo of some sort, but I'm not an expert in such things.

"Well, I hope you can put them to good use for us," I say, amused by his obvious love for himself.

"Don't you worry, little lady," Slade says with a wink and an over confident grin. "I'll do what needs to be done."

I turn to Aiden.

"Who's missing?" I ask him. "Because the last one isn't here."

Aiden looks confused. Obviously, he thought all of the Watchers were present. He looks around, taking inventory of those around us then sighs as he realizes who didn't show up.

"Jered isn't here," he says. "He probably didn't think he would be chosen after what happened last night. Plus, Malcolm hasn't exactly been shy about telling him just how incompetent he thinks he is."

"Then he must be the last one," I tell Aiden, tugging on his hand to follow me back to where Mason, Jess and Uncle Malcolm are still standing on top of the dune.

“How do you know that exactly?” Aiden asks, sounding mystified by my ability to pick and choose among the Watchers.

“They’re glowing,” I whisper, not wanting to be overheard by those we’re walking past.

“Are you serious?” Aiden asks, sounding like he thinks I’m making a joke.

“Yes,” I say, looking over at him. “I can see them glowing. That’s why it was so easy for me to pick them out. I think God chose them for me.”

“Doesn’t really sound like something He would do,” Aiden says, slightly confused by God’s participation in such a monumental event. “He normally stays out of most of our decision making.”

“Well, all I know is what I see. I just need to find Jered and see if he glows too. Then we’ll know for sure.”

“Is Malcolm glowing to you?”

“Yes.”

“What are you going to do when he asks where the seventh one is?”

“I’m not sure,” I say, hoping I can find a way without having to blatantly lie to my Uncle Malcolm.

When we come to stand in front of Mason, I ask, “Do you know where Jered is?”

“Are you serious?” Uncle Malcolm almost explodes. “He can’t possibly be one, Caylin!”

“I need to see him to be sure,” I reply, trying to be the calm before Uncle Malcolm's storm. “But I’m pretty positive he’ll be one.”

“Even if he is, that only gives you six,” Uncle Malcolm points out, making me cringe inwardly because I know he’s going to want an explanation about why I’m only choosing six Watchers.

I had hoped the question of the seventh one would be asked much later.

“Who is your seventh?” Uncle Malcolm asks directly.

“Maybe we only need six,” Jess answers for me, and I silently thank her. “We have no way of knowing when Levi will retake a body and who knows where Lucifer is or when he’ll show back up.”

“So what are the ones I chose supposed to do with the princes exactly?”

“We’ll discuss the details later with the ones you’ve chosen,” Mason says to me. “Right now you need to go see Jered. Aiden,” Mason looks at Aiden, “take Caylin to Jered’s cabin in Montana. He’ll probably be in the barn. He usually likes to take care of the horses when something is bothering him. While you handle that, I’ll gather the ones you’ve picked and take them to our villa. Meet us there when you’re done.”

“Ready?” Aiden asks.

“Yes.”

Aiden phases us and I find myself standing inside a rather large barn. It’s warm considering the time of year it is, and I have to assume there’s a heating system keeping it such a comfortable temperature. I hear the sound of a horse chomping on something solid come from one of the stalls, which has its door open.

“Easy does it, Samson,” I hear Jered say in a calm, soothing voice.

With Aiden by my side, we walk hand in hand up to the stall where Jered is.

“Jered,” Aiden calls out to give the man some warning of our approach.

Jered steps to the doorway of the stall and stares at us in confusion as we walk up to him. To say he looks stunned by our presence is an understatement.

"What are the two of you doing here?" Jered asks.

"You didn't come to us so we had to come to you," I tell him as I stare at the glow surrounding him.

"But…why?" He asks, still mystified by our presence.

"Because you're meant to help us," I tell him. "I choose you, Jered, to be one of the Watchers to protect my family."

Jered shakes his head.

"You don't want me," he says vehemently. "You could choose someone a lot better."

"Are you refusing to help us?" I ask.

"No, but why would you want me?" Jered says, doubly confused. "I've already failed you once. How do you know I won't fail you again? Why risk it?"

"It's not a risk," I tell him. "And I think the only person you need to prove yourself to here is you, Jered. I have faith in you."

"But why?"

“Call it a gut instinct,” I say, feeling that I shouldn’t mention the whole “glowing of the chosen” to too many people. “Will you help my family or not, Jered?”

Jered sighs deeply and looks down at the straw strewn haphazardly across the stall’s floor. He stuffs his hands in the front pockets of his jeans and remains silent for a time.

I patiently wait for him to come to terms with what I’m asking of him. Finally, he lifts his gaze to meet mine.

“All right,” he says. “I promise I’ll do my best for your family. I won’t fail you this time. I solemnly swear that to you.”

“I know you won’t fail us,” I tell him.

“So, what now?” Jered asks. “What do you need me to do?”

“You’ve been to Jess and Mason’s villa, right?” Aiden asks.

Jered nods. “Yes, I’ve been there many times over the past few years.”

“Mason is gathering up the others and taking them there. You should probably go ahead and phase to join the ones who have already been chosen.”

Jered nods and phases.

Aiden turns to me.

"Are you ready to hear the rest of Mason's plan?"

"Do I have a choice?"

Aiden grins. "No, I guess not."

"Then let's go so we can find out what needs to be done next."

Aiden takes the lead and phases us, but I don't make it to the villa with him.

I end up somewhere else.

I find myself standing on a patch of greener than green grass within a lush forest. The thundering screech of a large animal in the sky above instinctively makes me look up. Flying in the air as if playing with one another is an array of colorful dragons.

I know where I am.

The Garden of Eden.

The only reason I know it so well is because my father painted a mural of it in Mae's room.

"Hello, Caylin," I hear a familiar voice say to me.

When I look to my left, I see God standing beside me looking up at His creations as they fly over us high in the sky.

This is the first time God has ever wanted to speak with me one on one. Most of our conversations have always been in the presence of my parents. The only member of my family He ever wanted private conversations with was my mother.

“Why have you brought me here?” I ask.

God looks over at me with a closed lip yet understanding smile.

“I thought you might want to ask me something.”

“Why did you take the choosing of the seven out of my control?” I ask Him because I did want to know the answer to that particular question.

Aiden was right when he said God usually didn’t make our decisions for us. So, what was different about the choosing of the seven? Did He not trust my judgment?

“I didn’t choose them. They chose themselves.”

Now, I’m even more confused.

“What do you mean they chose themselves?”

“You were able to see their desire to be a part of your quest. That’s why they glowed to your eyes. Over all of those present, the seven of them wanted you to choose them the most.”

"But," I pause to think because one thing doesn't make sense, "Uncle Malcolm glowed."

"Yes, he did."

"He wants to stay?"

"It's not so much that he wants to stay here on Earth after your mother's passing, but Malcolm has always felt a need to protect her and her family. Deep down I think he knows he will need to stay until Anna is born. He just doesn't want to face that decision yet. He doesn't trust anyone else to do the job as well as he can. He fears the others will fail if he isn't here to lead them."

"Why can't my mother and I talk about Anna to anyone? My mom is having a hard time keeping her a secret from my dad. She feels like she's lying to him by not being able to mention her."

"I don't want Anna's identity revealed. Tell your mother she can speak about the child she met to your father, but she will not be able to reveal her name to anyone, neither will you."

"Why?"

"Because if you tell your chosen her name, they will keep waiting for an Anna to be born or worse yet they will keep trying to influence the name choice. So, you may speak of the girl but never say her name to anyone but your mother."

I nod, letting him know I understand.

It was better than nothing, and I hoped it would bring my mother some much needed peace.

"Now, go meet with your men," God tells me. "You all have a lot of work to do."

I look around me one more time because I have no way of knowing if I'll ever see the Garden of Eden again in my lifetime.

Just as I phase, I hear God say, "Be strong, Caylin."

What exactly was that supposed to mean?

CHAPTER EIGHT

As soon as I phase into the living room of Jess and Mason's Villa, Aiden is by my side.

"Where have you been?" He asks me, taking me into his arms and hugging me so tight, I'm not sure he ever intends to let me go. "You didn't have a phase trail for me to follow. I thought…"

"God needed to speak with me," I tell him, making sure he understands I was perfectly safe.

Aiden kisses the top of my head. His lips linger there for a long time before he finally loosens his hold enough for me to pull back from him slightly. The worried expression on his face breaks my heart, and I can only guess at what horrible scenarios his mind conjured up after my disappearance.

"What did my father want to speak to you about?" Aiden asks.

"He explained the choosing to me," I say in a whisper, knowing the others are nearby and not wanting them to hear more than they should. "And to tell me we have a lot of work left to do."

I look at the others in the room and see that everyone is present. I direct my gaze to Mason and Jess.

"I think it's time we learned exactly what your plan is," I say.

"Then why don't you all sit down while we explain," Mason tells the others in the room.

Everyone takes a seat either in one of the armchairs or the sofas. Aiden and I sit side by side on the couch facing the fireplace, which is lit, and crackling with warmth.

Mason goes on to explain to the Watchers how we intend to have Brutus make daggers from the remnants of the archangel crowns with Zack's daggers.

"That's where the rest of you come in and why I asked Caylin to choose you. Each of you will be given the responsibility of hiding one of the princes after he is placed into stasis, and you can never tell anyone where you've hidden him. You will each need to protect your prince until Caylin's descendant is born and is ready to take care of them."

"So why do we have to wait for this girl to be born?" Brutus asks. "Why not just find a way to kill them once we place them into stasis with the daggers?"

"Because our father needs something back from them that only she can retrieve, apparently."

"What could He possibly need from them?" Andre asks.

Mason pauses and looks at the group of angels around him.

"They stole something from Heaven after the war and our father wants it back."

No one says anything.

Finally, Jered asks, "Stole what exactly?"

"Yeah," Slade says, leaning back in the chair he's sitting in, and absently rubbing his left arm where the tattoo is, "if they stole something wouldn't we have known about it?"

"Are you saying God is lying?" Mason asks him.

Slade rolls his eyes. "Of course not. It just seems odd that none of us have ever heard about this theft."

"Maybe it was something God knew none of us could do anything about until now," Desmond says. "And we still can't really do anything, apparently, except set the stage for Caylin's descendent to do the real work."

"Do we know how she's supposed to take back what they stole?" Slade asks.

"No, not exactly," Mason admits. "But she will be born and she will stop them from doing something catastrophic according to our father. All we can do is make sure we keep them safe until the time comes for the girl to take care of them."

"So, Brutus is making the daggers?" Daniel asks.

"Yes," Jess replies. "We've already set that up to happen tomorrow. We feel it's important for all of you to be there when it happens. All of the vessels are coming to help as well."

"So we're assuming this will work," Desmond says, "but what if it doesn't? Do we have a contingency plan?"

"Not really," Mason admits. "But I don't have any doubts about this working."

"Is there anything else we need to know?" Andre asks.

"There's nothing else to tell," Jess says. "You all know about as much as we do now."

"So, after these daggers are made," Andre says, "I suppose we need to test them out?"

"Yes," Mason says. "Malcolm and I have talked about it. We need to draw out one of the weaker princes so we can test one of the daggers on him."

"And how do you plan to do that?" Aiden asks, but something in his voice makes me think he already knows the answer to his question, and he's not happy about the answer that's coming.

"We're going to use Caylin as bait," Mason says.

"No," Aiden says with such finality that a lesser man would have simply let the subject drop.

"There's not a better way to draw him out and take him off guard," Mason says as he turns his gaze to me.

"She shouldn't have to risk her life," Aiden says. "It's not right."

"She'll be guarded," Uncle Malcolm says. "We won't be so far away from her that we can't act quickly. Do you honestly think I would put her in any real danger?"

"Is anyone here going to ask me what my opinion on the subject is?" I ask, feeling like my fate was being decided for me without my consent yet again.

Aiden squeezes the hand he still holds, and I look over at him, my heart breaking from the worry on his face.

"I don't want you to put your life in danger," he says, and I can almost hear him begging me to say I won't do what they want.

"Nothing's going to happen to me," I tell him. "Remember, I've already seen our future. I'll be all right."

I look over at Mason and Uncle Malcolm.

"Have you picked a prince to test?"

"Yes. Belphagor will be the easiest to trap."

"The prince of sloth," Slade says derisively. "She's in no danger then. I could probably knock him out with my pinky toe."

"When do you want to do it?" I ask.

"We'll make the daggers tomorrow and test the first one on Belphagor on Monday. We've had Watchers tracking his movements and know his routine. I don't foresee any problems that we'll have to contend with. It shouldn't take very long."

"Good," I say. "The sooner we take them all down the sooner Aiden and I can start our future together."

"How did *you* end up with someone as wonderful as her?" Desmond asks Aiden in a friendly, teasing manner. "You know you don't deserve her right?"

"So you keep telling me," Aiden says in mock irritation.

"Well, I don't do it often," Slade says, "but I have to agree with the leprechaun about this one. You don't deserve someone so … *good.*"

"Anyone else want to tell me how much I don't deserve Caylin?" Aiden asks in exasperation.

"Well we could," Andre says with a sly grin, "but what would be the point in being so repetitive?"

I giggle because I know they're all just teasing Aiden. Unmercifully? Yes. But all in good fun.

"Jealousy doesn't become you, gentlemen," Aiden replies, giving back a little of what he's getting. "And if we're through here, I think I should take Caylin back home so she can tell her parents what's happened. I'm sure they're worried."

Aiden and I stand.

Jess comes over to me and gives me a hug.

"We'll be over tomorrow afternoon to get you," Jess tells me.

She stands back from me and smiles, but I can tell it's forced. She's worried about me and can't seem to hide it. I wouldn't want her to. It shows me how much she cares.

"I'll see you all tomorrow," I say to the group at large.

Everyone says good-bye and I squeeze Aiden's hand.

"Ready?" I ask him.

He nods and I phase us.

I phase us home, but I make a slight detour and phase us to my studio first.

I don't have to tell Aiden why I've brought us here. He instantly wraps his arms around me, and I melt against him. I need to feel him. I need to be alone with him for just a little while before I have to go inside and explain everything that's happened to my folks.

I bury my head against his chest and take in a deep breath.

"How are you doing?" Aiden asks, worry for me in his voice.

"I'll be fine," I say, not moving my forehead from his chest, just closing my eyes and feeling him, soaking in his nearness like a dry sponge does water.

"I just want things to be over," I say. "But I have a feeling things have just begun, especially after what God said to me."

"What do you mean?" Aiden asks. "Did He say something to you that you didn't tell us about?"

I lift my head from Aiden's chest and look up at him.

"Right before I phased he said 'be strong'. It sounded…ominous."

"He probably meant it to be encouraging," Aiden tells me, trying to smile. "My father has never been very good at *not* sounding ominous when He speaks."

I decide not to say any more about it. Aiden's worried enough about my welfare. I don't need to add to it.

"I just need one more thing before we go inside," I tell Aiden, leaning against him and wrapping my arms around his neck.

"Wow, it's really hard to read you sometimes," he says with a playful smile.

"I know. I'm such a closed book to you, but I'm trying to open up a little."

Aiden chuckles and lowers his head until our lips meet.

The kiss is gentle, not one meant to evoke a passionate response. It's more a physical pledge of our love for one another.

We don't linger long over the kiss because I need to go tell my parents what's happened.

And the sooner I tell my mom about Uncle Malcolm and Anna the better.

When we phase into the house, I find my dad in the kitchen preparing supper, and my mom and Mae in the living room putting a large floor puzzle of a fantasy castle together. They both immediately stop what they're doing when they see us. My mom picks Mae up and my dad turns off the stove. I sit them both down at the dining table and tell them what happened.

"It's a good plan," my dad says. "But I'm a bit surprised by some of your choices. I never thought you would pick Slade or Jered."

"Why?" I ask.

"Well, Slade can be rather annoying, and Jered is new to being trustworthy."

"I didn't tell the others this," I say, "but God told me the reason they glowed was because they were the ones who wanted to be chosen the most."

"Maybe you inherited something from your grandfather that let you see how they felt," my mom suggests. "You know Jess is able to see auras surrounding certain people. That could be the reason you saw them glow."

“I didn’t think about that as being the reason but it makes sense. And mom,” I say, “Uncle Malcolm glowed too.”

My mother is silent for a moment as if digesting this new bit of information.

“You’re sure?” She finally asks, tears coming to her eyes. “He wants to stay?”

“God said he probably hasn’t admitted it to himself yet, but that he feels like no one else can do the job of keeping our family safe like he can. I don’t think he realizes he’s already made the decision. So, stop feeling guilty about having to ask him to stay because I think he’s already mentally preparing himself to do it after you die.”

My mother does cry, but they’re relieved tears this time, not sad one.

“I guess I should have known he wouldn’t trust anyone else to protect your family. My asking him to do it is probably just a formality to let him know the decision he’s already made is the right one.”

“Yes, I think so too.”

I fall silent because I can’t think of anything else to say.

"Well," my dad says, taking my silence as his cue, "do you know how to cook, Aiden?"

"Uh," Aiden looks confused by the unexpected question. "Can't say I've done much of it."

My dad stands from his chair. "Then why don't you go change clothes and come back. I'll give you a quick lesson. You're going to need it if you plan on marrying my daughter one day."

"And... why is that exactly?" Aiden asks, even more confused.

"Because, unfortunately, my daughter inherited her mother's proficiency in the kitchen. If the two of you intend to ever eat or feed your children, at least one of you needs to know how to cook and not burn your home down."

"Dad," I say, drawing out the word and feeling completely mortified by him revealing one of my shortfalls to the love of my life.

Aiden wasn't supposed to know about my imperfections so soon, at least that was the way I thought about it anyway.

Aiden looks at me and smiles.

“Then I guess cooking lessons will be helpful,” he says. “I’ll go change.”

Mentally, I’m thinking “do you have to change?” Because I really like looking at Aiden in his princely outfit. But, I guess a black feathered cloak isn’t exactly the safest thing to wear near a gas stove. Though, I don’t see anything wrong with him just taking it off and cooking half naked. What would be wrong with that?

“I’ll be right back,” Aiden says to me before phasing.

My dad returns to the kitchen and mom, Mae and I go back to finish the floor puzzle in the living room.

“Mom,” I say in a whisper as we’re sitting on the floor across from one another, “God told me you could tell dad about meeting Anna, but neither of us will be allowed to mention her name to anyone.”

I go on to explain why He’s laid down that particular rule.

“It makes sense He wouldn’t want them to know her name,” my Mom says after my explanation. “And thank you for telling me. I hate not sharing everything with your father. It makes me feel like I’m lying to him.”

"Have you always shared everything?" I ask. "Isn't there anything you've kept secret from him?"

"No, not really," my mother says. "Though there were a few things concerning your Uncle Malcolm I wish I had kept to myself."

"Like what?" I ask, completely intrigued by this little window into my mother's past with Uncle Malcolm.

"It's probably not something I should tell you," my mother says, looking uncomfortable all of a sudden.

"Why? Is it that bad? What did the two of you do?" I ask, my mind racing with the possibilities.

"Well, it's nothing *that* bad," my mother says, obviously sensing my mind is coming up with things far worse than reality.

"I let your Uncle Malcolm kiss me a long time ago before your father and I were married. It was one of the few things I wish I had kept to myself."

"Well...how was it?" I ask, finding this new piece of information about my mother's past extremely interesting. "And did dad go ballistic when he found out?"

"I'm not going to lie and say the kiss wasn't... interesting. But no one can make me feel like your father does with a simple kiss. And your dad made it known to your Uncle Malcolm that such a thing would not be tolerated again."

I have a hard time wrapping my mind around the fact that my mom and Uncle Malcolm kissed in a romantic way. Over the years, I've seen them kiss each other's cheeks, but those kisses were innocent and quick, simply meant as a show of affection.

"Was dad the first boy you kissed?" I ask.

"No, he wasn't the first."

"Who was?"

"My friend Will."

My brother's namesake wasn't mentioned very often. I think it hurt my mother too much to think about him. From what I understood, he sacrificed himself in an attempt to stop Lucifer from taking control of her body. As an ordinary rebellion angel, Will simply wasn't strong enough to stop Lucifer. But, apparently his self-sacrifice garnered him a special place back in Heaven.

So, my mother has kissed three men in her life while I will only have kissed one in mine. Honestly, I'm ok with that. I can't imagine anyone even coming close to making me feel the way Aiden does when he kisses me. He is the only man I will ever kiss and the only man I will share my heart with. I lift my hand to the crystal pendant around my neck and start swaying it back and forth along its chain, thinking about the one who gave it to me.

Aiden phases back into the house, standing behind the chair he was sitting in at the dining table before he left. He's dressed simply in a pair of jeans and a white V-neck t-shirt. How can someone look just as good with clothes on as he did half-dressed?

"Ahh, just in time to watch me make the pasta," my dad says to him waving Aiden into the kitchen.

Aiden looks over at me and smiles. I can tell he likes the fact that my father is taking the time to show him how to cook for us. And a small part of me is guiltily thankful that he's willing to learn. I love to eat but hate to cook. And, my father is right. I did not inherit his innate ability to whip up something even coming close to being remotely edible.

My father even taught Uncle Malcolm how to cook once upon a time, which was a miracle unto itself. A miracle they both survived the ordeal anyway.

Supper turns out to be one of my father's simpler meals: spaghetti with meatballs and homemade tomato sauce, salad and knot yeast rolls. My mother has to drag my brother Will away from his video game, but finally we're all sitting around the table as a family and eating supper together.

It feels right to have Aiden with us. It's almost like he's always been a part of our family.

After the meal, Aiden and I clean up, allowing my parents to spend some time with Mae and Will. As I hand the dishes to Aiden to place them in the racks in the dishwasher, I can't help but feel at peace by doing such a menial chore with him. It's something a couple would do together and further proof, to me at least, that we belong with one another.

While I'm wiping down the countertops with a rag, Aiden leans against the kitchen island and asks, "Would you like to go out on a real date tomorrow night?"

I stop what I'm doing and look over at him.

"Do you think we'll have time?"

Aiden shrugs. "I don't see why not. Making the daggers shouldn't take all day. And I owe you a do over date considering how our last one ended."

"That wasn't your fault," I tell him.

"I know. But, it wasn't exactly the way I imagined our first date ending either."

"And how exactly did you see it ending?"

Aiden smiles. "I saw it ending with you in my arms kissing me until I almost reached my breaking point. I have hopes that's the way this one will end."

"Then I accept your invitation," I tell him. "And I guess we'll see if it ends the way you imagine."

"I don't have any doubts that it will," he says rather cockily.

I smile back at him. "Well, now I'm just going to have to make you work for it."

"Will I enjoy this work?"

I shrug. "Depends I guess."

"Then I look forward to any challenge you set in my path," he tells me. "There isn't anything that I won't do to have you just the way I see you in my mind by the end of the evening."

"How should I dress?"

"Dress up. I want to take you somewhere nice, beautiful."

I smile. Every time Aiden calls me 'beautiful', it makes my heart sing. And for him to want to take me on a real date, shows me how much he cares for me and wants to treat me with the respect I deserve.

"But, right now, I should be going," Aiden announces. "You and your family will probably want to get to bed soon."

I don't want him to go, but I know he's right. I'm not sure what all tomorrow will entail, but I do know it will end well. Of that, I have no doubt, no doubt at all.

Aiden says his goodnights to my family, and I walk him out to the front porch. There's no way I'm letting him leave without him kissing me first. In my mind, it's imperative that we make that a necessity anytime we separate.

Once we finally pull apart, Aiden says, "You do make it hard to leave you."

"Good," I say. "Because I don't want you to ever think it's easy on me either."

Aiden smiles and kisses me gently on the lips.

"I'll see you tomorrow, beautiful. Sweet dreams."

Aiden phases and I stand there determined to fill my dreams with a certain angel.

CHAPTER NINE

The next morning Mason brings Leah and Joshua over to have breakfast with us. I'm thankful to him for knowing I would need my friends close by me that day.

Mason tells me, "Jess and I are high-jacking your boyfriend for some actual work this morning. So I thought Leah and Joshua could make up for him not being here."

"What work?" I ask.

"Hunter."

I don't need any more clarification than that. I know what they intend to do with the changeling who took over Hunter's identity. The Hunter Manning I knew doesn't exist anymore, and I am more than happy to see the demon who killed him pay for what he did to a decent guy who just happened to fall in love with the wrong girl.

"Good luck," I tell Mason, giving him my full blessing.

Mason nods, not needing to say anything else about the matter.

While we're at the table eating the buttermilk-chocolate chip pancakes my father made for breakfast, I get a text message on my phone from Aiden.

Sorry I couldn't come over this morning, but Mason told me he explained things to you. Have you picked out what you will wear tonight?

Uh, no. But I've got it handled

I'm sure whatever you wear you will look beautiful, Beautiful. Was that too redundant?

Absolutely not! Say it as many times as you want...

Ok, Beautiful...See you later

"Mom, do you think JoJo would mind me calling her?" I ask.

"No," my mom says, taking her plate of pancakes from my dad, "but why do you need to speak with her?"

“Aiden is taking me out tonight, and I want something new to wear. JoJo has the best clothes.”

“You know she’s not your own personal closet,” my mom says.

“Honestly?” Leah says. “I tried to buy a dress once and JoJo heard about it. She called me crying, Ms. Lilly. She thought I didn’t like her designs anymore. So, don’t think you’re bothering her by asking her for clothes. She gets really emotional if you *don’t*.”

My mom laughs. “Well, since you put it that way, Leah. I guess you had better call her, Caylin. We certainly don’t want our little French seamstress to have her feelings hurt.”

I find JoJo’s number on my phone and call.

“Mon Cher,” JoJo says when she answers, “what is wrong?”

Odd that she would automatically assume something is wrong.

“Nothing’s wrong, JoJo. I just need a dress for a date with Aiden tonight.”

“Oh!” She says excitedly. “Come, come then. I am at my studio in New York.”

“Have you eaten breakfast yet?” I ask.

"Uh, no, Mon Ami. Why do you ask?"

"I'll bring you something then."

"Oh, Brand cooked? I am salivating already. Hurry, hurry!"

"Be right there."

My father obviously heard my promise to JoJo. He quickly makes her a plate for me to take.

"Do you want to go with us?" I ask my mom.

"No, I told your Aunt Tara I would watch Ella and Linc while she and Malik took care of something this morning. You kids go ahead."

Joshua and Leah hold hands and Leah lays her free hand on my shoulder.

I phase us to JoJo's New York studio and find her alone in the large open space. Bolts of fabric and vacant worktables dot the area. A large glass wall faces toward Central Park giving the room an almost outdoorsy feel.

"Do you ever do anything but work?" I ask JoJo as we walk over to her worktable. I see she's designing a pantsuit on one of her headless mannequins.

"Idle hands are the devil's playground," JoJo jokes. "And Lord knows that man can have a field day."

JoJo's eyes fall to the plate in my hands.

"Oh! Pancakes! I do so love them."

I set the plate on her table, and she immediately takes the clear wrap off and lifts the plate to her delicate little nose, inhaling the aroma.

"Heaven!" She says with a giggle. "Pure Heaven!"

We let JoJo eat her meal, and I fill the three of them in on what happened the day before. We're in no rush. And to be honest, I don't want to stop and think about what Aiden, Mason, and Jess are doing right at that very moment. I want Hunter's murderer destroyed, but I definitely don't want to know the details. The less I think about it the better.

After JoJo is through, I ask, "So what amazing creation do you have for me to wear?"

JoJo crooks her little finger at me, and we walk into a separate room where there are a line of mannequins displaying a myriad of dresses.

“Every young woman needs a little black dress,” JoJo tells me, walking to one of the mannequins.

It’s wearing a sleeveless, seam-sculpted dress with cutouts on the neckline and a center front slit at the bottom.

“It’s gorgeous and simple,” I say, walking around the dress and seeing that there is a long zipper in the back.

“How come you’ve been giving Caylin such grown up clothes lately and still have me dressing like Mary Poppins?” Leah complains, obviously envying me for getting such a … well… sexy dress.

“Because you are still too young for such a dress. Caylin is practically a woman.”

“I wouldn’t mind you wearing a dress like that,” Joshua says, eyeing the dress with undisguised interest.

“Which is exactly why I will not be designing such a dress for Leah any time soon,” JoJo says resolutely. “She is too young for you to be drooling all over her.”

“So you don’t mind Aiden drooling all over Caylin?” Leah asks, seeing this as a double standard.

"Aiden is a man who can control himself," JoJo says. "Joshua is a regular human boy who thinks with his hormones first instead of reason. So, no, I do not mind Aiden drooling after Caylin because I know he will behave like a gentleman with her. Joshua… sorry my little love…but you are simply too young and human to be trusted completely."

I have to smile at JoJo's sense of logic because it's very true. "Thanks, JoJo. I'll take it."

JoJo puts it into a hanging bag for me to take back home.

"So you'll be there when we make the daggers this afternoon?" I ask JoJo. "That's what they told me last night. That all the vessels will be there to help."

"Oh yes, Mon Cher. I will be there. I have made something for the daggers and for the other Watchers."

"What did you make for the Watchers?"

"Smaller versions of the protective anklets. Since the princes know what they do, it was decided something else should be done to protect them."

"What do you mean?"

JoJo looks uncertain. “I’m not sure it is my place to tell you, Mon Ami. Perhaps you should ask Mason or your Uncle Malcolm that question.”

I wasn’t sure I liked the look on JoJo’s face. Why did she look so apprehensive in telling me what the plan was? What was so terrible that she thought maybe it was better if I didn’t know?

Right after lunch, Aiden, Mason, and Jess phase into our living room.

I walk over to Aiden and wrap my arms around his waist.

“Did you have any trouble finding the changeling?” I ask him.

“No. He barely put up a fight,” Aiden reassures me, kissing the top of my head.

“Everything is ready,” Jess tells my parents. “Hopefully, it won’t take very long to make the daggers.”

“I’ll go with you,” my dad says. “Lilly will stay here with the kids.”

“Are you ready?” Aiden asks me as I take a step away from him.

“Yes. I want to put all of this in the past as soon as possible.”

I walk over to the kitchen island and grab the box with the remnants of the archangel crowns.

Aiden takes my hand when I walk back to him and phases us.

I soon find myself standing in Brutus' workshop on his island. It's a large wood building with massive double doors at the front facing the blue-green waters of the Mediterranean Sea and shuttered openings along the walls to let the cool ocean breeze flow through the open space.

My chosen Watchers are already present talking amongst themselves, at least most of them. Jered seems to be the odd man out and standing by the open doors looking towards the sea.

"Brand!" Desmond says, walking over to my father and shaking his hand. "I'm glad you came today. We haven't seen you much lately. You're looking happy and.... older...."

My dad smiles. "Happens when you turn mortal, Desmond."

"Ahh well, guess I won't know anything about that for a while yet."

"No," my dad says, almost looking sorry for Desmond. "I guess you won't."

"Pfft, mortality," Slade says, "completely overrated."

“Not everyone is cut out for it,” my father agrees.

“Well, after this last mission is over,” Daniel says, “I plan to do what you and Mason have done: find someone, settle down and have a family. I can’t think of anything I want more from this life.”

“I have a feeling it will be a long time before any of us can think about doing that, my friend,” Andre says.

“It’ll probably take that long just for you miscreants to find women who will put up with you,” Uncle Malcolm tells them with a teasing grin.

“You’re one to talk,” Slade says. “I’m not sure there'll ever be a woman born who you’ll love more than your own ego. She would have to be a saint or something.”

“I have no desire to fall in love,” Uncle Malcolm proclaims. “It’s not exactly a goal in my life. Besides, it’s not like I have trouble finding companionship when I want it.”

“Like your latest one?” Desmond asks. “Haven't I seen her on the cover of some magazine?”

“Seems like all of your *companions* are models or actresses. Ever thought about dating an ordinary human?” Daniel says.

"When did this become a time to delve into my love life?" Uncle Malcolm complains. "I think we have more important things to concern ourselves with. Where are the vessels?"

"They're at our home in Cypress Hollow," Mason says. "I'll be right back with them."

Mason leans over and kisses Jess on the cheek. "Be right back. Keep the boys in line if you can."

"I'm not a miracle worker," Jess grumbles.

Mason winks at her and phases.

I look over at Jered to see that he is still looking out towards the sea, seeming intent on ignoring the teasing the others enjoy so much.

"I'll be right back," I tell Aiden, letting him know I want to speak with Jered alone.

As I reach Jered's side, he drags his eyes away from the crashing waves along the rocky shoreline and looks over at me.

"Are you sure you made the right choice by choosing me, Caylin?" He asks, still looking unsure of himself. "I'm just not like the others."

"And you say that like it's a bad thing," I tell him which makes him chuckle. "Yes, I made the right choice picking you. Stop second guessing yourself, Jered."

"I'll try to stop," he promises. "But it's become my nature to second guess myself. If I had done more of it sooner, maybe I wouldn't have been on the wrong side at the beginning of this fight."

I couldn't argue against that logic.

"But, you found your way back from that," I remind him. "It takes a lot of strength to want to become a better person. Look at Aiden. He did it, and now he's happier than he's ever been. It can happen for you too, if that's what you want. I think you're stronger than you give yourself credit for being, Jered. Stop doubting yourself so much because I don't have any doubts in you."

Jered smiles wanly, and I can tell he's pleased by my praise, but I fear it will take a long time before he truly believes in his own judgment again.

I notice Mason phase in with the rest of the vessels. All of them have their respective talismans with them.

I sigh because I suddenly have a sinking feeling that making the daggers won't be as easy as they seem to think it will be.

“Are you ok?” Jered asks me. “You seem worried about something.”

“I just hope this works,” I confide. “The plan seems too easy, and if I've learned anything about our lives, it's that nothing comes without a price.”

“Sometimes the easiest path is actually the right one.”

I look at him and raise my eyebrows at him. “Do you really believe that or are you just saying it for my benefit?”

Jered chuckles. “I’m going to plead the fifth on that question.”

“Yeah, that’s what I thought,” I sigh.

“It’ll work,” Jered says, turning to face the others as I look at them too. “You have a blessed life. I have a feeling things will go as planned.”

I nod, hoping Jered is right.

“Leah,” Brutus says, “come over here please.”

Leah walks over to Brutus who is standing beside a large stone forge.

“Caylin,” he says to me, “bring the box with the crown pieces please.”

Once we're both there he instructs us further.

"Now, place the box on the coals," he tells me.

"But the box is wooden," I say, completely confused. "Won't it just burn up in the fire?"

"It's an artifact from Heaven," Brutus tells me. "It won't simply burn up like an ordinary box would. I believe it will be strong enough to withstand Leah's fire."

Trusting his knowledge about such a thing, I place the box on the coals within the fire pit of the forge and flip the lid open.

"Leah, are you able to control the intensity of your fire at all?"

Leah nods. "Yes, I can control it a lot better now than when I first learned what I could do."

"Good, then start a slow burn and let's see what happens."

Leah points the palm of her hand toward the fire pit and a stream of orange flames issue forth, enveloping the box. I watch, much like everyone else, to see if the silver crown pieces begin to melt. Unfortunately, they don't.

"Make it hotter," Brutus tells her. "Keep making it hotter until you can't anymore."

Leah nods and continues to heat the box. Five minutes pass before Leah says, “That’s as hot as I can make it.”

Still, the crown pieces haven’t melted.

“Well,” Slade says, “we could always gut the princes and stuff the pieces inside them, might actually be more fun.”

“Wait,” Jess says, pulling out her sword from the baldric on her back. “We have one more thing to try.”

Jess goes to stand beside Leah, her sword igniting with orange flames. She places the blade of her sword into Leah’s fire stream. Where Jess’ sword meets Leah’s flames, the fire turns blue.

I look back at the silver pieces in the box and see them begin to melt.

“Zack!” Brutus says, waving him over. “Make a dagger and drop it into the silver.”

Zack walks over to Brutus and rubs his right hand over the dagger tattoo on his left arm, magically pulling out a real dagger. He stands next to the forge and drops it into the silver.

Brutus picks up a long pair of tongs and places it in the box. He pulls the dagger out, and I’m relieved to see it’s covered with the silver. But, the silver slowly begins to drip off and Zack's dagger disintegrates into sand.

"Now what?" Andre asks.

"We need something to bind the silver to the dagger," Brutus says, rubbing his head while he racks his brain to think of the solution.

A little voice inside my head says, "*Blood binds*."

"Wait," I say. "I think we need blood."

"Please don't tell me we need to make a virgin sacrifice," Slade moans. "Those were hard enough to come by back in the days when saving yourself for marriage was expected. I can't imagine how hard finding one now a day will be."

Leah and I look at each other and just smile.

"No, it's something that was said to me in Heaven by someone," I say vaguely, not wanting to mention Anna to those gathered. "God wanted me to know that '*blood binds*'. I didn't understand it at the time, but I think it must have something to do with making the daggers now."

"But whose blood?" Jered asks.

"Mine maybe?" I ask. "Since it was said to me?"

"No," Jess says, "I don't think so."

Jess looks around at the other vessels gathered.

"I think it means us," she tells them. "The crowns belonged to us. Maybe they need our blood to bind to the daggers."

"Let me try it first," Rafe volunteers, walking up to the forge. "Anyone have a knife handy?"

"Here," Joshua says, pulling out a little Swiss army knife from one of his pants pockets and tossing it to Rafe.

Rafe makes a small slit on his right index finger and holds his hand over the box until a few drops of his blood mixes with the now bubbling silver. When he's done, he folds his finger into the palm of his hand, and I see his hand glow blue as he heals the wound.

"Ok, Zack make another dagger," Brutus instructs.

Zack pulls out another dagger and drops it into the box. Brutus gets his tongs and pulls the dagger out. We all watch breathlessly to see if the silver will hold this time.

It does.

Brutus places the dagger in a tub of water to cool it off then pulls it back out.

It doesn't look very sharp to me.

"I'll grind it down to sharpen it," Brutus tells me, obviously seeing my doubt.

Rafe holds up the Swiss army knife. "Who's next?"

Chandler comes forth first and one by one, all the vessels give some of their blood to make the daggers.

I feel sorry for Leah when it's her turn. Not only does she have to keep her fire going, but she has to have her finger cut by Rafe. Thankfully, he heals it quickly after she's given the remaining silver her blood to make the last dagger.

Once all seven of the daggers are made, no silver remains within the box, which makes me think that whatever remained of each archangel's crown was soaked up by each dagger one by one.

As I look down at the line of seven daggers, I feel a bit overwhelmed by the task ahead of us.

How are we ever going to trap all seven of the princes? And what price will we have to pay to get the job done?

CHAPTER TEN

After the daggers are made, Brutus places them all in a black felt lined silver box. He takes them to JoJo who is setting out long, thin strips of black leather on one of the worktables nearby.

"What are those for?" I ask her, watching as she picks up one of the daggers and begins to wrap the leather tightly around the hilt.

"They are to make sure those devils cannot grab hold of the daggers," she tells me. "If they do, they will regret it!"

I smile because I've never seen JoJo look so feisty.

"What will happen to them?" I ask, wanting to know what booby trap JoJo has planned for the princes if they try to grab hold of one of the daggers.

"Zzzzzz," JoJo says, play-acting at electrocution while holding the dagger by the hilt. "They will let it go quickly enough. I assure you, Mon Cher."

"JoJo," Uncle Malcolm says, walking over to the table. "Did you bring what we discussed?"

“Oui,” JoJo says, nodding her head to a black velvet drawstring bag sitting on the table in front of her. “They are all in there. I made them as small as I could.”

Uncle Malcolm picks the bag up and looks inside.

“Thank you, JoJo. They should work just fine.”

“What's in there?” I ask, remembering JoJo say something about making smaller version of the anklets for all the Watchers.

Uncle Malcolm digs into the bag and pulls out what is indeed a smaller version of the anklets, which are about the size of a nickel.

“What is that going to fit on?” I ask, not seeing how it would be able to even fit around a Watcher’s pinky finger.

“It's not going to fit on anything,” Uncle Malcolm says. “But it will fit inside something.”

“Inside?” I ask, not understanding what he's talking about.

Uncle Malcolm looks me in the eyes. “Inside our bodies, Caylin. Unless they tear us to pieces, they won't be able to find them there. Each Watcher will get one of these and put it inside themselves somewhere. It'll hurt like hell, but we regenerate quickly enough. This way no one else will know the exact location of the talisman except the Watcher it belongs to.”

I glance over at Aiden who is speaking with my dad and Andre about something. I don't like the idea of Aiden having to insert a foreign object into his body, but it's better than the alternative. And I decide then that I won't ask him where he places the talisman because it's information I don't need to know. What if one of the princes tried to make me tell them? Ignorance was a far better alternative.

"What about me?" I ask. "Do I need to put one of those things inside me too?"

"No, Cher," JoJo says. "It was decided I would make you and your family something different. Perhaps not as concealable, but hopefully less noticeable than thc anklets."

JoJo lays down the dagger she is working on and picks up her purse from the floor beside the stool she's sitting on. From her purse, she pulls out what looks like a jewelry box. She lifts the lid and shows me a row of silver rings etched with a decorative ivy design.

"Each ring's core is made of leather," JoJo tells me. "And for the little ones," she says, pulling out a drawer beneath the layer of rings, "I have made these guardian angel necklaces which have a piece of leather I enchanted sandwiched in between the medallions."

It's certainly not foolproof, but neither can my mortal family insert strange objects into their bodies and not have adverse reactions to them being there.

Uncle Malcolm goes around to the Watchers present and hands them their protective talismans. Aiden is the last to receive his. He stuffs it into the back pocket of his jeans and looks over at me. He smiles at me reassuringly, like I shouldn't worry about what he has to do with the talisman.

Yeah, right, like I'm just going to forget he has to stuff that thing into his body somewhere like he's a Thanksgiving Day turkey.

I hate the circumstances the princes have forced us into, but I find grim satisfaction in the knowledge Anna will be born to take care of them one day and take back what they stole from God.

I wish her the best of luck in kicking their asses, literally.

Aiden walks over to me and takes one of my hands into one of his, gently pulling me off to the side away from the others.

"Slight change in plans for tonight," he tells me, and I hear a warning in his voice as if he doesn't like the change but there's nothing to be done about it.

"What change?" I ask, bracing myself for the answer.

“We’re still going out, but,” Aiden says hesitantly, “it’s been decided two more Watchers will be going with us for safety’s sake.”

My heart sinks. “Why?”

“Just a precaution,” he tells me. “In case a prince tries to attack, it’s better to have back up than not. And I’m not taking any chances with your life, Caylin. There seems to be enough of that already as it is.”

“Aiden,” I say, reaching up with my free hand to caress his cheek, “I won’t be in any danger tomorrow. Uncle Malcolm would never put me in a situation where he thought I might get hurt.”

“All I want to do is take you somewhere safe so you don’t have to deal with this ugliness,” Aiden tells me, turning his face slightly to kiss the palm of my hand, his warm lips linger against my skin for a moment before he turns his face again and settles his cheek there once more.

“I’m not going to run from a fight,” I tell him. “That’s not the way I was raised. You fight beside the people you love, not abandon them until all the dirty work has been done for you. You need to know that about me. I don’t run.”

Aiden nods, a faint, accepting smile on his lips. “I know. And I do love that about you. But, I still want to protect you from what’s coming. I can’t help it. And you need to understand that about me, Caylin.”

“And I love that about you,” I reply, garnering a real smile from him. “Maybe that's why God chose to put us together. The combination of both of our stubbornness is bound to produce some interesting children.”

I see a faint blush appear across Aiden's cheeks at the mention of us having children together and smile.

“Why do you blush so much around me?” I ask him, finding it incredibly adorable but at the same time odd that someone like me can make someone as ancient as Aiden blush like a school girl.

I rub my thumb against the heightened color across the cheek I still hold and watch in amazement as it becomes even pinker after my question.

“I'm not completely certain,” Aiden admits as I let my hand drop back down to my side. “I'm pretty sure I've never blushed in my life until I met you. I guess some of the things you say and do just take me by surprise. I don't expect them from you.”

"Like me looking at your butt at the reception?"

I didn't think it was possible, but Aiden's whole face turns red as an apple. It was totally worth asking the question to see his reaction to it.

Aiden laughs nervously. "Yes, I would say that was extremely unexpected from you."

"Why?" I ask. "I'm just like everyone else."

"No," Aiden says looking at me like I might have forgotten who I am, "you're not like everyone else. There's no one like you in this world or any other world, beautiful."

"Why? Because my grandfather is an archangel and my father was a Watcher?"

"Well, that certainly qualifies you to be unique," Aiden admits, "but that's not really what I was talking about. You're the only woman I love. Since the moment I saw you, you've become my everything."

I feel on the verge of tears and immediately stop them because what Aiden says doesn't deserve tears. I raise up on my tiptoes and hug him around the neck.

"Could you be more perfect?" I whisper in his ear.

“I think I can be for you,” he replies.

I can't do anything to prevent the tears this time, and I don't try to hold them back because I want Aiden to know how much what he just said has moved me, and that I will never take his pledge for granted.

Leah comes over to my house to help me get ready for my date with Aiden. I have no idea where we're going, but I do know I have the perfect dress for anywhere he wants to take me.

“I still can't believe she gave you this dress,” Leah says enviously, standing by the full-length mirror the dress is hanging from.

“She trusts Aiden,” I reply, putting the last touches of my make-up on and brushing out my hair. “What do you think? Hair up or down?”

Leah walks over to me as I turn to her in the chair at my vanity table.

“Definitely up,” Leah says. “It makes you look more mature that way.”

“Can you do it?” I ask. “I'm horrible at making it look right in an up-do.”

“Sure, you got some bobby pins somewhere?”

I pull out a drawer in my vanity table and take out a small clear plastic box of bobby bins.

Leah starts to style my hair, and I watch her in the mirror as she sets to work.

“Leah,” I say, deciding to broach a question I've been debating about asking, “remember that day I first called Aiden?”

“Sure,” she says, concentrating on what she's doing to my hair as she lifts it up into a loose bun.

“You said Aiden wasn't exactly ‘the poster boy for abstinence’. How exactly did you know that?”

Leah meets my gaze in the mirror with a bobby pin hanging out of the corner of her mouth and all my hair in her hands. Her eyes are as big as saucers like she just got caught doing something she shouldn't.

“Just knew,” she says lamely with an even less convincing shrug.

I immediately know she's hiding something.

“Spill it,” I tell her. “Don't make me tickle you unmercifully until you can't breathe. You know I can do it...”

Leah rolls her eyes at me, completely undaunted by my threat.

“I saw him with a couple of girls once,” Leah says. “Well...I guess I didn't technically *see* him with them but heard him with them.”

“Where?”

“It was right after I connected with Uriel for the first time. Jess and Mason took us all to their villa for that. Aiden was placed in charge of looking after us. And let me tell you, he's a lot more approachable now than he was back then. I guess it might have been because he still had the blood cravings. I’m sure babysitting a bunch of tasty humans wasn’t the easiest thing for him to do.”

“So…what is it that you heard exactly?”

Leah shakes her head slowly. “Trust me, you don't want me to describe any of that. I've pretty much put a mental block up to keep that stuff out of my head. You're better off not knowing, Caylin.”

I sit there and watch Leah continue to style my hair.

“Do you think...” I start but end up biting my lip unable to finish my question.

“Think what?” Leah prods, trying to get me to say the rest.

I take in a deep breath.

“Do you think I should go further with Aiden than just kissing?”

Leah narrows her eyes at me in the mirror suspiciously.

“How far exactly?”

I hesitate and finally whisper, “All the way.”

“Why?” Leah asks in alarm. “Is he hinting around at it or trying to make you feel like you should?”

“No, no, no,” I say, making sure she understands the idea is totally mine. “If anything, he's the one wanting to take things extra slow. He's scared to touch me because he doesn't want us to go too far too fast.”

“Then why are you even thinking about going all the way?”

“I don't want him to feel like he’s missing out on that part of his life,” I admit. “He's used to so much more than just kissing. What if he starts to get bored with it?”

“Has he acted bored?”

I giggle. “No. Most definitely not bored.”

“Then why are you worrying about it? Plus, this is Aiden we're talking about. The man who waited three years just to be able to talk to you, Caylin. The odds of him ever getting bored with you are astronomical! With everything you have to worry about, this should *not* be one of them.”

I know Leah’s right. The logical part of my brain does at any rate. But, for Aiden, sex played an important role in his life. Maybe if we just went ahead and broke down that barrier he wouldn’t feel like he had to treat me with kid gloves.

It’s something to think about at least.

Something that might even help…

CHAPTER ELEVEN

After I'm dressed and ready for my date with Aiden, Leah walks downstairs with me where I plan to wait for him to pick me up. To my surprise, I find Aiden already in my home standing in the living room talking to my dad.

"I didn't know you were here," I say to Aiden as I walk over to him.

When Aiden's eyes find me, his lips part slightly, and I hear a small, almost imperceptible gasp issue from his mouth.

I can't help but grin because Aiden looks just as gasp worthy to me. He's dressed in a nice dark blue suit, white shirt, and matching silk tie. He styled his hair and has it gelled up out of his face but still a bit wavy, not slicked back.

Out of the corner of my eye, I see Slade and Jered sitting at the dining table. They soon stand to their feet, like most gentlemen with proper manners do when a lady enters a room.

My dad's eyes narrow on me. I get the impression he doesn't whole-heartedly approve of the dress I'm wearing, but he doesn't say anything.

When I reach the two of them, I smile because I'm not quite sure what else to do in the awkward silence that's permeating the room.

"Do I need to bring a coat?" I ask Aiden, thinking this a reasonable question to break the sudden tension.

Aiden clears this throat. "No, we'll be phasing straight into the restaurant."

"Where are you buying us dinner anyway?" Slade asks, as he and Jered join us.

I smile at Jered and he immediately grins back. I'm glad to see he will be one of the Watchers accompanying us that evening. It shows a level of trust from Aiden that I believe this particular Watcher needs.

"El Celler de Can Roca," Aiden tells Slade. "Have the two of you been there before?"

"Who with good taste hasn't?" Slade asks with a cocky grin.

Aiden looks to Jered. "Have you been to that location?"

"Yes," Jered answers simply.

"I reserved two tables there for us," Aiden says.

"Where is it exactly?" I ask.

"Girona, Spain," Aiden tells me. "It's one of the best restaurants in the world. I thought you might enjoy it. They serve some rather unique dishes there."

I smile. "I'm sure I'll love it."

But it's not because of the food, I think to myself. Aiden could have taken me to the local McDonalds, and I would have had a wonderful evening. As long as I get to spend some private time with him, I don't care where we go.

"I'll be sure to have Caylin back by ten," Aiden tells my dad. "I believe that's her curfew?"

"I don't have school tomorrow," I say, hoping this reminder will garner me an extra hour. "Tomorrow is President's Day. No school."

My father grins tight lipped at me because he sees through my little ploy for added time with Aiden rather easily.

"All right," he says, "you can stay out until eleven tonight but no later."

I smile and lean over to kiss my father on the cheek.

"Thanks, Dad. I won't be late."

"No, she won't," Aiden promises.

"Then the two of you have a good time," my dad says. "I'll stay up until you return home."

"Ok," I tell him, "I'll see you when I get back."

"Text me later," Leah says. "I'll get your mom to phase me back home. And since no one else has said it yet, you look gorgeous. Have fun!"

"Thanks," I tell her before turning to Aiden and holding out my hand to him to let him know I'm ready to leave.

He takes my hand into one of his, and I instantly find us standing inside a unique looking restaurant.

"Ahh, Mr. Keles," a dark complected, black haired man dressed in a nicely tailored black suit says as he walks up to us with his hand held out for Aiden to shake.

"Hello, Jerico." Aiden shakes the other man's hand. "Thanks for getting us tables on such short notice."

"Anything for you, my friend," Jerico replies as his gaze drifts in my direction. "And who is this vision of loveliness?"

"Jerico, I would like to introduce you to Caylin Cole."

Jerico holds his hand out to me palm up. I place my hand into his and he bows at the waist lightly brushing his lips across the top of my hand.

"A pleasure to finally meet you, Ms. Cole. I was beginning to wonder if you were simply a figment of Mr. Keles' imagination." Jerico says letting go of my hand and standing back to his full height.

"A figment?" I ask, slightly confused.

"He has often spoken of a single beauty who stole his heart. I am just happy to see he can finally be with you instead of sitting at one of my tables pining for someone he was forbidden to have any contact with."

"You make me sound like a sad sap," Aiden says slightly embarrassed.

"Well, no sadness for you tonight, my friend. I have had the chef prepare the very best for you and Ms. Cole."

Jerico looks behind us and waves to someone.

"Take care of Mr. Keles' friends, Miguel. I will take care of our special guests personally."

I look behind us and see a waiter, presumably Miguel, escort Jered and Slade in the opposite direction from us.

"Please follow me, Mr. Keles and Ms. Cole," Jerico says.

"I thought they were supposed to stay close," I whisper to Aiden as we walk behind Jerico.

"If anything happens they will be," he assures me, "but they don't need to be right next to us to provide added security. Plus, this is a public place. The more public the place the less likely the princes will try to bother us."

The restaurant is simply decorated but beautifully so with sleek modern looking furnishings. In the center of the dining room is a wall made of glass, which looks out onto a small, lit garden. Jerico pulls out one of the chairs at the table for me to sit in while Aiden sits across from me.

"I hope you enjoy your first visit with us, Ms. Cole," Jerico says before bowing to us and leaving.

The table is illuminated by a single spotlight over the table. The table itself is covered by a long white tablecloth. We each have our own setting of fine bone china, a crystal glass and silverware wrapped in a pristine white cloth napkin.

When I look at Aiden sitting across from me, I suddenly begin to feel the walls of my stomach tighten in nervousness. He must notice the change in me because he rests his arm on the table and holds his hand out to me palm up. I place one of my hands into his and he squeezes it reassuringly.

"What's wrong?" He asks gently.

"I just realized this is like a real date."

Aiden chuckles softly. "Yes, it is a real date, beautiful."

"I know it's silly but the thought just made me feel nervous all of a sudden."

"Why?" Aiden asks, rubbing the pad of his thumb in a circular pattern over the top of the hand he holds.

"I'm not sure," I admit with a small shake of my head. "I guess because it makes us seem so official."

"That's a good thing, isn't it?" Aiden asks, a touch of worry added into the question, like maybe he's wondering if I'm not ready for all this yet.

I squeeze his hand. "Yes, it's the best thing in the world, Aiden. The very best thing."

Aiden smiles and I see his posture relax in relief.

A waiter brings over a small, potted tree to our table. It reminds me of a bonsai tree my Aunt Tara once tried to take care of. The operative word being 'tried'. It died a month after she got it.

"Please, enjoy," the waiter says, leaving the miniature tree with us.

I look at it and think it's a cute decoration. Then Aiden picks off one of the olives hanging from the bottom limbs of the plant and pops it into his mouth.

"The olives are an appetizer," Aiden says after he swallows. "They're caramelized and stuffed with anchovy."

Aiden picks off another olive and leans towards me to bring it to my lips. I open my mouth, and he drops it on my tongue. The olive is tasty but that isn't what makes me smile. I liked the natural way Aiden just fed me. It showed a level of intimacy only lovers would share.

I pull off an olive and reach across the table. Aiden's eyes stay focused on me as my fingers touch his lips, and I drop the olive into his mouth. Before I can take my hand away, he gently grabs it by the wrist and brings it back to his mouth to suck off the lingering butter on my fingers.

I have to take in a deep breath just so I don't pass out from the increased beating of my heart.

When Aiden finally does lets my hand go, I want to tell him not to because I don't want him to stop. Aiden smiles at me, and I realize he knows exactly how he just affected me. It makes me wonder if what I was thinking earlier is true. Does Aiden miss having sex? Is he asking me without words if I'm ready for the next step? Or is this just part of his plan of a slow seduction?

I have no way of knowing. I'm just not experienced enough to read between the lines.

The next dish served to us is what the waiter calls the World on a Platter.

It's composed of five canapés, which he tells us represents the world. He patiently explains to me what some of them are. The first represents China and is a cone of pickled vegetables with plum cream. Another one is a ceviche broth from Peru. Mexico is represented with guacamole, tomato water, and coriander. And the Moroccan portion is composed of a yogurt concoction with almond, rose, honey saffron, and spices.

While we eat this, Aiden strikes up a conversation about Yale and if I've found a place to live near the college yet. We end up discussing our plans for our time there, and I discover Aiden has signed up for all the same classes as I have.

"How did you know what classes I would be taking?" I ask him as the waiter takes away our dishes and says he will be back with the main course.

Aiden smiles. "I had a spy within your midst."

I sit there for a moment to think, but it doesn't take me long to figure out who fed Aiden the information.

"Jess."

Aiden nods.

"That's why she was so interested in helping me decide what classes to take," I say. "I wondered why she cared so much."

Aiden shrugs. "She knew my plan and figured I would want to be able to go to your classes with you."

I make a note to myself to give Jess a big hug the next time I see her.

Our faithful waiter brings over our main course. He tells me it's a signature dish of the restaurant consisting of Iberian suckling pig with artichokes, decorated on top with artichoke flowers, orange, lemon, and beetroot arranged in the middle of the dish to look like a beautiful flower.

While we eat, Aiden informs me that after he steps down from being the head of the Memphis Watcher Headquarters, Mason plans to place Jered in the position.

"I'm sure that doesn't make Uncle Malcolm too happy," I say.

"No. He isn't happy about it, but he isn't our leader yet either."

"So, Mason must really trust Jered if he plans to place him in charge of one of the headquarters."

"Mason has always tried to help Jered. I think he feels sorry for him more than anything. And, over the past few years, they've become friends. It took a while for Jered to stop craving blood enough to be around humans again. Mason was the one who helped him the most during his darkest days."

"Who helped you?" I ask, knowing Aiden would have gone through a similar experience in order to earn his forgiveness.

“Desmond,” Aiden tells me. “He was one of the few who thought I was worth saving. We were friends before the fall and before I chose to become what I became.”

Alongside my note for Jess, I make another note to thank Desmond for being such a good friend to Aiden.

After we finish our meal, I expect our waiter to bring a dessert but he doesn’t. Instead, Aiden stands from his chair and comes around to mine to pull it out for me so I can stand too.

“Are you taking me home?” I ask, thinking it’s way too early for that.

“No, we’re going to my house in the Bahamas for dessert,” he tells me.

I see Slade and Jered walk towards us.

“Enjoy your meal?” Jered asks me.

I smile. “Yes, I did. How about you?”

Jered gives Slade a sideways glance. “It was interesting.”

“So,” Slade says, “beach house now, right?”

“Yes,” Aiden says. “The places I showed you earlier.”

Each man nods and phases.

“What places?” I ask.

"I showed them each spots outside the house where they would have good vantage points to keep an eye on things."

"So, we'll be alone inside?" I ask, my heart beginning to race because I remember Aiden's vision of how this evening is supposed to end.

Aiden takes my hand and phases us to the living room of his home.

"Yes," he says, a sly grin stretching his lips as he turns to me.

"And now that you have me here," I say looking up at him, "what exactly do you plan to do with me, Aiden?"

"Feed you?" He asks, like he hopes I won't be too disappointed by his answer.

"Feed me what exactly?"

Aiden pulls me alongside him as he heads to the sleek, modern kitchen at the back of the house.

He opens up the freezer section of the large stainless steel double door refrigerator and pulls out a tub of chocolate and a tub of vanilla ice cream. From the refrigerator section, he pulls out a jar of maraschino cherries, canned whipped cream, chocolate sauce, and caramel syrup.

“Ice cream sundaes?” I ask.

“Yes,” Aiden says, walking over to one of the glass wall cabinets and pulling out two white bowls then grabbing some spoons out of a nearby drawer. “I’m not a cook yet so I couldn’t exactly make you anything edible. I thought this would be something we could do together.”

I smile because I think it’s sweet of Aiden to come up with this plan. It’s not something I would have expected him to arrange for us to do together.

I look down at what he has and ask, “So, where are the nuts?”

Aiden sets the bowls and spoons in front of me on the kitchen island before looking up at me.

“Nuts?” He asks, like the concept is foreign to him.

“You know the little can of toasted pecans.”

“I don’t have any,” Aiden says slightly worried. “Do we need them?”

“It’s better with them,” I say.

“Any grocery store should have them, right?”

“Yes, they should.”

Aiden holds his hand out to me, and I soon find myself standing at the back of a small, mostly empty of customers, grocery store.

"This way," Aiden says, holding my hand tighter and walking quickly down the aisle we are on.

A girl wearing a red vest is stocking one of the shelves.

"Hmm," Aiden says looking at the empty shelf. "It looks like they're out."

"Can I help…," the girl says as she turns around but seems to utterly lose her train of thought when she sees Aiden.

Aiden smiles at her, and I fear we've lost her after that because her eyes look completely glazed over as if she's just been placed into a trance and all she can do now is stare at Aiden with her mouth slightly ajar. I just pray she doesn't start to drool on herself.

"Hi," Aiden says, looking down at the nametag on her vest, "Jean. How are you doing this evening?"

Jean just nods at Aiden. Frankly, I'm surprised she's retained even that limited motor function because it's obvious she's fully lost the ability to speak.

"Jean," Aiden says, "this lovely lady and I really need a can of those toasted pecans that you put on ice cream sundaes. Would you happen to know if you have any in the back? Possibly needing to be stocked?"

Jean closes her mouth and the glazed look in her eyes fades a fraction.

She clears her throat and says, "I can go see."

"We would really appreciate your doing that for us. Thank you, Jean."

Jean practically runs to the back of the store. I'm not sure if she's walking so fast because she wants to help Aiden out as quickly as possible or if she just wants to get back as soon as she can. Either way, I find myself immensely amused by her reaction.

"I take it you never had any trouble getting a date," I tell Aiden.

Aiden looks down at me. "No, not really."

He doesn't say it in arrogance, just fact.

"And I suppose women rarely said no to you when you…wanted more than just a kiss from them?"

Aiden continues to look at me. His eyes are contemplative, like he's wondering why I'm asking such a question. He finally decides whether to answer.

"I never heard no," he tells me. Still, no arrogance, just fact.

"And your last time being with a woman was the day I first called you, right?" I ask.

"Yes," he says with no hesitation, "why are you asking me these questions, Caylin?"

I'm saved from answering his question by the out of breath return of Jean and our can of chopped roasted pecans.

"Here you go," she tells Aiden holding out the can to him.

Aiden takes the offered can.

"Thank you, Jean. We truly appreciate your help."

"Sure," Jean says, smiling from ear to ear as she openly looks Aiden up and down. "Anytime. Anytime at all."

Aiden turns me towards the front of the store where the cash registers are located.

He seems to be in a hurry because his pace is much faster than before.

He quickly pays the cashier and tells her to keep the change. Without bothering to conceal what he is, he phases us back to his home. Once there, he sets the can of chopped pecans on the kitchen island beside the other ingredients for our ice cream sundaes.

Aiden lets go of my hand and begins to take off his jacket and then his tie. He walks over to the dining table in the room and drapes both items on the back of a chair there. He turns around to face me and unbuttons the top three buttons of his shirt.

"Now," he says looking at me with his hands on his hips and legs slightly spread apart, "why the questions back there? What is it that you really want to know, Caylin?"

The way he's standing, and the way he just asked his question makes me feel like I probably shouldn't have brought the subject up. But, the can of worms are open now and there really isn't any putting them back in.

"I've been wondering if we should just go ahead and make love sooner rather than later," I admit.

Aiden stares at me. He just stands there and stares at me hard without saying a word, without changing his facial expression.

I'm not sure he's going to say anything until finally he asks, "Have I done something that would make you wonder such a thing? Have you felt any pressure from me at all that would make you think I expect that from you?"

"No," I say, "you haven't done anything."

I see Aiden's shoulders sag in relief after hearing my statement.

"Then, why are you even bringing it up?"

"Because you're a man who is used to having sex with anyone he wants, anytime he wants. How long are you going to be satisfied with just kissing, Aiden? It's already been a really long time since you had sex, and you told me how important it was to you in the past. I just don't want you to think you have to find it somewhere else."

Aiden continues to stare at me for a little while before closing his eyes and lowering his chin to his chest. He remains like that for quite a long time, and I worry that something's wrong with him. He just stands there unmoving, not talking.

Finally, he lifts his head and opens his eyes to look at me.

My heart instantly aches against the walls of my chest because of the pain I see in his soul. His usually happy blue-green eyes are swimming with unshed tears as he looks at me.

"I'm sorry," he says to me. "I'm sorry I've made you think you would ever have to give yourself to me like that just to keep me faithful to you. I guess I hoped you would trust me more than that."

Now I'm the one who is stunned.

"I didn't say that," I tell him. "I never said I didn't have any faith in you."

"Yes," he says in a whisper, "you did. Maybe not in so many words but that's exactly what you're thinking. You think that I'll become so frustrated sexually that I'll go find someone else to satisfy that need. I guess…I guess I hoped you would think better of me than that, Caylin."

I take a step forward to go to Aiden but he puts up a hand to stop me.

"No," he says, "we need to come to an understanding about this first."

"Forget about what I said," I beg. "Please, Aiden. The last thing I wanted to do was hurt you. I just thought…"

But I can't finish my statement because it's only now that I understand how stupid I was. How could I have thought I needed to have sex with Aiden to keep him? He's right. That's exactly what I was thinking. But that's not what true love is built on. It isn't centered on a base physical need. It's founded on mutual respect and trust. And now the man I love thinks that I don't trust him when he's someone I have complete faith in.

"I've had sex, Caylin," he says. "I've had a lot of it in my time. And yes, I admit, I want to make love to you. I want to bring you pleasure. I want to be the man who awakens that side of you. But, making love to you comes in a distant second to what I really want from you."

"What do you want?" I ask breathlessly, on the verge of tears myself because I can't stand the thought that I've made Aiden second-guess my love for him.

"I want you," he says. "I want all of you, not just your body. I want to know you so well that I can silently finish your sentences in my head. I want to become a part of your soul that you can't live without. I want you to know you can trust me with all that you are, and that I will always respect your thoughts and opinions. I want to be someone you can share your hopes and dreams with and not worry that I will ever ridicule any of them. I don't just want to become your lover, Caylin. I want to become your best friend. I want to be the person you willingly share every aspect of your life with and not feel like you have to lose any part of yourself to do it. I thought we were heading in that direction but now I feel like we've just taken a giant leap backward."

"Don't say that," I beg. "Please don't even think that."

"But you don't trust me," he says, wiping at his eyes with the back of one hand. "And I'm not sure how to fix that."

"I do trust you," I tell him openly crying now.

And then I think of something that will prove it.

I walk up to him and pull Jess' bracelet off my wrist.

"Put this on," I tell him, even though I see him shaking his head at me. "You made me use it. Now it's your turn. Ask it to tell you how I feel. I did it when you asked me to do it. I think you owe me the same courtesy, Aiden."

Aiden sighs and reluctantly holds out his right arm to me so I can put the bracelet on. I slip it onto his wrist and grab hold of his hand.

"Please," I say to him, as I look him in the eyes, "please ask it to tell you how I really feel about you."

Aiden stares down at me for a long while, as though he's bracing himself for what he's about to learn.

I know when he asks the bracelet how I really feel about him because his grip tightens on my hand.

I watch as his eyes widen in wonder. I know he feels how deeply ingrained inside my soul he already is. I can't imagine my life being complete without him in it and sharing every aspect of me: mind, body, and soul. I want to be his best friend too. I know he's had a hard life and all I want to be is his sanctuary. I want to be the one person in the world he can come to and just feel happy and safe with. And, I know he feels my faith in him to be the man I need by my side in sad times and in happy times. I trust him completely with all that I am.

"I trust you," I tell him, making sure he understands that simple fact. "I'm so sorry I made you doubt that. I think I just let my own insecurities overrule my better judgment. I'm still mostly human, Aiden. I'm not nearly as perfect as you might want to make me out to be. I'm going to make boneheaded mistakes like this again. Not on purpose though, just remember that. And please, never doubt that I trust you completely. And never, ever doubt how much I love you."

Aiden doesn't say anything. He just pulls me into his arms and holds me.

"I don't deserve the way you feel about me," he says, tightening his hold on me. "But, I'll take it."

I hold him just as fiercely and sigh.

CHAPTER TWELVE

After we both pull ourselves together, I feel the tension between us has fade. I think Aiden is still a little hurt by what I did. But, by making him use the bracelet to feel the depths of my love and trust in him, he seems to be slowly recovering.

After we make our ice cream sundaes, I sit on one of the stainless steel stools at the kitchen island while Aiden stands across from me on the other side.

A large glob of caramel is covering my spoon, and I pick it up and begin to suck on it to get the caramel off. My eyes just happen to wander to Aiden, and I see him staring at me as I work the spoon in and out of my mouth.

"What?" I finally ask, wiping at my mouth thinking I must have something on it to make him stare at me so intensely.

Aiden shakes his head and directs his gaze down to his ice cream sundae.

"Nothing," he says.

"No, do I have caramel on my face or something? What's wrong?"

"I don't think I should say anything considering the conversation we just had."

I admit. It takes me a few seconds to figure out what he's talking about, but I finally do.

I feel my cheeks grow warm as I stab the spoon in the ice cream and pick up a large portion of the chocolate and stuff it into my mouth.

"This help break the image?" I ask in an ice cream muffled voice.

Aiden laughs. "Uh, yes, most definitely."

I smile and swallow the ice cream in my mouth before I choke on it.

After we finish eating, Aiden tells me he has a new movie for us to watch in the living room. I happily follow him because I hope this becomes the promised part of the evening where a lot of kissing is supposed to happen.

I sit on the chaise lounge while Aiden finds the movie on his holographic TV. After it starts, Aiden lays on the lounge chair propping his back firmly against the back of it with one leg bent up and the other straight out. I sit beside him and he wraps his arms around me seeming content to just hold me while the movie starts.

I see the movie playing, but I have a hard time concentrating on what's happening. I keep wondering when Aiden will make his move. A half an hour into the movie, he still hasn't done anything, and I begin to wonder if he's changed his mind about the way he saw this evening ending because of what I did earlier. I thought 'watching a movie' was just code for 'hey, let's go make out'.

I let the movie play on for a little while longer until I just become completely frustrated.

I turn to Aiden and find that he isn't actually watching the movie either. He's watching me.

"Why haven't you kissed me yet?" I ask him, not seeing any reason to beat around the bush with him.

"I'm not sure," he admits, and I hear the confusion in his voice as he confesses this to me.

"Is it because of what I said earlier?" I silently beg him to say that isn't the case.

"Yes," he answers truthfully. "I guess I'm scared I might inadvertently do something that makes you think I want more than just kissing from you."

I sigh.

"Then maybe we should just talk about when we think we want to do that," I say, thinking this a reasonable solution. "When do you see us making love, Aiden?"

"Honestly?" He says. "I've always thought we would wait until after we were married."

"Is this because of Uncle Malcolm's threat?" I ask, voicing my suspicion.

Aiden smiles. "No. This decision has nothing to do with Malcolm or his threat. It was an empty threat anyway. He just wanted to make sure I understood something like that with you shouldn't be taken lightly."

"So you really want to wait until we're married?" I ask.

Aiden nods. "It seems like the right thing for us to do."

"So when do you see us getting married?"

Aiden shrugs. "I'm not sure. No time soon though."

"Well, I need a time frame," I tell him, not seeing this as an odd request. I'm a planner. I like to plan things ahead of time. "Everyone knows we'll be getting married and having babies at some point. It's already been predestined. So, I don't see any reason for us to wait very long."

"You're only seventeen," Aiden points out.

"And my mother was only eighteen when she and my father got married."

"That was a slightly different situation," Aiden says. "She thought she didn't have much longer to live. She almost didn't."

"Then, how long are you going to make me wait, Aiden?"

Aiden smiles at my question, and I think he's pleased by my eagerness for us to start our married life together.

"Can you give me at least a year before we set a firm date?" He asks. "I want at least that long with you where sex isn't even a factor in our lives."

"Why?"

"To prove something to myself mostly," he admits. "To prove that I've actually changed and don't have to have sex to have a relationship with a woman."

"Ok," I say. "I can live with that. But, I need you to kiss me, Aiden. This is killing me."

In one swift movement that's part phasing and part brute strength, Aiden has me lying on my back on the chaise lounge underneath him in the blink of an eye.

"Wow," I say completely impressed by the maneuver, "that was fast. I didn't even see you move."

"War Angel, remember? Being able to move fast was sort of a requirement."

I lift my hands to either side of his face, and he lowers his head until I can feel his breath against my lips. He presses his lips to mine tentatively, kissing my top lip then my bottom and finally teasing my lips apart with his tongue and gently plundering my mouth. After a while, I feel his hands glide up my sides and stop at my breast. In one smooth motion, he slides his hands underneath my back, lifting my chest up slightly. His mouth leaves mine and travels down one side of my exposed neck in a trail of small, wet kisses.

"Have I told you how sexy you look in this dress?" He asks, trailing kisses across my clavicle to the other side of my neck.

“No,” I say breathlessly because breathing isn’t exactly high on my list of priorities at that moment.

“You look very sexy, Caylin Rayne,” Aiden murmurs before going lower and kissing the exposed flesh revealed by the cut outs of the dress over the top of each breast.

Aiden lifts his head back to mine. When he looks into my eyes, I notice he looks almost drugged which makes me smile as his lips find mine again. I like knowing I’m Aiden’s drug of choice.

After a long while, we each finally need time to catch up on our breathing and simply lie in each other’s arms enjoying the warmth our bodies make pressed together.

Aiden slips off Jess’ bracelet from his wrist and places it back on mine.

“Thank you for sharing yourself with me like that,” he says.

“I have nothing to hide from you,” I tell him. “If you ever want to know what I’m thinking or feeling, I will always tell you the truth. We don’t need a bracelet to do that for us anymore.”

“Then tell me what you’re feeling right now,” Aiden says, gliding his hand up and down my exposed arm.

“I feel safe and loved,” I tell him.

"Good. That's the way I always want you to feel when you're with me."

I tighten my arms around Aiden and continue to lay my head on his chest completely content to just listen to the steady beat of his heart.

I feel the hand he's been using to glide up and down my arm venture down to between my arm and side and slide up to my rib cage. His fingers start to move there quickly which makes me start to laugh from the tickling sensation.

"Stop!" I tell him.

He does stop for a second. "I didn't realize you were so ticklish, beautiful."

"Well, now you know," I say, mistakenly thinking that would be the end of the subject.

Aiden's fingers begin to move against my side once more but even faster now.

"Aiden!"

Just like before our make out session, he does his phasing maneuver, which puts me beneath him and completely at his tickling mercy.

Well, two can play at that game.

I phase to move him beneath me and straddle his waist, which makes my dress bunch up around my hips. I grab both his arms by the wrists and pin them above his head with one hand. I'm slightly stronger than he is which means he can't move unless he phases.

"My turn," I tell him, as I use my free hand to begin tickling him all over his torso.

"I surrender!" he finally laughs after a full minute of my tickling torture, unable to take it anymore. "I surrender!"

I hear snickering behind me and stop my fun with Aiden to look over my shoulder.

Standing there watching us are Jered, who looks completely mortified to even be in the room, and Slade who is leering at my exposed lower section and obviously the one I heard snickering.

I quickly phase behind the back of the chaise lounge so I can lower the hem of my dress from being bunched up around my hips.

"Sorry for our intrusion," Jered says in earnest. "We heard Aiden yell and thought there might be trouble."

"No need to apologize," Aiden says standing from the chair. "It's about time for me to take Caylin home anyway."

"You might want to freshen up a little bit," Jered says to me, pointedly looking at my hair.

I look at Aiden. "Bathroom?"

He comes to me and takes my hand leading me down a hallway to the first room on the right.

Just before I'm able to let go of his hand to go in by myself, Aiden tugs on my arm until I'm brought up firmly against him.

"I think you look beautiful," he tells me, kissing me on the lips and setting my body on fire. "Even if your hair looks like a rat's nest."

I slap him playfully on the arm and giggle.

"I'll be out in just a minute," I say, closing the door behind me.

When I look into the mirror over the vanity, I literally gasp. All of Leah's hard work has been destroyed and my hair does resemble an untidy nest of some sort.

I deftly take out all the bobby pins and toss my head down to run my fingers through my hair since I don't have a brush handy. I decide then that I might need to start carrying a small purse around with a spare brush and lipstick for occasions just like this. I know my father will be waiting for me when I return home and cringe a little on the inside.

It's obvious what Aiden and I have been doing. It's not exactly as if I can hide the now down hair and bare, swollen lips. But, I figure my dad has already assumed such a thing was happening. I'm sure he and my mother weren't exactly innocent of make out sessions when they first fell in love. I just hope he doesn't make a big deal out of it.

When I go back to the living room, Aiden has my high heels dangling from one of his hands.

"Did you want to put them back on?" He asks me, holding them up.

I shake my head. "No, I would just end up taking them off again as soon as I got home."

I hold out my hand to take them from him.

"Gentleman," Aiden says to Jered and Slade, "thank you for your services this evening. We do appreciate your help."

"Anytime," Jered says.

"Yeah," Slade says with a sly smile, absently rubbing the top of his left arm "anytime I can hear you scream for mercy like a little girl is totally worth the inconvenience."

"Goodnight, then," Aiden says, choosing to ignore Slade and phase me home.

My dad is sitting in the living room reading something on his tablet. He looks up at us, and I watch as he sweeps his eyes down the length of me taking in my disheveled appearance.

"Have a nice evening?" He asks me, not in a knowing way but genuinely interested if my night was fun.

"It was a wonderful evening, Dad."

My father stands and shakes Aiden's hand.

"Thank you for getting her home exactly on time," my dad tells him.

"I will always try to keep my promises to you, Brand," Aiden says.

"I'm sure you will," my dad replies.

Aiden turns to me and leans down to give me a kiss on the cheek.

"Sweet dreams," he says to me. "I'll see you tomorrow."

"Ok," I say, not wanting him to leave but knowing he has to. "See you tomorrow."

Aiden phases.

"So," my dad says, sitting back down on the couch, "did you enjoy the food? It's been a long time since I went to that restaurant. What did you eat?"

I go on to tell my dad a PG-13 version of my evening with Aiden. I decide to omit the drama and the making out part of the night however. That's really something I would discuss with my mother, not my dad.

"So, have you and Aiden discussed your future together much?" He asks.

"We did talk about it some tonight," I tell him. "We talked about when we might want to get married."

"Married?" My dad asks in alarm.

"Don't worry," I tell him quickly. "We're not going to even talk about it again for at least another year. That's what Aiden wants so that's what we're going to do."

"Why does he want to wait a year before you even talk about it again?"

"He wants to prove to himself that he can have a real relationship with a woman without being in it for the sex. And you might as well know that he and I won't be making love until after we're married. He was very adamant about wanting to wait."

"Well," my dad says looking contemplative, "I can't say I saw that coming. Considering his track record, I was concerned he might try to accelerate that part of your relationship together before you were ready."

"The exact opposite," I tell him. "If anything he wants to go extra slow. So, don't worry, Dad."

"I wasn't exactly worried," he says. "I knew Aiden wouldn't do anything to you that you didn't want him to. But, I *am* relieved to hear he respects you enough to not treat you like the other women he's been with. It shows how much he loves you, and I'm happy to see that."

Involuntarily, I yawn.

"Go on up to bed," my dad says leaning over and kissing me on the cheek. "You've had a busy day and tomorrow won't be any less so."

"Ok, night, Dad."

I don't even bother to walk up the stairs. I just phase to my room and quickly change out of my dress into some comfortable pajamas.

I crawl under my covers and grab my phone to send a text to Leah. She doesn't respond so I assume she's probably already asleep.

I decide to send Aiden a text.

Thank you for the wonderful evening, minus me being stupid. Other than that it was a perfect real date

He replies back almost immediately.

No need to thank me, beautiful. I had a wonderful time too, minus you being stupid lol. Now get some sleep. We have a busy day tomorrow. I love you with all my heart, for now and always.

I love you too. Goodnight.

I put my phone up and turn my light out before snuggling even further underneath my covers.

I'm worried about the next day because it will be the first real test of one of the daggers.

I just pray that it works.

CHAPTER THIRTEEN

The next morning I wake up to find a little warm body lying in bed with me. I'm not sure when Mae came to my room, but I snuggle up with her basking in the innocent aura that perpetually surrounds my baby sister. Pure innocence is what Mae represents to me. We're all special in our own way, but for some reason, Mae has always been able to bring joy to anyone she's around. I guess it's her gift. Lord knows she's had Uncle Malcolm wrapped around her little finger since the day she was born.

I notice a silver chain around her neck and reach around to the front until I feel the outline of the little guardian angel pendant. I'm thankful she's wearing it, but at the same time, I'm sickened by the fact that she needs to. The necklace will protect her from the prince's archangel power, but they could kill her just as easily by a vast assortment of natural means. She's mostly human after all. It doesn't take much.

My phone vibrates indicating I have a text message. I pick it up from my nightstand and read the message.

Good morning, beautiful. I hope you had sweet dreams last night. Was just thinking about you and thought I would see if you were up yet.

I smile and my heart aches with joy because I like knowing Aiden is thinking about me.

Yes, I'm awake and cuddling with Mae in my bed.

Is it bad of me to say I wish I was Mae right now?

You want to be a three-year-old little girl?

Ok, I giggle. It's funny!

No, beautiful. I want to be lying next to you with your arms around me and whispering just how much I love you in your ear.

Will that be how we start every morning after we're married?

Start, yes. But I hope we can add a little bit more to that by then.

How can he make me blush and not even be in the same room with me? I stare at the text and don't respond right away.

Did I say too much?

No, I'm just smiling

Oh…good. I hope I can always make you smile.

I hear a soft knock on my door.

"Come in," I whisper.

My mom peeks in.

"Ahh, I thought she might be in here," my mom says, walking into the room.

"She must have come in some time during the night. I didn't even notice until I woke up."

My mom comes to sit on the side of my bed, and I notice the silver ring she's wearing on her right hand.

"How did your date go last night?"

I tell my mother about everything that happened the night before.

"Well, I won't sit here and lie by saying I'm not disappointed in what you thought you needed to do to keep Aiden. And I agree with him. You should have trusted him more."

"I know. I was stupid," I admit. "But we got things straightened out."

"So are you all right with his wishes about waiting until you're married?"

"Yes. I don't have a problem with that. He's right. We have a lot to learn about one another and there really isn't any reason to rush things. We'll be together forever."

My mom smiles. "I wasn't so sure in the beginning about Aiden. Your father and I were worried about him being your soul mate. Honestly, we didn't know if he was good enough for you. But, I should have known to trust God's judgment. I'm not sure I could have picked anyone more perfect for you. I'm glad you have him in your life."

"Me too," I tell her, unable not to smile about the man in my life.

My phone buzzes reminding me that I was talking with my Mr. Perfect before my mother came in.

"Do you want me to take her?" My mom asks, nodding her head to Mae.

"No," I tell her. "She'll wake up soon on her own. And I like holding her."

My mom stands. "Ok. Come down for breakfast when you get ready, sweetie."

I nod to her and she walks out of my room.

I look at the text on my phone.

Hello?

Sorry, my mom came in and we had a talk. She thinks you're perfect for me by the way.

LOL…. That isn't something I ever thought a mother would think about me concerning her daughter. But, I'm glad Lilly approves of me. I think your father is finally accepting me too.

It's not like he has a choice…

No, only you can make the final decision.

That decision was made the first time I saw you, Aiden.

Ok, now I'm smiling.

Good. Can you come over for breakfast?

Not this morning, beautiful. Malcolm promised that I could go with him to scout out Belphagor. I want to know what the plan is before I place you in harm's way.

Do you know what time I'll be needed?

Sometime around lunch from what I was told.

Then I won't see you until then?

I'm afraid not. But, I love you. I will miss you until I see you again.

I'll miss you too. Come to me when you can...

I will. I love you

I love you more.

I love you most.

I love you infinity...

Ok, you win.

No, we both win, Aiden.

Yes…we do. See you later, beautiful.

I put my phone back on the nightstand and hug Mae close. I'm not completely sure what the day will bring, but I do know my safety isn't something I need to worry about. Uncle Malcolm would never place my life in any real danger, and Aiden would kidnap me himself if he thought there was even a remote possibility of me being hurt.

By the time Aiden and Uncle Malcolm come to get me, I'm a bundle of nerves. I'm not nervous because I'm worried about my safety. I'm worried that I might make a mistake and completely screw something up.

Aiden comes straight to me like we're tethered by an invisible elastic string and takes me in his arms.

"Are you ready?" He asks me.

"I guess," I say hesitantly, not really sure what will be expected of me on this mission.

"You have nothing to worry about, Caylin," Uncle Malcolm tells me coming to stand beside us. "Belphagor will be the easiest of the princes to capture. He's just that stupid. That's why we've targeted him first."

Aiden lets go of me and my mom walks over to give me a reassuring hug.

"Don't worry," she tells me. "You'll do fine."

I should have known it would be my mother who knew the true worry I had.

"What exactly is it that I have to do?" I ask Uncle Malcom.

"Shop."

I feel sure I misunderstood. "Shop? Like go around and buy stuff?"

"Yes," he tells me. "Belphagor has been living in New Orleans since the Tear was sealed. Around this time every day, he goes to the French Market to have lunch. The plan is for you to walk around the market and shop. He'll notice and come to you without you having to do anything. While you act as a distraction, I'll phase in and take him down with one of the daggers."

"And it's going to be that simple?" I ask, thinking there has to be something that he isn't telling me. There has to be a catch, right? We're talking about one of the most powerful creatures on earth, an archangel. Surely, it won't be that clear-cut.

"It will be that simple," Uncle Malcolm promises me.

I nod, trusting what he says. "Ok, I guess I can shop and try to act normal."

I grab my brown leather cross body purse and slip it on.

"Here," my dad says, pulling out his wallet from his back pocket, "use cash."

I take the stack of bills he hands me and place them inside my purse.

Aiden takes my hand, twining our fingers together. "Ready?"

I nod and he phases us to New Orleans.

I find myself standing outside the entrance to the French Market. I see numerous stalls within the open marketplace with vendors selling all sorts of items ranging from fresh produce to clothing and jewelry.

"Ok," Aiden says, turning to me, "just walk around for a while. He won't be here for at least another 15 minutes so try to stay calm and just buy whatever you want like you're on an actual shopping trip."

I nod, trying my best to relax but still feeling nervous.

"It'll be fine," Aiden reassures me. "And I'll be watching to make sure nothing unexpected happens. We all will."

"Who does 'we all' include?"

"Besides Malcolm and me? Jered, Slade, Daniel, Andre, Brutus, and Desmond. We're all here to make sure nothing strange or unexpected happens. But, this should be fairly straightforward. It's basically just a snatch and grab. You're just the distraction to take him off his guard while he tries to figure you out."

"Do you think I'll be that much of a distraction for him?"

Aiden smiles. "You distract me all the time."

Aiden leans down and gives me a chaste kiss on the lips.

"Don't worry, beautiful. Everything will be fine. I would never let anything bad happen to you."

I nod and Aiden phases, leaving me alone.

At least, that's the way it feels. I know he and the others are a safe distance away watching me, but that fact does nothing to stop the nervous butterflies in my stomach.

I walk into the French Market and start to browse the various vendor stalls there. The smell of freshly brewed coffee and the music from a small jazz band nearby fills the area I'm in. I buy a pair of pink glittery mardi-gras masks for Mae and Ella to play with from one of the vendors. In another stall, I find something that reminds me of Aiden.

It's a double stranded black braided leather bracelet with a silver infinity charm in the middle. I'm sure he's watching me buy it so giving it to him as a surprise probably isn't an option anymore. But, I don't care. At least he knows I'm thinking about him.

"Is that for a special someone?" A man standing beside me asks.

I look over at him and instantly know he's Belphagor because Jess' bracelet grows warm around my wrist. Only someone who means me harm would cause the bracelet to send out its warning.

I guess I didn't expect Belphagor to be so dashingly handsome. Shouldn't he have horns or something jutting out of the top of his head? But then again, the princes simply took whatever human body they wanted. Why would you choose an ugly one if you didn't have to?

"Yes, it is," I tell him.

Belphagor crosses his arms over his chest as he studies me, and I notice something on one of his hands. It's a raised circular brand with archangel writing embossed across it. But, I don't understand the significance of the word.

"Levi said you were dangerous," he tells me looking me up and down. "But I just don't see how an innocent little thing like you could be of any danger to us."

"Did you see what I did to him?" I ask, thinking that should be evidence enough of the threat I pose. "I don't suppose you happen to know where Levi is now, do you? He and I have some unfinished business."

Belphagor gives me a toothy grin. "Do you now? Think you can finish him off? I highly doubt it. Not even Lucifer can do that."

"Has Levi taken on a new form?" I ask, trying to get as much information as I can before Uncle Malcolm shows up.

"Not yet. But when he does, I would be careful if I were you. He seemed rather put out by the inconvenience. And Levi really isn't someone you want to piss off."

Uncle Malcolm phases in so close to Belphagor's back that when he slips the dagger into the prince I don't even realize he did it, much less anyone else around us. The only thing that gives it away is Belphagor's look of surprise just before he closes his eyes and begins to slump forward. Uncle Malcolm wraps an arm around Belphagor's waist to hold him up against him.

"Go home," he tells me just before he phases.

I immediately phase home as instructed. My mom and dad are by my side almost instantly.

"How did it go?" My dad asks, trying not to sound anxious but not being able to hide it very well.

"It was quick," I say in total disbelief. "He didn't seem to see it coming at all."

Aiden and most of the others phase in just a few seconds later.

"Are they all going to be that easy?" I ask Aiden, completely dumbfounded that we took down a prince so effortlessly.

Aiden walks over to me, and I already know the answer to my question by the strained look on his face.

"No," he says regretfully. "Belphagor has never been very bright. The others will be more of a challenge because they're smarter and more cunning. Plus, they'll soon realize Belphagor is missing which means we've lost the element of surprise now."

I look over at my group of chosen and notice someone missing.

"Where is Daniel?" I ask.

"Malcolm is handing Belphagor over to him now," Aiden tells me. "Daniel will be in charge of hiding him until the girl from our family line is ready to deal with him. And he'll be the only one who knows his location, just like Mason planned."

"So, now what do we do?" I ask.

"Mason and Jess will let us know when it's time to attack the other princes," Aiden tells me. "For now, we just sit and wait."

"Is that why they weren't with us today?" I ask. "Because they're planning what we do next?"

"Yes. They're scouting the next prince."

“The next victim you mean,” Desmond says with a grin as the others walk over to join us.

“Belphagor has always been the pussy of the group,” Slade says snidely. “The rest will be just as easy though.”

“You shouldn’t underestimate them,” Jered tells Slade, a grave undertone of warning in his voice. “You might think they’re simple minded because they’ve followed Lucifer for this long, but they are not. I assure you. Belphagor was the exception to the rule because of his nature. The others will not be taken so easily.” Jered looks to Aiden. “They might even go on the offensive even more aggressively now.”

“More aggressively?” I ask. “Just how much more aggressive can they get?”

“I’m not sure,” Jered tells me, and I can see his worry over not knowing written plainly on his face. “But if they learn Belphagor was taken by us, they will know we have access to something formidable. I just hope they don’t jump to the conclusion that our secret weapon is you, Caylin.”

Everyone falls silent, like they don't know what to say about what Jered just said. It's not until there's a knock at the front door that the quiet is broken.

My Aunt Tara peeks her head inside.

"Oh good," she says, opening the door wider, bringing in two handfuls of plastic white shopping bags, "most of you are here already. Why don't some of you angels be useful and go out to my car to bring in the rest of the groceries for me?"

Jered and Brutus immediately head outside to do my Aunt Tara's bidding.

"Are we having a party?" I ask, mentally visualizing a calendar to make sure today isn't my mother's birthday.

"Kind of," my mother says to me. "Your Aunt Tara and I thought it would be a good idea if we got to know the Watchers you chose a little better. They'll be in our lives for a long time. It would probably be a good idea if we all became friends."

I couldn't argue against the idea. I did want to get to know my chosen a little better. They would be in our lives and the lives of mine and Aiden's descendants until Anna was born. Essentially, they would become a permanent part of my family. It was a reminder to me just how special my particular family was. We weren't just tied together by blood. We were bound to one another by choice, by loyalty, and by love.

Now, we had six new members. I just hoped my unconventional family didn't end up feeling any growing pains from the additions.

CHAPTER FOURTEEN

It always amazed me how my father could teach almost anyone how to cook, *except* for my mother and me. I guess we just weren't gifted with that particular gene. My dad and Aunt Tara take charge of the food preparations for our impromptu get together. Jered, Brutus, Desmond, and Andre watch them prepare the meal in hopes of picking up a few culinary tips. Jered seems to be the most interested, but, unfortunately for him, he looks as helpless as me in a kitchen.

"You would think Jered's never cooked before," I say to Aiden as we sit at the dining table and watch the others ask my dad and Aunt Tara questions as they cook.

"I would imagine cooking is as new to him as it is to me," Aiden says, looking over at the others in the kitchen like he wants to join them for the lesson being given.

"Why is that?" I ask. "I mean you've been around a long time. Why haven't you learned how to cook by now?"

Aiden looks back at me. "Because human food wasn't what I survived on, Caylin."

I instantly realize how stupid my question was. Of course cooking would be new to Aiden and Jered. Both of them had survived on human blood as their main source of sustenance for a very long time.

"I'm sorry," I tell him. "I wasn't thinking."

Aiden shakes his head at me. "No, don't be sorry for forgetting what I was. I'm glad you can."

"But I should have been more thoughtful," I say.

Aiden grins at me. "When you were in the French Market, I got the feeling you were thinking about me. Was I wrong?"

"No," I tell him, unable to suppress a smile, "you weren't wrong at all."

I reach over for the little purple shopping bag with his bracelet in it. When I take it out, Aiden automatically stretches his left arm towards me so I can put it on.

"It made me think of what I texted you this morning," I tell him, fastening the bracelet around his wrist and finding that it's a perfect fit. "I thought you might like it."

Aiden looks at the silver infinity symbol on the front of the bracelet and smiles so bright his whole face lights up.

"Thank you," he tells me. "I love it, and I love you."

I look at Aiden with only one thought in my mind, getting him alone somewhere and kissing him until he can't think straight. He seems to be able to read my thoughts because he chuckles and holds his hand out to me.

"Not yet," he tells me, even though I can tell by the sparkle in his eyes that he wants to do the exact same thing.

I place my hand into his, and he squeezes it.

"Why not?" I ask in a whisper.

"I would feel like I was disrespecting your parents if we ran off and did that right now," he tells me. "They want us all to spend some quality time together. And even though there's nothing more that I want than to kiss you until you beg for mercy, now isn't the time. Later. I promise."

"Mercy?" I ask, wondering just what Aiden has in mind to bring me to the brink of saying such a word.

"Yes, beautiful," Aiden murmurs, a new promise lighting up his eyes, "mercy."

"You know that's completely unfair, right?" I ask. "Saying something like that to me but making me wait to find out how exactly you'll make me want to ask for such a thing."

"Well, that's part of the fun," Aiden tells me, a sexy smile tilting the corners of his mouth up. "Anticipation is half the pleasure."

"More like torture if you ask me."

Aiden chuckles and brings the hand he holds up to his lips. I expect a simple kiss, but my heart does a somersault inside my chest as Aiden presses his lips against the middle knuckle and gently licks it with his tongue.

"Are you kidding me?" I whisper breathlessly.

Aiden just smiles and winks at me. "Later, beautiful. I promise. And I will always keep my promises to you."

I sigh, completely frustrated because I know there isn't anything to be done about it now.

The front door opens and Uncle Malcolm and Slade walk inside the house. Uncle Malcolm is carrying a silver metal box in his hands with some wires hanging from it. I knew he and Slade were outside doing something, but I wasn't sure what. They both come over to us, and Uncle Malcolm places the box in front of me on the table like he's handing me a gift.

I just stare at the strange contraption not having a clue why he's giving it to me.

"What is it?" I finally ask.

"I took the governor off your car," he tells me. "We thought it was time."

I look up over at my dad standing in the kitchen and see him grin at me. Then I look at my mom sitting in the living room with Mae and Ella as they play with the masks I bought them. She winks at me and smiles.

I look back down at the box and realize what's really sitting in front of me. My freedom.

They haven't just made it so I can go faster in my car. They're telling me they trust me to use my own judgment now. They've done their best to prepare me for my life, but the time has come for me to start making decisions for myself.

"Thank you," I say to all three of them, knowing they understand I'm not just thanking them for removing the governor. I'm thanking them for having faith in me to know what's right.

"Can I take your car for a spin?" Slade asks anxiously.

"No!" Uncle Malcolm and I answer at the same time.

"Sorry," I tell Slade, "I promised Uncle Malcolm no one would drive my car but me."

Uncle Malcolm digs in his front pocket and pulls out his set of keys, throwing them over to Slade.

"Take my Bugatti if you want to go for a joy ride," Uncle Malcolm tells him.

Slade smiles like a teenage boy given his first car and heads out of the house. We don't see him again until lunch is ready to be served.

"Are Jess and Mason coming for lunch?" I ask later when we're all sitting down to eat at the table. Aiden holds my chair out for me as I sit down.

"No," he tells me. "But they said they would contact us when they have a plan set for the next prince."

Brutus leans over to grab a piece of fried chicken but soon gets his hand slapped away by Aunt Tara.

"Now you of all people should know we need to say grace before we eat," she tells him as if he's a child needing to learn some manners.

Brutus sits back in his chair, eyes wide in what appears to be shock at the admonishment. I seriously doubt Brutus has ever been slapped so readily by anyone in his life much less someone almost half his size.

"I'm sorry," he says.

"Well, that's all right, hon, but in this family we say grace before we eat together. Understand?"

Brutus nods his head and Slade snickers.

Aunt Tara raises her eyebrow at Slade which, amazingly enough, seems to make him uncomfortable and causes him to immediately wipe the smirk off his face.

"Let's all bow our heads and give some thanks back," Aunt Tara says.

I can't help but smile as all the Watchers do exactly what Aunt Tara has instructed without question or argument.

"Dear Lord," my Aunt Tara says, "we give thanks for this food in the nourishment of our bodies. We thank you for guiding

Caylin in picking out these angels of mercy to watch over her family in the years to come. Please help them accomplish what it is you need them to do. And Lord, if you could teach Slade a little more humility, I think we would all appreciate it. Amen."

This time the other Watchers at the table snicker at Slade's expense.

"Why should I be humble?" Slade grumbles to Aunt Tara. "I'm perfect."

Aunt Tara tilts her head at Slade. "Hon, ain't nobody perfect in this world but God, and I hate to tell ya but you are not him."

Slade just rolls his eyes at Aunt Tara and grabs a roll off the platter in front of him. The end of the prayer seems to be most of my chosen's cue to descend upon the feast on the table as if they haven't eaten in days.

"Jered, hon," Aunt Tara says, scooping out some mustard greens from the bowl in front of her, "you've been the most quiet of the bunch. Are you feeling all right?"

Jered nods, trying to look under Desmond's arm at Aunt Tara as his fellow Watcher is scooping up some mashed potatoes from a bowl on the other side of him.

“Yes. I’m fine,” he tells her. “I’m just not used to being around so many people at one time I guess.”

“Well, if you’re gonna be a part of this bunch,” Aunt Tara tells him, eyeing the seemingly ravenous Watchers around her, “you need to get over your shyness, or you’re never gonna get anything to eat when they’re around.”

I decide to just wait out the others grabbing at food, but my Aunt Tara has other plans.

She stands from her seat, puts two fingers in her mouth and whistles, gaining the attention of the angels at the table.

“You boys need to just sit your butts back in your chairs and start acting civilized. You can’t just grab for food over people. Hasn’t anyone taught you to pass bowls around the table and take turns?”

My chosen sit back in their chairs looking properly chastised.

“Now,” Aunt Tara says, picking up the platter with the corn bread on it. “Who wants some cornbread?”

It takes a little while for everyone to get what they want, but at least I don’t feel like I’m in the middle of a food fight between the Watchers.

The lunch goes by smoothly. I'm glad to see all of my chosen seem to get along with one another, even though Jered doesn't quite seem as comfortable as the others in his new role. But, it all feels right. I sense we're becoming closer just by spending this time together and eating with one another. I hope to be able to do this with them all on a regular basis because I believe it's important we stay close to one another and become an integral part of each other's lives.

While we're cleaning up the dishes afterwards, I hear Will say to Slade, "Do you know how to play pool?"

"Kid, of course I know how to play pool. I know how to do just about everything."

"Man, you think you could play a game with me? Maybe I could learn some moves from you. And just so you don't feel like you're wasting your time with me, I've got some money. We could place a wager on the game to make it more interesting for you. I'm sure you'll win it, but it would be worth it to learn from the best."

I stop clearing the table and look at Will. He looks at me and winks before returning his doe eyed attention back to Slade.

I know what he's doing, but I can't believe he picked Slade to do it to.

My father taught Will how to play pool as soon as he could hold a cue stick in his hands properly. He's the best pool player I know, and I can't believe he's picked Slade to hustle!

"Now why are you just handing your money over like that to him, Will?" Linc asks in exasperation, obviously a willing accomplice in Will's little game.

"Well, I hate to take your money, kid," Slade says hesitantly.

"No, no," Will assures him. "Trust me. Once I learn your moves I'll make it back tenfold."

"Well, I'll tell you what. Just to make it fair, I'll double whatever you put down to give you an added incentive."

"Wow, really?" Will says so convincingly in mock amazement I'm left speechless by his acting skills. "That would be awesome! But, I'm pretty sure your money is safe from me."

Slade smiles and puts a hand on Will's shoulder.

"Come on then, show me where the pool table is, and I'll show you how to win from anybody."

Will, Linc, and Slade head up stairs, and I see Desmond, Andre, and Brutus follow behind them to watch. Uncle Malcolm is sitting on the living room floor with Mae. She's trying to put her pink glittery mardi-gras mask on his face. He smiles for all he's worth as he watches the others go to the second floor where the game room is. I feel certain he knows exactly what Will is up to.

My dad comes up to me. "Wonder how much he'll win from them."

"Are you ok with what he's doing?" I ask.

My dad chuckles. "If they let a thirteen-year-old boy hustle them so easily, it might be a good lesson for them all."

I giggle because I know he's absolutely right.

I see Jered walk out to the front porch alone and wonder what it's going to take for him to feel like he's a part of the group.

While Aiden is learning how to make my favorite chocolate fudge from Aunt Tara in the kitchen, I slip out to the front of the house to speak with Jered.

I find him sitting on the porch swing in a contemplative mood, just staring down at his hands clasped loosely in his lap.

"Mind if I join you for a little while?" I ask him.

His head snaps up like he didn't even realize I was outside with him.

"No, of course not," he tells me.

I go to sit next to him on the swing.

"Why didn't you join the others upstairs?"

"And be hustled by your little brother?" Jered says with a chuckle.

"Ok, so now I know who the smart one of the bunch is," I say, not even trying to suppress a giggle.

Jered sighs. "I guess I'm just not that trusting anymore. Though, I might go up there just to see Slade lose for once."

"I think it'll be good for him to be humbled by Will."

"Certainly won't hurt," Jered agrees.

We sit in a comfortable, mutual silence for a while.

"Do you mind if I ask you something?" Jered finally says.

"No, I don't mind. Ask me anything."

"How did you know I would be one of your chosen? I mean you could have just picked anyone who showed up in the desert. What made you seek me out in particular?"

"Because I knew you were supposed to be one."

"But how?"

"Can you keep a secret?" I ask.

"Of course. Nothing you say to me will be repeated."

"I didn't really choose you guys. You chose yourselves."

Jered looks at me in complete confusion. "I'm afraid you've lost me."

"When it was time for me to choose, those of you who wanted to be chosen the most glowed to me. It was almost like you had a permanent spotlight on you. Your auras showed your need to help me and my family."

Jered falls silent and contemplative again for a while.

"I guess that makes sense," he finally says. "I did want you to choose me."

"Then why didn't you come to the desert?"

Jered shakes his head. "Because I didn't see the point in it. I felt certain you wouldn't consider me since Malcolm distrusts me so much. And, I know how much his opinion means to you."

"Ok, it's my turn to ask *you* something," I say.

"Anything."

"Why did you want me to choose you so badly?"

Jered sighs heavily. “Everyone has had to earn their forgiveness in one way or another. I hoped this mission would be my way to earn mine. I still hope it is. And it’s not just my father’s forgiveness that I’m seeking. I need to feel like I’ve done some good to earn it. I think that’s how it is for all of us. We angels are the worst when it comes to guilt complexes.”

“I totally agree with you on that,” I tell Jered with a smile, knowing how much it meant to Aiden to earn his forgiveness after the Tear was made, and he was given the opportunity.

“Our father would probably forgive us if we just asked Him to, but I think He knows we need to feel like we’ve done something to earn it or it means nothing.”

“I can understand that,” I tell him. “Having something handed to you doesn’t mean as much as working for it.”

“Exactly.”

The front door opens and Aiden steps out. I feel my breath catch in my throat when I see him, but I’m becoming used to that now. Just the sight of him seems to take my breath away.

“Hey,” he says to us, “are you ready for dessert?”

I want something sweet against my tongue, but it's not exactly the chocolate cream pie my father made for us to eat.

"Sure," I say, standing from the porch swing and turning to look at Jered. "Coming?"

"No," Jered says, "I think I would like to stay out here for a little while longer, if that's all right."

I nod, letting him know I understand.

Just then Daniel phases onto the front porch.

"Oh, sorry," he says startled to find us all there. "I didn't want to just phase into the house without having permission."

"Did everything go all right?" Aiden asks. "Did you have any trouble stashing Belphagor?"

Daniel shakes his head. "No. No trouble. I just felt like I needed to watch over him for a while before I left him there. I wanted to make sure the dagger's effect wasn't temporary."

"Well, we have some leftovers if you're hungry," Aiden tells him. "And we're just about to have dessert."

"Leftovers sound great," Daniel says with a smile.

Aiden and I begin to walk Daniel inside the house, but I chance a glance back at Jered before I go in and see that he's crawled back into his own little world again.

I hope in time he will come to realize he was chosen for a reason and accept that his fate is now in his own hands.

A couple of hours later, just as it's starting to get dark outside, I decide to check on Will in the game room. Aiden and I go up just to make sure he's survived his devious plans to separate Slade from his money.

When we get up there, Will is standing beside the table with his partner in crime, Linc, standing behind him holding a wad of cash in his hands greedily counting their profits. I see Jered finally decided to join the group also and smile at him so he knows I'm happy to see him there with the others.

Desmond seems to be the latest victim to Will's skill with a pool cue.

"Couldn't have given me a little warning that your brother was a pool shark, Caylin?" Slade asks as he comes to stand beside Aiden and me.

"Well, I could have warned you," I say, "but would you have believed me if I had?"

Slade laughs. "No, probably not. I guess I've learned to not underestimate a half-pint."

Will looks at Slade and smiles. "Never underestimate a Cole, either. We rarely lose."

"I'll try to remember that," Slade says with a shake of his head, apparently still having trouble believing he just got swindled by my little brother.

"Besides Jered, who had the good sense to stay out of all this, I'm the last Watcher standing," Desmond says as he concentrates to make his next shot but scratches.

"Not standing for long," Will tells him, going to the pocket that Desmond shot the cue ball into and taking it in hand.

Will goes on to call his next three shots to clear the table of all his solid colored balls.

"And that just leaves the 8 ball in the corner left pocket," he says, taking his aim and sinking the called ball into its designated pocket.

Desmond groans and hands over a stack of bills to Will.

"I thought I had you, little man," Desmond says, ruffling Will's dark hair into a mess, but Will doesn't seem to mind much.

Why should he? He just won a pile of money from my chosen.

Desmond lays his pool cue on the table and walks over to Aiden.

"How about coming out with us for a pint?" Desmond says to Aiden. "It's been ages since we did anything together."

I look up at Aiden and see uncertainty on his face.

"Why don't you go?" I tell him, hoping to alleviate any worry he has that I wouldn't want him to leave me. "You should go spend some time with your friends."

"Are you sure?" he asks me. It's then I know he wants to go.

"Absolutely," I tell him, standing up on my tiptoes and giving him a kiss on the cheek. "Go have some fun."

"There," Desmond says, "you have the blessing of the only person who matters." Desmond turns to the others in the room. "Anyone else up for a pint of ale?"

"Are you dragging us to that hole in the wall in Cardiff?" Andre asks.

"Of course!" Desmond says like Andre shouldn't have even needed to ask. "Why would we go anywhere else?"

"I'm in," Brutus says.

"Me too," says Daniel.

"How about you, Jered?" Desmond says. "I think you're the only one who might have money left to pay for it all."

"I'm not sure where it is," Jered says, not looking completely certain he wants to go.

"No worries," Slade says placing a beefy hand on Jered's shoulder. "I'll escort you there myself."

Aiden turns to me.

"I'm not sure what time I'll be through," he tells me, not having to mention out loud that this means he probably won't be able to keep his earlier promise of making me say 'mercy'.

"Another time," I tell him. "Go have fun with your friends."

Aiden leans down and kisses me lightly on the lips.

"I'll text you later," he promises.

"Ok."

The Watchers phase for their night of revelry, and I turn to my little brother and Linc.

"So," I say crossing my arms in front of me, "just what exactly do you plan to do with your ill-gotten gains from this evening?"

Will places a hand over his heart and feigns a look of hurt.

"Ill-gotten? I'll have you know I worked hard for that money. And it's not like I cheated them. They had a fair chance to win."

"But why did you want the money, Will?" I ask. "What did you need to buy that mom and dad couldn't give you money for?"

It wasn't like my parents weren't filthy rich. None of us kids had ever *not* gotten whatever we needed.

"I wanted to buy mom a gift with my own money instead of the money dad gives me to go get her something with," Will says. "This way she'll know it's from me."

I can't help but smile. "That's actually kind of sweet, little bro."

Will shrugs. "Can't help it. I'm just a big softy."

"What did you need so much money for though?"

"You'll just have to wait for her party to find out."

I don't push Will for more information. He seems to want to surprise my mom and the rest of us so I decide to let him keep his little secret.

We spend the rest of the evening with just immediate family. At one point, Mae talks Uncle Malcolm into going outside to swing her on one of the dragons hanging from the pink castle play set he built her for Valentine's Day. I decide to go out with them for a little fresh air.

As Uncle Malcolm is swinging Mae, he asks, "So, did you like your own castle on Valentine's Day?"

I smile as I lean against the side of the rainbow slide.

"Yes, I did. Thank you for helping Aiden design it. And thank you for having a talk with him about kissing me."

"Someone had to talk some sense into the boy," Uncle Malcolm grumbles. "I didn't see any point in him denying you something you wanted just because he felt the need to deny himself. It wasn't your fault he used to be a blood sucking nymphomaniac."

"Uncle Malcolm," I say rolling my eyes at his description of Aiden before he met me.

“Well, it’s the truth,” Uncle Malcolm defends, “and the only reason I had a talk with him is because I knew he wasn’t like that anymore. If anyone has been an example of how true love can change a person, it’s Aiden.”

“Did you really threaten to kill him when he first saw me?”

“Yes, I did,” Uncle Malcolm answers with no shame attached to the words. “And I would have done it if your mother had given the ok. Luckily, for the two of you, she didn’t.”

“Higher, Uncle Malcolm!” Mae urges.

“Uh, you Cole women,” Uncle Malcolm says with a shake of his head, “so demanding, even at a young age.”

“We just know what we want,” I tell him with a smile. “There’s nothing wrong with that.

Uncle Malcolm looks over at me and continues to shake his head, but I see a hint of a smile tug at the corners of his lips.

Unfortunately, it doesn’t last long.

Uncle Malcolm suddenly stops Mae’s swinging and looks off toward the woods to the right of the house. He quickly grabs Mae off the swing and hands her to me.

“Go inside. Now!”

He phases before I can ask why.

I look down at Mae just before I'm about to phase us inside the house.

But Mae phases first and not into the safe confines of our home.

She follows Uncle Malcolm…

CHAPTER FIFTEEN

I don't hesitate. I follow their phase trails and find myself standing in a clearing within a dense forest. The moon is full and high in the sky, illuminating the scene before me.

When I get there, I see Uncle Malcolm fighting off five cloaked Watchers. The fighting is almost too fast for my eyes to follow. They seem to be using a combination of just plain brutality and phasing in an attempt to get the upper hand on one another. Uncle Malcolm seems to be trying his best to break through their lines to reach something behind them. I look over and see what it is he's after.

Mae.

Mae is being held by one of the Watcher's children who are already transformed by the rise of the moon into a werewolf. The wolf stands tall, well over six feet high, on its backward legs as the other four werewolves around him cower off to the side away from him and Mae. Mae is watching Uncle Malcolm fight and crying hysterically. I'm not completely sure if she's crying because Uncle

Malcolm is fighting or because she's scared. But, the wolf holding her doesn't seem to have any intentions of harming her, at least not yet. I assume it won't do anything to her until it's given the order to by its father.

I can't just phase over to her because I'm somewhere I've never been before. I have to make it through the line of Watchers to reach my sister, which seems to be the same dilemma Uncle Malcolm is facing.

I pray the fight Uncle Malcolm is putting up is enough of a distraction to allow me to pass by unnoticed and get to Mae.

As I try to sneak by, two of the Watchers abandon the fight with Uncle Malcolm to suddenly phase into my path, forcing me to stop dead in my tracks.

"Get out of my way!" I tell them. "I don't want to hurt you."

Neither man says a word. One phases in front of me and the other behind. Both lunge at me at the same time. My hands burst into blue flames, and I grab each of them by an arm, easily breaking their appendages at the elbows until their arms are bent completely backward and they cry out in pain.

"Leave *now*," I tell them both through clenched teeth, barely able to hold back the rage I feel towards them, "or I swear to God I *will* destroy you."

Both Watchers phase over to their children and grab them before they phase away from the fight.

Seeing what I did causes one of the three Watchers Uncle Malcolm is still fighting to phase over to the wolf holding Mae.

"Give the child to me!" the Watcher orders.

I immediately assume the wolf holding Mae must be this Watcher's child.

I watch this interaction between the Watcher and his child because I know Uncle Malcolm has his fight well under control when I see two heads roll off to the side and the corresponding bodies crumple to the ground at his feet.

"Rolph!" Uncle Malcolm says to the Watcher. "Leave her alone!"

The Watcher ignores Uncle Malcolm almost completely as he continues to stare at cursed offspring.

"Give me the girl, Tristan!" The Watcher demands.

Mae has stopped crying now since Uncle Malcom's fight is over. It's then I know the fighting was the true cause of her distress, not the fact that a werewolf is holding her.

Mae looks at the wolf and lifts one of her tiny hands to the top of his head. She begins to pet him between his eyes. The wolf looks startled when she first touches him like he isn't used to being treated with such gentleness. But, as she continues to glide her little hand across the pale hairless skin covering his head, I can see a calm settle over the wolf as he begins to relax under her comforting caress.

"Tristan!" The Watcher screams on the verge of hysteria. "Give her to me!"

The wolf looks at its father, and I see a slow transformation take place as its eyebrows lower and it bares its teeth at the Watcher with a menacing growl. He brings Mae closer to his chest in a protective hold.

Mae looks over at the Watcher and narrows her eyes at him as she says, "You are a bad man."

I almost want to laugh at the surprised look on the Watcher's face at her admonishing words. Mae turns back to look at the wolf.

"Come on, puppy," Mae says. "I'll take care of you."

And she phases.

"What the hell…." Uncle Malcolm says, voicing exactly what I'm thinking.

I can see where she's phased to, our living room in Lakewood. I don't worry too much about Mae because I know my mother can take care of the werewolf if it poses a threat back home.

Rolph stands there in what appears to be stunned silence. Finally, he turns to face Uncle Malcolm.

"How was she able to turn him against me?"

Uncle Malcolm crosses his arms over his chest.

"Maybe your hold over him wasn't as strong as you thought," he says. "What exactly was the purpose of this little attack, Rolph?"

"I asked them to bring you here," I hear a strange male voice say behind us.

Uncle Malcolm is instantly by my side, and we face a man I've never seen before together.

He's tall with shoulder length blonde hair and a short beard and mustache covering his face. His blue eyes practically glow in the dim light from the moon telling me I'm standing in the presence of someone powerful.

The stranger looks at Rolph.

"Leave us, but don't go after your son…"

"But…" Rolph begins to protest.

"Do not argue with me!" The stranger orders. "Now leave!"

Rolph grunts but phases as the stranger orders. The two remaining werewolves are in the process of placing their father's heads back on their bodies. I'm not sure how long we have before the Watchers are able to regenerate, but I don't intend to stay in the area long enough to find out.

"Hello, Lucifer," Uncle Malcolm says.

I feel the hair on the back of my neck stand up on end as I fully realize who is standing in front of me.

"Malcolm," Lucifer says before he directs his gaze to me. "Well, aren't you just the spitting image of your mother when she was your age."

"What do you want, Lucifer?" Uncle Malcolm asks almost as if he's bored with the conversation already. "I seriously doubt you brought us here for polite chit chat or to reminisce about all the times we've kicked your ass."

Lucifer looks back at Uncle Malcolm.

"Well, I only intended to bring *you* here, Malcolm. I didn't realize I would also gain the pleasure of having Ms. Cole present as well. But, since she's here, I suppose I can deliver my message to her personally instead of using you as a little messenger boy."

"And what is it exactly that you want to tell me?" I ask, finding my voice but still hearing it tremble slightly. I just hope Lucifer doesn't notice.

He smiles indulgently at me, and I know he realizes how intimidated I feel in his presence. An advantage I definitely don't want him to have over me.

"I was going to tell your over protective uncle here to inform you that you've declared a war on us you will never win. You should stop now while you're ahead. Levi is still trying to recover from losing the perfectly good body you destroyed. And I'm not sure what it is you've done to Belphagor, but I do know I can't call him to my side anymore. That in itself tells me whatever you're able to do must be very powerful. My brothers think you have an ability we don't know about yet. But, I don't share their suspicions. I think you've been given access to something by my father. Is my assumption correct, little monkey?"

"What did you steal from Heaven?" I ask in return, hoping to turn the tables and unbalance him.

My question seems to hit the desired nerve because Lucifer's eyes widen in surprise.

"So, He finally told you about that, did He?" He asks in a whisper.

"What did you take Lucifer?" Uncle Malcolm asks. "What does our father want back from all of you?"

"If He wanted you to know that I suppose He would have told you, Malcolm. But," Lucifer's brow wrinkles in confusion, "why only give you half the information? Why not tell you the whole story?"

Apparently, none of us has the answer to that particular question and silence reigns supreme. Only the wind rustling through the leaves of the trees surrounding us breaks the quiet.

“Are we done here then?” Uncle Malcolm asks. “I would really like to go wash the blood of your Watchers off of me as soon as possible.”

“Yes, we’re through for now,” Lucifer says as he directs his gaze to me again. “I hope to not see you again, Ms. Cole.”

“I guess we’ll just have to see what the future holds for the both of us,” I tell him.

Lucifer phases.

“Well, that was interesting,” Uncle Malcolm says.

“Don’t you mean terrifying?” I ask, still trying to shake off being in the presence of someone who just seemed to ooze pure hatred.

“It’s been a long time since I felt any sort of intimidation in his presence,” Uncle Malcolm tells me. “I mostly just feel pity for him now.”

“Why?” I ask, finding it hard to believe Uncle Malcolm could pity someone as formidable as Lucifer.

“Jess almost got him to ask for our father’s forgiveness once,” Uncle Malcolm tells me. “She was so close, but he let his pride get in the way, as usual.”

"Do you think he'll ever be that close again?"

Uncle Malcolm shrugs his shoulders. "Really not high on my list of priorities at the moment. But, this little meeting did tell me something."

"What's that?"

"That we've scared him," Uncle Malcolm says. "Well, as scared as the devil himself can get anyway. If he didn't think you presented a threat, he would have just left things alone, but he felt compelled to give you a warning instead."

"Is that good or bad?"

"Good in a way," Uncle Malcolm says, "and bad in others."

"That's not very reassuring."

"No," Uncle Malcolm agrees, "it isn't. But, there's not much else to be learned here now. Why don't we go see if your mother has killed Mae's new pet yet or not?"

Uncle Malcolm and I both phase to my home and find a scene I don't think either of us expected to be met with.

Mae is sitting in the middle of the living room floor in my mother's lap with the werewolf lying flat on his back in front of them. Mae is petting his head and singing *Somewhere Over the Rainbow.*

“What the hell…” Uncle Malcolm says, repeating his exact same words when Mae first phased back home with her new pet in tow.

“Why are you covered in blood, Uncle Malcolm?” Will asks, openly staring at the blood splatter on Uncle Malcolm’s body and clothing.

“Just a little tussle with a few Watchers,” Uncle Malcolm tells him.

My dad comes up to me and takes me into his arms, hugging me fiercely. I almost think he has his Watcher strength back his embrace is so strong.

“Are you all right?” He asks, leaning away from me to look me over and make sure I don’t have any visible wounds.

“I’m fine, Dad. I didn’t get hurt.”

My dad looks over at Uncle Malcolm, taking in his appearance.

“Why don’t you go shower and come back,” my dad suggests. “We’ve got things handled here for now.”

"Do you want me to take him to the cell Sebastian used to stay in at my house?" Uncle Malcolm asks staring at the werewolf with complete distrust.

"That won't be necessary," my mom tells him. "He won't harm us."

Uncle Malcolm lifts a dubious eyebrow at the whole scene but doesn't try to argue with my mother.

"Well, I'll make sure the door is locked down there just in case you need to phase him into it quickly, dearest."

My mother nods, letting Uncle Malcolm know she heard him, but from the look on her face, I can tell she's convinced we won't need to put the werewolf in the cell.

After Uncle Malcolm phases home to wash up, I ask my dad, "So, what exactly are we supposed to do with him?"

My dad shrugs. "Just keep him calm tonight, I think. When he transforms back into his human form in the morning, I guess we'll ask him what it is he wants to do. So, what happened, Caylin? Where did the three of you go?"

I tell my family exactly what transpired after Mae followed Uncle Malcolm's phase trail.

"I wish you'd had a dagger with you to stab that…" my mother pauses because I think she was about to say a term not suitable for the tender ears of young children, "person."

"Yeah," I agree, "me too. That would have been a big one of the seven down."

"The most difficult one to find," my father agrees as he watches Mae fall quiet in my mother's arms and lay her small head against her shoulder. "Lilly, she needs to go to bed."

My mom gets up from the floor and the werewolf follows her with his eyes, keeping a watchful eye on Mae.

"Come on," my mother tells it before looking at my dad. "I'll sleep in Mae's room tonight. I'm pretty sure he'll follow us up there and just sleep on the floor."

"I don't like this, Lilly."

"It'll be all right, Brand. Trust me."

"I always have."

"Then don't worry," she tells him. "I know what I'm doing."

My father sighs heavily but nods his agreement.

"At least let me sit in there with my shot gun."

My mother smiles. “If that would make you feel better then do it. But, I don’t think it’s necessary.”

“What’s not necessary?” Uncle Malcolm asks, phasing back to the house with wet hair and wearing a white silk pajama set with the shirt completely unbuttoned.

My mother tells him the plan.

“Well I’m sitting in there too,” Uncle Malcolm declares in a voice that says he isn’t going to accept any argument from my mother or father on this matter.

“Fine,” my mom says in a resigned voice, “you two do what you want, but it isn’t necessary. He won’t harm us.”

With Mae cradled in her arms, my mom heads up the stairs with the werewolf following close behind.

My father walks to his study to get his shotgun out of the safe, and Uncle Malcolm follows behind the werewolf up the stairs.

Will and I soon find our own beds. No matter what might have happened this evening, we both still have school tomorrow.

It’s not until I crawl into bed that I see the ten missed messages from Aiden on my phone.

I take a deep breath and text him back.

Hi

He answers back immediately like he had his phone in his hands just waiting for me to text him.

Is everything all right?? I almost came over but didn't want to look like a psycho boyfriend who needed you to answer every text I sent. Are you safe?

I'm fine. Uncle Malcolm and I just had a little adventure is all.

Why do I get the feeling this little adventure wasn't of the fun variety?

Because you are very intuitive where I'm concerned.

What happened?

I hesitate to reply back. I have a feeling Aiden might go ballistic when he learns what happened. But, we promised each other that we wouldn't keep secrets from one another, and I'm not about to be the first one who breaks that pact.

I met Lucifer tonight.

Where are you now?

My bedroom.

Before I know it, Aiden is standing beside my bed.

"What happened?" He asks, sitting on the side of my bed and bringing me into his arms.

His hug rivals my father's in intensity.

"I'm fine," I reassure him. "I wasn't hurt."

Aiden just holds me for a moment longer before letting me go so he can look me in the eyes.

"Caylin, what happened?"

I go on to tell Aiden exactly what happened.

"I don't like it," Aiden says, standing from the side of my bed as he starts to pace back and forth. "Lucifer wouldn't waste his time unless he thought you were a real threat. He's basically placed a bull's-eye on your forehead, Caylin. And you can bet every minion under his control will be targeting you now, if not under his direct order than to prove themselves to him."

"It'll be all right, Aiden. I'm not scared."

Aiden stops pacing and stands there staring down at me.

"You should be," he tells me. "You should be very scared, Caylin. I'm not sure what it is Jess might have seen in him to think he could change, but I've only ever seen pure evil from Lucifer. In the war in Heaven, hc was the most vicious of us. The most ruthless. And his hatred for humans is what fuels his power here on Earth. It sounds like you've just reached the top of his hit list. That isn't a spot you want to occupy."

"I'm not going to say I'm not scared by him," I admit. "But I'm not going to let my fear of him control me either. If I did, he would definitely win, Aiden. And I refuse to go down without a fight."

Aiden comes to sit back down on the side of my bed. He takes one of my hands into one of his.

"Please," he almost begs, "promise me you won't take any unnecessary chances."

"I promise not to take any unnecessary chances."

"And promise me you won't run off like that again without taking back up with you. You were so lucky tonight, Caylin. You could have been seriously hurt."

"I had to go," I say, not understanding why he doesn't understand that. "Mae could have been in danger. I didn't have time to gather up a cavalry."

"A couple of minutes wouldn't have made much of a difference," Aiden argues.

"It only takes a second to break a neck," I tell him, hoping he understands the reality of the situation I faced. "Are you seriously telling me you wouldn't have done the exact same thing I did?"

"That's not the point."

"It's exactly the point. You're going to have to get over your fear of me getting hurt, Aiden. I'm strong. You know that. I'm even stronger than you are."

"But you're also human," he argues. "You can die. You don't have our regenerative powers. I have had my head ripped off but still managed to come back after the damage healed itself. You can't do that, Caylin. Yes, you're stronger. Yes, you're just as powerful as your mother, but you're also human. You're mortal. And I can't lose you," he says, squeezing my hand.

I lose some of my growing irritation because the look in Aiden's eyes breaks my heart. Just the thought of losing me dims the light in them.

I squeeze his hand back.

"I promise I won't take any unnecessary risks. You won't lose me. Not anytime soon at least. Not until we're old and grey with a ton of grandchildren running around us."

Aiden tries to smile, but I can see how forced it is. He's still worried.

He lifts his free hand and traces the edge of my cheek. He leans in and kisses my lips so lightly I barely feel it.

"Is that the best you can do?" I ask him, hoping to tease him into a better kiss than that.

"It is while I'm in your bedroom," Aiden tells me. "Get some sleep, beautiful. I'm not sure what will happen tomorrow so you need to get as much rest as you can."

I crawl under my covers and Aiden straightens them across my chest.

"Sweet dreams," he says to me, turning off the lamp on my nightstand.

"Will you stay with me?" I ask him, not wanting to be alone just yet. "At least until I start to snore. Then you can leave."

I hear a soft chuckle come from Aiden as he sits back down on my bed.

"I'll wait," he promises.

I reach out a hand to him and he clasps it gently.

When I close my eyes, I sigh in contentment because I know the man I love is watching over me.

CHAPTER SIXTEEN

When I wake up the next morning, I smell the sweet aroma of apple cinnamon muffins and bacon. I notice the door to my room is wide open which is strange because I never leave the door open at night. I sit up in bed and hear familiar voices coming from the kitchen.

One of the voices definitely belongs to Aiden.

I quickly get out of bed and phase to the kitchen.

I find Aiden there flipping an egg with a spatula in a pan on the stove with my dad standing beside him watching.

"You need to control your strength and do it more gently," my dad tells Aiden. "You broke the yolk by flipping it too hard."

Aiden's mouth quirks to the side. "Hmm, yes, I see that."

"What are you doing here?" I ask, drawing Aiden's attention away from the pan.

"I invited Aiden to stay for breakfast," my dad says, being the one to answer my question instead.

"Stay?" I ask.

"I never left your room last night," Aiden tells me. "After what happened to you yesterday, it didn't feel right to leave you all alone."

I look at my dad assuming I'll see steam coming out of his ears at any moment by this knowledge, but he doesn't look phased by it one bit.

"Aiden kept the door open all night," my dad tells me. "I saw him in there when I went to check up on you, and we had a talk."

I'm not sure what all the 'talk' entailed, but I guess things such as the proper etiquette while in my bedroom were discussed.

"And you were ok with him staying?" I ask my dad.

"I understood his motivation," my dad replies.

Aiden smiles at me, and I notice him staring at my hair.

Self-consciously, I run my fingers through it and know instantly why he's staring at it. It's a total mess.

"I should probably go get ready for school," I tell them, phasing before Aiden can take a permanent mental picture of me with my rumpled pajamas and messy hair.

I quickly jump into the shower and get ready for school. I wear my usual uniform combination of plaid skirt, white shirt, blazer, tie and knee high black boots. I grab my backpack from my desk and head downstairs.

Just as I exit my room, I literally run into a half-naked man I've never seen before. He was towel drying his hair as he came out of the bathroom and obviously didn't see me.

Without even thinking about, I drop my backpack to the floor and grab the man by the throat as I slam him hard up against the wall.

"Who are you?" I demand.

My mother phases to my side almost instantly.

"Caylin, put him down. He's Mae's wolf."

I look into the stranger's handsome face and am immediately drawn to his blue eyes. They hold the same sadness of the wolf from the night before. Slowly, I loosen my grip and step away from him.

"Sorry," I say, briefly taking in his muscular form and tanned skin being exposed in his shirtless state.

He's only wearing a pair of blue jeans, and his short blonde hair is standing straight up from his head like it's permanently gelled that way.

"No, I'm sorry for running into you," he says. "I should have been watching where I was going."

I look over to my mother, and I see her shake her head slightly. She knows I want to ask questions, like why the heck is this guy still here, but apparently my mom doesn't want to discuss it in front of him.

"Tristan," my mom says, "I put some more clothes in the guest room I showed you. Feel free to wear whatever you want. It's all yours now."

"Thank you, Mrs. Cole."

"Call me Lilly, Tristan."

Tristan nods but he doesn't look like he'll be very comfortable addressing my mother so informally.

"I'm sorry I scared you," Tristan tells me. "I'll try to watch where I'm going next time."

He turns away and walks to the guest bedroom, shutting the door behind him.

"Why is he still here?" I ask my mother as I pick my backpack up and we walk downstairs together.

"He doesn't really have anywhere else to go," my mother answers.

"I thought he would go back to his father."

"He can't."

I stop descending the stairs halfway down.

"What do you mean he can't?" I ask.

"When he defended Mae against his father last night, he broke his bond to him. He's no longer connected to his father anymore."

"So, what…he's like a lone wolf now or something?"

"More like rogue."

"Does that mean we have to keep him forever?"

My mother smiles. "You make him sound like a dog Mae picked up off the street and brought home."

"He kind of is, isn't he?"

"Yes and no, I guess. He isn't our pet, but he's formed a bond to Mae."

"What kind of bond?" I ask, downright suspicious of this wolf's motives.

“I’m not completely sure yet,” my mom admits. “Malcolm wasn’t certain what it meant either. No wolf has ever broken the bond with their father before. I’m not even sure Tristan understands what happened last night. So, let’s give him some space and time, ok? He did protect Mae. We owe him a debt of gratitude for that.”

“How long is he going to be staying here?”

“Just until he figures out what he needs to do next. I don’t think it will be for very long.”

I don’t like it, but I can’t exactly argue that Tristan didn’t save Mae’s life last night either. Who knows what his father would have done to Mae if Tristan had handed her over to him. I didn’t want to think about it, and thanks to Tristan we didn’t have to find out.

We’re half way through eating breakfast when Uncle Malcolm comes over dressed in his usual teacher garb of suit, tie and black rimmed glasses. He’s carrying a pink pastry box in his hands, and I know he’s already been to Paris that morning to buy my mother her favorite chocolate croissant rolls. He’ll do it every morning of her pregnancy until she gives birth. It’s tradition.

"So, where's the dog?" Uncle Malcolm asks, snatching a piece of bacon off Will's plate as he hands my mom her box of croissants. Mae climbs up on her chair seat and holds her arms out to Uncle Malcolm until he comes to get her.

"Tristan," my mother says as if correcting Uncle Malcolm, "is up in his room."

"His room?" Uncle Malcolm questions with a raised eyebrow, settling Mae against his hip while he looks at my mother. "Lilly, you aren't seriously going to let him stay here, are you?"

"Do you have a better idea?" My mom questions. "He's basically homeless now because of us."

"Nonsense," Uncle Malcolm scoffs. "He made his own decision. Besides, I can set him up somewhere out of our way where he won't hurt anyone."

"We're not going to just abandon him, Malcolm."

"But dearest, he could be a danger to all of you. Let me take him somewhere. I'll make sure he's well taken care of."

"No."

And that pretty much ended the discussion. Whenever my mother said no, she meant it. Uncle Malcolm was well aware of this fact and didn't try to argue his point any further.

There's a knock on the door and Leah pokes her head inside.

"Morning everyone," Leah says, walking in with Mason and Jess following in behind her.

Mason is carrying a black garment bag over one arm with JoJo's signature hot pink 'A' stitched on it, and Jess looks like she's prepared for war. She's dressed in her white leather outfit. She has her sword strapped to her back in its baldric, plasma pistol in its holster strapped to her right thigh and two new belted sheaths against each hip that I haven't seen before. Each sheath holds one of the silver daggers in it.

"So Malcolm told us you had an encounter of the Lucifer kind last night," Jess says to me, giving me a brief hug after I hand my dad my dirty breakfast dish.

"Yeah," I say. "I'm not sure how you could stand being around him, Jess. He gave me the creeps."

Jess lets out a half laugh. "Lucifer is an acquired taste, I guess. But, I'll do my best to make sure you don't have to deal with him again. Honestly, you and Malcolm are the first of us to see him since the Tear was closed."

Jess pulls out one of the silver daggers hanging on her hip from its sheath.

"I want you to keep this with you," she says, handing me the dagger.

"I don't think I'm supposed to take weapons to school," I tell her and realize how stupid it sounds coming out of my mouth after I say it.

"Don't worry, kiddo. No one is going to search you for weapons. Just stick it in one of your boots. If one of your classmates happens to see it, just tell them it's a stage prop or something. And Malcolm will be there in case any school official asks you about it. If Lucifer sees you as a threat now, there's no telling what he might send after you. This will at least give you an upper hand in case it's one of the princes."

"Is that for me?" Aiden asks Mason.

Mason hands Aiden the garment bag. "JoJo said it should fit."

"Did you need clothes for something special?" I ask Aiden.

"I'm going to school with you," he tells me. "But, I needed to go in without anyone being able to see me. This outfit is like Jess'. I can turn invisible when I'm wearing it."

"We're both going with you today," Jess tells me.

"Not that I'm complaining," I say, "but shouldn't school be a safe place for me? Aiden told me they never attack in public areas."

"Usually not," Jess agrees, "but we have no way of knowing how desperate they are right now. Anything can happen. I'm mostly going to make sure there aren't any more changelings in your school. I'm really the only one who can see them since their auras are different. After I do a sweep, Mason and I will be heading after one of the princes today."

"Alone?" I ask.

"No, Zack, Chandler, Jered, and Andre will be going with us."

"Do you need me?" I ask.

Jess shakes her head. "No, we can take care of Amon ourselves. Once we have him, that'll only leave us five more to take down."

"I'll be right back," Aiden tells me before he phases.

I assume he's gone to one of his homes to change clothes.

"I'm sorry. Am I interrupting something?"

All eyes turn to Tristan standing just outside the kitchen in his jeans and a buttoned up blue green plaid shirt.

"Puppy!" Mae says, before scrambling down from Uncle Malcolm's hip and running to Tristan like he's her long lost best friend.

Tristan bends down on one knee as Mae runs up to him and wraps her little arms around his neck. She hugs him fiercely before pulling away.

"Come play with me," Mae says, taking one of his hands with her own.

Tristan looks uncertain and directs his gaze to my mother as if asking for her permission.

"She won't be satisfied until you do," my mom tells him. "You might as well get it over with."

Tristan grins and stands up to follow Mae's lead into the living room and straight to her Victorian dollhouse.

"So…" Jess starts in a whisper, "what's up with that? Why does Mae seem so attached to the wolf?"

My mom shrugs. “I’m not sure, but whatever the connection is it seems to have saved her life last night.”

“Have you talked to Tristan about what happened?” Uncle Malcolm asks.

“A little,” my mom answers. “Basically, he just said he felt an overwhelming need to protect Mae, even from his own father.”

“I’ve never heard of a wolf disobeying their father,” Mason says as he watches the two of them in the living room. “The bond is usually so strong they follow any order their father gives, especially when they are in wolf form.”

“We’ve always been able to keep the wolves at bay,” my mom says. “Even Caylin saw her effect on the wolves with the Watchers who attacked Aiden.”

“True,” Brand said. “I remember Abby telling me how much you affected her when she was in wolf form.”

“And the wolves when Tara and Malik were attacked that Halloween,” my mom reminds my dad. “They did what I told them to do.”

“But that’s not the same as a wolf severing his bond with his father,” Mason points out.

My mom watches Tristan and Mae playing by the dollhouse.

"I just don't feel any danger from him," my mom finally says. "I don't think he would hurt Mae or anyone else in this family for that matter whether he's in wolf form or not."

"I have to agree with Lilly," my dad says. "I don't sense any malice from him. He just seems lost more than anything else."

"Well," Uncle Malcolm says, crossing his arms over his chest as he watches Mae and Tristan play, "if he doesn't behave himself I can always get him a leash."

"Malcolm…" my mom says in her 'warning' voice.

"Just making the offer, Lilly," Uncle Malcolm says with a shrug.

Aiden phases back and I literally do a double take at his outfit.

It's black. It's leather. And it's tight.

"I think JoJo thought I was a bit smaller than I actually am," Aiden says, self-consciously rubbing at the thighs of his pants as if the action will magically cause the leather there to stretch an inch or two.

Personally, I think they fit perfectly because I absolutely can't stop staring at Aiden.

I feel Uncle Malcolm's index finger slide underneath my chin gently tilting my head back up.

"Eyes up," he whispers to me, and it's only then that I realize my gaze wasn't exactly directed to the most proper spot on Aiden's person. But, it definitely stood out to my eyes.

I try to shake off the effect Aiden is having on me, but I feel almost drugged because my head is spinning. When I look back over at Aiden, I swear he's blushing.

"We should head to school," Uncle Malcolm says, his words acting like cold water in my face. "Otherwise, we'll be late."

"Aiden and I will phase there ahead of you," Jess tells me. "I'll be invisible, but I'll stay there until I'm certain there aren't any changelings around."

I nod. "Ok. Be careful."

Aiden doesn't say anything to me, but he does wink and smile before he phases him and Jess to my school.

When Leah and I arrive there, I immediately wonder how I will know where Aiden is.

It's not until I'm at my locker to grab one of my books that I know Aiden is nearby.

I feel someone play with the back of my hair, but when I look behind me, there's no one there.

I turn back to face the inside of my locker and whisper, "Is that you?"

"Yes," he whispers back.

"Are you going to act as my shadow today?"

"Yes," he says, and I can hear a distinct smile in his voice.

"I hope you don't get too bored."

"Never."

I close my locker and head to my first class.

As I sit in my American History lecture, I wonder where Aiden is. But, how am I supposed to figure that out?

Then I have an idea.

I find a clear page in my notebook and write, *Are you there?*

I feel Aiden wrap his hand around mine and guide my hand to write, **Yes.**

I wish I could see you

Why? Do you like the outfit that much?

I do like the outfit. I'm not going to lie about that. But, no, I want to see your face.

I hear a slight creaking of leather before I feel a hand underneath my desk grab the hand I have resting in my lap. Before I know it, I feel Aiden's face pressed against my palm. His warm breath tickles my skin, but just being able to feel him and 'see' him with my hand makes me smile.

I don't smile just because I can feel him. I'm smiling because he's showing me yet again just how much he loves me. Not that I had any doubts about that fact, but a girl likes to know she's worth having someone sit on a cold hard floor, crouched uncomfortably beneath her desk just so she can feel the face of the man she loves.

After a while, Aiden kisses the center of my palm and his face is gone.

Thank you

Anytime, beautiful.

When lunch rolls around, I feel like Aiden is wasting his time watching over me. I feel sure he would be of more use to Jess and Mason in helping them take down Amon.

"Are you hungry?" I ask him as I sit at the table.

"No," he says from behind me, and I feel him play with the back of my hair a little bit, like he needs to touch me.

"I like that," I tell him.

"Good."

Leah, Will, and Linc join me soon after.

Will starts to wave his hands in the air around me looking like a wacked out mime.

"What are you doing?" I hiss at him.

"I'm trying to figure out where he is," Will says.

Suddenly Will's chair is pushed further up to the table.

"Stop," Aiden warns.

Will silently mouths, "O-K."

Linc snickers at Will.

"Dude, you should know better. Aiden's a War Angel. He could have your noodle for breakfast if he wanted to."

Will rolls his eyes at Linc.

"He wouldn't do that to me."

Will makes his statement with so much confidence I have to ask, "What makes you think that?"

"Because I'm your brother and you guys will be getting married. We're like family now, which makes me like his little brother too. There's no way he would hurt me."

Well, I couldn't exactly argue against that logic.

Even though I can't see him, I know Aiden is probably smiling about what Will just said. I get the feeling family will be very important to Aiden. The total respect he shows my parents tells me that he won't expect anything less from our own children. And to be honest, that's exactly what I want. I always imagined me having the same relationship with my own kids that my parents have with Will, Mae, and me. We've always felt loved and taken care of, yet, at the same time, given just enough freedom to slowly come into our own and become the people we are meant to be.

When I walk into Uncle Malcolm's class, I sit in my usual desk. After everyone has entered the room and the door is closed, I hear a slight creak of leather beside me and know Aiden has just sat down in the desk Hunter used to sit in every period. I'm reminded that this fight with the princes has already claimed a casualty. An innocent boy who could have had the world at his feet when he became a man. But, his attraction to me led him to an early grave. I feel a pang of guilt as I realize how different Hunter Manning's life would have turned out if he had never met me.

"I hope you all did your assignment this weekend," Uncle Malcolm tells the class.

It's only then that I realize I didn't actually do the project, but surely Uncle Malcolm will cut me some slack after the weekend I just had.

"Caylin," Uncle Malcolm says, "why don't you start us off on today's assignment?"

Hmm, I guess trying to save the world doesn't get you out of homework in Uncle Malcolm's class. Thankfully, I have a memory so perfect I can remember things I haven't read in years.

I stand up and go to the front of the class.

"I hope you all have your chosen poems memorized," Uncle Malcolm says. "And I want you to recite them with a little feeling. Don't just say the words like you're reading a shopping list. Put a little emotion into what the writer of the poem is trying to make you feel. Caylin, which poem did you pick?"

"You said we could pick any poem we wanted, right? Even if it wasn't by an English poet?"

"Yes. That's what I said. Which did you choose?"

"I chose one by an American poet by the name of Ella Wheeler Wilcox. Its title is *I Love You.*"

As I stand in front of the class, I direct my gaze to where I know Aiden is sitting. I wish I could look into his eyes as I recite it, but I try to put as much of my feelings for him into the words as I can to make up for not being able to see him. The poem is a little racy in parts with talk about wet mouths and warm young bodies in each other's arms, but the part I want him to hear most and know that it comes from me is how he sets my heart on fire.

When I'm through reciting my poem, I have to take in a deep breath just to calm the beating of my heart. Every word, every syllable I just uttered was meant only for Aiden. Even though I can't see him, I feel sure he understands the poem was meant as a small gift from me to him.

"Thank you, Caylin," Uncle Malcolm says. "You may sit down."

I go back to my seat and as soon as I sit down, I feel Aiden's lips press lightly against my right cheek. It makes me smile.

The rest of the period goes by rather boringly. At least until the last student gets her chance to recite her chosen poem.

"Keri," Uncle Malcolm says, "it's your turn."

Keri gets up and goes to stand in front of Uncle Malcolm's desk.

"I have chosen to recite a poem by Pablo Neruda. He was a Chilean poet, and he also won the Nobel Prize for Literature a long time ago."

"And which of his poems did you choose for us today?" Uncle Malcolm asks from his perch on the corner of his desk.

"I chose…" Keri turns towards Uncle Malcolm and says dramatically, "*I Do Not Love You Except Because I Love You.*"

"Oookay," Uncle Malcolm says, looking a little worried by Keri's selection. "Proceed when you are ready, Keri."

Keri clears her throat and goes on to recite her poem.

The poem starts slow by talking about how much the person in the poem loves this other person. Keri slowly inches her way closer to Uncle Malcolm as she says the words and then, rather melodramatically spreads her arms out wide as she says 'I hate you deeply and hating you bend to you'.

Uncle Malcolm leans back away from Keri as far as he can without falling off the edge of the desk.

Keri's rendition of the poem is very intense. She continues her recitation, all the while staring into Uncle Malcolm's eyes. I almost want to laugh at the expression on Uncle Malcolm's face. He doesn't seem to know how to react to Keri's sudden dramatic performance, which seems meant just for him. If I didn't know any better, I would say he looks… scared.

When Keri falls to her knees in front of him almost screaming 'I will die of love because I love you', I think she actually renders Uncle Malcolm speechless, something that doesn't happen very often.

Once Keri is through reciting the poem, she stands to her feet and just looks at Uncle Malcolm. She's slightly out of breath from her theatrics as she waits for Uncle Malcolm to make a response to her poetic plea.

"Thank you, Keri, for that…rather manic interpretation of Mr. Neruda's poem. Please, retake your seat."

Keri goes back to her seat but continues to stare at Uncle Malcolm.

"And on that note," Uncle Malcolm says, raising a dubious eyebrow, "class dismissed. I'll see you all tomorrow."

I pick up my books and head out of the room.

I feel Aiden grab hold of my right elbow and gently guide me somewhere. He steers me towards a door stenciled with the words 'supply closet' in black.

I look around to see if anyone is watching, but no one seems to be paying me any mind. I quickly open the door and feel Aiden grab me around the waist pulling me inside and shutting the door behind me.

In the pitch black of the closet, I feel Aiden press my body firmly against him as his mouth finds mine easily in the darkness. He kisses me like a man who hasn't eaten in weeks, and I'm his first taste of food. His mouth ravages mine not only stealing my breath but also stealing every thought inside my head because all I'm able to think about is how his mouth feels against mine. His passion for me in that moment is almost like a physical presence in the room with us. I feel his want and his love for me in the kiss, and I don't want it to end.

It's only the screams from my classmates that is able to break through the spell Aiden is weaving around me.

Their cries of terror tear us away from one another. I immediately reach for the doorknob to see what's going on but Aiden stops me.

"Stay here," he orders. "Let me see what's happening out there first."

"They need help," I argue. "It might be a fire."

"If it is, I'll know soon enough. Please, Caylin, just stay here for a few seconds."

"Fine. Go!"

Aiden phases and I stand there in the dark for what seems like forever but is actually only about ten seconds.

Aiden is soon beside me again.

"What's going on?" I ask. "What's happening?"

"The princes are attacking."

CHAPTER SEVENTEEN

I reach for the doorknob, but Aiden grabs my wrist to stop me.

"You can't go out there," he says, almost yelling at me.

"Innocent people are in danger because of me, Aiden. I have to help them."

"Let me take care of it, Caylin, please."

"I don't run," I tell him. "And I don't hide. Either fight by my side or get out of my way!"

Aiden's hold on my wrist slackens, and he twines the fingers of our hands together instead.

"Side by side then," he says, sounding resigned to the fact that whether or not he helps me I'm going out to fight.

I open the door and see my classmates frantically running away from something coming down the other end of the corridor towards them.

Aiden, who is fully visible now, and I step out of the closet to face what's coming.

I'm not completely sure what I'm seeing at first.

Baal is walking down the hallway with two creatures who look like oversized wolves. Their fur is fluffy and a pristine white, but it has an orange glow to it as if it's on fire. Their soulless eyes are jet black like pieces of coal and staring straight at me.

"What are those things?" I ask Aiden.

"Hellhounds," he tells me, and I can hear the dread in his voice. "Whatever happens, don't let them bite you."

"I didn't have any intentions of letting them bite me, but why are you making a point of saying it?"

"Their bite is poisonous. You'll live the rest of your life feeling like your whole body is on fire. And that's not even the worst part."

"It gets worse than that?" I ask sarcastically. "Maybe you should just tell me the best way to kill them."

"Rip their heads off," Aiden says. "Your archangel power might work too. I don't know exactly. It's not something I have much experience with."

"Are the two of you trying to strategize together?" Baal taunts as he comes to a halt halfway down the hall with his beasts staying close to his sides. "How sweet. You know a couple who dies together gets to drift off into the ether in each other's arms. Wouldn't that be the epitome of a tragic love story?"

"Neither of them will be dying today," I hear Uncle Malcolm say behind me.

An eruption of frightened shrieks from the student body of my school echo down the hallway. They seem to be coming from each end of the building.

"Caylin," Uncle Malcolm says, "go find Leah. Aiden, go up front and see what's causing the commotion there."

"We can't just leave you here with him," I say, not liking the idea of splitting up.

"The more time you spend standing here arguing with me the more people will die because of this," Uncle Malcolm says to me in a controlled voice. "Now go!"

I know he's right, but it doesn't mean I have to like the idea of us being separated from one another.

I look over at Aiden. "Be careful."

Aiden nods. "You too, beautiful."

I phase to the back of the school where the Olympic size swimming pool is. Leah would have been at swim practice this time of day. It doesn't take me long to know she's in trouble.

One of her fireballs shoots over the water of the pool like a meteor and blasts the inner wall of the school, setting it ablaze with flames I know will be close to impossible to put out by conventional means. Leah's fire isn't like normal earthly fire. It can last ten times as long and burn a thousand times as hot. I look to see what or who she's firing at but see nothing there except a burning wall.

The fire alarm in the school begins to blare its warning siren and the sprinkler system switches on.

Through the deluge of water, I see Leah crouched down behind the stands against the outer wall with the other members of her swim team. It's only then I realize the cat's been let out of the bag. The kids at our school will soon know we're not your ordinary run of the mill students. I just hope none of them has to pay for that knowledge with their lives.

I phase over to Leah, which seems to startle the girls cowering beside her.

"What are you shooting at?" I ask Leah as I frantically scan the room for any signs of danger.

"Mammon was here," Leah tells me.

"Can you put the fire out?"

Leah shakes her head. "Not without my staff to help me control it."

I sigh because there's nothing to be done about it now, and there just wasn't enough time to worry about the school burning down. In fact, it might help get more of the students out of the building faster with the water pouring out of the sprinkler system and the deafening shriek of the alarm reverberating against the walls.

"Everyone grab hold of me," I tell the seven girls crouched around Leah. It seems like there should be one more girl to fill out the swim team, but I'm not certain.

They all look at me as if they're not sure I can be trusted.

"If you want to live," I tell them resisting the urge to yell at them, "come here and touch me so I can get you out of here."

"Come on girls," Leah tells them. "Caylin will protect us."

To Leah, they listen and finally gather around me.

“Hold on,” I tell them and phase them to Mama Lynn’s living room.

“Let go of me,” I tell them, but one doesn’t let go. “Leah, you need to let go of me.”

“No.” She says stubbornly. “I’m going back with you.”

“I don’t have time to argue about this,” I tell her, snatching my arm out of her grasp.

I phase back to the pool, but not before Leah grabs me again and phases with me, only then letting go.

“Damn it, Leah!” I yell, grabbing her again, but she just yanks her arm out of my hand before I can phase her back to safety.

“Don’t curse at me, Caylin Cole,” Leah says, looking just as frustrated with me as I am with her. “You’re not the only one who can fight them. I’ve done it once. I can do it again.”

“Yet, we always manage to come back,” a voice from the other side of the pool mocks.

We both look to see a man holding Keri, the girl from my English Lit class, by the throat three feet above the ground in front of him. Apparently, she was the missing swim team member because she’s still dressed in her swimsuit.

"Put the girl down, Mammon," Leah says, pointing the palm of her hand straight at the prince.

"Or what?" He asks snidely. "You're going to kill me? I bet I kill this *thing* first."

Mammon tightens his grip around Keri's throat, and I hear her begin to gag.

"Aren't you acting a bit childish, Mammon?" Leah taunts. "Or do you really have to hide behind a little girl? Afraid I'll fry your ass again like I did in Antarctica?"

"That body was rotting anyway," Mammon says, still holding Keri like a shield in front of him. "It just gave Lucifer incentive to release me from it so I could find a new one. Do you like this new form my little firecracker?"

"It's certainly younger and prettier to look at," Leah says. "Finally got better taste in bodies?"

While Leah taunts Mammon, I try to decide what to do. I have two options. One, I can phase over there and save Keri. Two, I can phase over there and stab Mammon with the dagger Jess gave me this morning and hope I can pry Keri out of Mammon's grip afterwards. Thankfully, a third option presents itself.

Uncle Malcolm phases in, grabs Keri and phases out, providing me with just the distraction I need. As Uncle Malcolm phases away with her, I crouch down to pull the dagger out of my boot where I stashed it earlier this morning and phase over to Mammon, stabbing him in the calf with it. The prince instantly falls to the ground.

Leah runs over yelling, “You got him!”

I stand up and look down at Mammon. My eyes are drawn to his outstretched hand, and I see a brand there similar to the one Belphagor had but this one says something different. I still don’t understand the significance of the word but make a note to tell someone about it later.

“But what do I do with him now?” I ask.

“I’ll take care of him,” Uncle Malcolm says, favoring his right leg as he bends down to pick Mammon up and toss him over his shoulder.

I look down at Uncle Malcolm’s leg and notice a lot of blood. His clothes have various rips everywhere but the material over his lower right leg is completely shredded.

“What’s wrong with your leg?” I ask him.

"Nothing," Uncle Malcolm says with a stone cold face.

I instantly know he's lying.

"I'll be right back," he tells us before phasing.

He's true to his word and returns a few seconds later, minus Mammon.

"We need to find Will and Linc," I tell Uncle Malcolm.

"I sent them home as soon as all of this started," Uncle Malcolm says. "I'm afraid my cover is blown here though. Too many people saw me phase."

"Leah's swim team saw us use our powers too," I inform him.

"Well, nothing to be done about it," Uncle Malcolm says, resigned to the fact that people know about us now.

"Where is Aiden?" I ask Uncle Malcolm.

"Still at the front of the school as far as I know," he says.

I grab Leah and phase us to where Aiden should be.

We find Aiden grappling with a man I have to assume is one of the princes since his hands are surrounded by blue flames. Their fighting is furious, and so fast I can't tell exactly who is winning.

Their split second phasing gives the illusion that they're blinking in and out of existence.

"How can we help him?" I ask Uncle Malcolm, feeling like we should do something but not knowing what.

"We'll just get in the way if we try," Uncle Malcolm says to me. "Or worse yet, accidentally hurt Aiden instead of Asmodeus."

"Do you have another dagger with you?" I ask Uncle Malcolm.

"No."

Leah shoots a fireball off to the right of us, and I hear a grunt of pain, which is the only thing that could draw my attention away from Aiden's fight with the prince.

Walking around both corners of the school are two groups of students, ten on each side. But, I know why Leah shot her fireball at them. Walking in front of the students, as if leading them towards us, are hellhounds.

"Caylin," Uncle Malcolm says, "you need to leave. We're out numbered."

"Changelings?" I ask, needing to know if that's what happened to the students converging on us.

"That would be my guess since they're being led by hellhounds," Uncle Malcolm says, unconsciously rubbing at his right leg and grimacing.

Leah shoots off two more fireballs in front of each group in an attempt to halt their progress, but it only stops them for a few seconds before they start walking towards us again.

"I'm not leaving Aiden," I say.

Uncle Malcolm turns to me and grabs me by the shoulders roughly.

"Caylin, listen to me. Take Leah and go home," he shakes me slightly to emphasize what he's telling me to do. "We're out numbered!"

"Not anymore."

Uncle Malcolm and I look to the bottom of the stairs leading to the landing we're standing on and see the cavalry.

Jess, Mason, Andre, Desmond, Brutus, Chandler, and Zack have come.

Jess pulls out her sword from the baldric on her back and it immediately ignites with its orange flames.

I see Chandler take out his talisman, Jubal's flute. He begins to play a tune, and I start to feel something stir within my soul making me feel invincible all of a sudden. I notice the changelings walking towards us have slowed their pace and the hellhounds are whining like Chandler's music is hurting their ears.

Jess turns around and surveys the situation we find ourselves in.

"You take the left and I take the right?" Jess asks Mason.

"Sounds like a plan," Mason replies.

"Jess," I say, "Aiden."

I don't need to say any more than that.

"Chandler," Jess says looking at the fight between Aiden and the prince, "take care of not-so-prince-charming over there to get him off Aiden's back."

Chandler looks over at the fight Aiden is having with the prince just as Jess and the others split up to charge the changelings and hellhounds.

Chandler's gift of music allows him to influence the emotions of others. With his talisman, he's able to weave more than one tune at a time. I have to assume he's weaving three now. One to make his comrades-in-arms feel invincible. A second to make those they're fighting against feel weak. And a third to do something to Asmodeus which makes him push Aiden away from him so hard it propels him into the air just before the prince phases away. Aiden's body flies over my head and through the outer wall of the school with such force, it makes the whole building tremble.

Taking into account the intensity of the blow and the trajectory of Aiden's body, I phase back to where the pool is and find him floating in the water face down. I jump in to grab him and phase him out. When I have him lying on his back, I notice his neck is broken. How do I know this? Because his face is against the concrete and his mass of curly black hair is facing me. I grimace slightly at the sight, but force myself to lift his head enough to twist it back in the right orientation.

I sit there and wait. I'm not sure how long it will take Aiden to regenerate enough to fix his broken neck, but I don't remain alone for long.

Uncle Malcolm finds me.

"Is he all right?" Uncle Malcolm asks, limping over to us.

"His neck was broken," I tell him. "But I put it right. How long will it take for him to heal on his own?"

"A while," Uncle Malcolm says. "We should go see Rafe to speed things up."

"What about Jess and the others? We can't just leave them."

"They have things under control," Uncle Malcolm tells me. "And Leah will burn the school to the ground to hide what really happened here today."

"But what about the kids who saw everything?"

"Let's leave the explanations to Jess and Mason. They're used to covering things like this up. I'm sure they'll think of something believable to explain what happened."

Uncle Malcolm grimaces slightly as he bends down to pick Aiden up into his arms.

"What's wrong with your leg?" I ask him again as I stand up. I grab hold of one of his arms so he can phase us all to Rafe's at the same time.

"It's nothing for you to worry about," Uncle Malcolm says, phasing us to Rafe's office in his Sierra Leone medical clinic.

Uncle Malcolm lays Aiden down on Rafe's mostly clear desk.

"Could you go find Rafe, Caylin?" Uncle Malcolm asks, sitting down on the small wooden chair in front of the desk.

I know my Uncle Malcolm. He wouldn't be asking me to go get Rafe and wouldn't sit down when there were things that needed to be done unless something was seriously wrong with him.

I don't waste any time. I rush out of the room and find Rafe in the infirmary speaking to one of his colleagues at the clinic.

As soon as he sees me, he runs towards me.

"Your office," I tell him, not wanting to waste time with pleasantries when two of the most important men in my life need his help.

When we are back in the office, Uncle Malcolm is passed out cold in the chair, and Aiden is still unconscious. I tell Rafe about Aiden's neck being broken.

Rafe walks over to a corner of his office to retrieve his talisman, Moses' staff.

"And what's wrong with Malcolm?" Rafe asks me as he begins to pass the staff over Aiden's neck to speed up the healing process.

"I'm not sure," I tell Rafe as I kneel down in front of Uncle Malcolm to examine his right leg.

I rip away what's left of the shredded pant leg and gasp at what I find.

I know what happened. And from what Aiden told me about such a wound, I'm surprised Uncle Malcolm could function much less keep fighting afterward.

"He was bit by a hellhound," I tell Rafe.

"He was what?" Rafe asks as if he's sure he misheard me.

"Bit by a hellhound," I say again, examining the large puncture wounds in Uncle Malcolm's calf. The lacerations are oozing a black substance, but I have no idea what it is. All I know is that it smells sulfuric.

Rafe leaves Aiden and comes to examine Uncle Malcolm's wound like it takes higher priority.

"This isn't good," Rafe says gravely. "I'm not sure I can heal these wounds."

"Why not?"

"From what I was told, Lucifer is the one who made the hellhounds. Their bites aren't just bites. They're more like curses."

"Like a spell?"

"Sort of, but worse. It's like being marked by Lucifer himself. It's meant to drive the person insane to the point where they'll do almost anything to end the pain they're in. When a person reaches that breaking point, Lucifer will come and offer them an end to their suffering in exchange for their souls."

"Rafe," I say in desperation, grabbing his arm, "you have to try. We can't let him go through that much pain. And I refuse to lose him to Lucifer like that!"

I feel like I'm on the edge of despair, and Rafe is the only who can pull me back.

"Of course I'll try," Rafe says like it's a forgone conclusion. "But, I don't want you to get your hopes up that it'll work. There's no guarantee. This is the first time I've ever seen this type of wound. My only knowledge is based on what Mason told me when we first saw the hellhounds a couple of years ago."

"Please," I beg fully crying now because I don't want to lose my Uncle Malcolm, "just help him."

"I'll do what I can," Rafe promises.

I stand up to give Rafe room to work on Uncle Malcolm and walk over to Aiden, who is still unconscious. Aiden's breathing is normal, and he simply looks like he's asleep. I know he'll be ok and try not to worry about him too much.

Uncle Malcolm's condition worries me more. He's not just my Uncle. He's more like a second father to me. I can't lose him like this, and I refuse to think he'll lose his soul to Lucifer because of a fight that was solely caused because of me.

Jess and Mason suddenly phase into Rafe's office.

"We thought you might be here when we couldn't find you at the school," Jess says, coming to stand by me. I know she wants to take me into her arms, but she's covered in so much blood she wouldn't be able to do it without drenching me in it too. "How are you holding up?"

I shake my head and look at Uncle Malcolm, tears spilling freely down my face.

"He got bit, Jess," I tell her as Mason walks over to see what Rafe is trying to heal.

"Damn," Mason says, sighing heavily when he sees the extent of the wound.

Rafe starts to shake his head in dismay. "I can heal it to an extent but the wounds are simply refusing to close up."

Jess walks over and looks at the bite marks.

"What if we cauterize them?" She asks Mason, drawing out her sword.

"It'll seal the physical evidence of the curse, but I'm not sure if it will stop his pain."

"Then I say we don't have anything to lose," Jess says as her sword bursts into flickering orange flames as its power ignites. "Stand back, Rafe. We should probably do this while he's still out."

I watch as Jess touches the tip of her sword's blade to each of the wounds on Uncle Malcolm's leg. Almost like magic, they seal up and black scar tissue forms over the punctures. Once Jess is through, Rafe passes his staff over Uncle Malcolm's leg one more time for good measure.

"I think that's all we can do," Rafe says with a resigned sigh.

Mason picks Uncle Malcolm up and cradles him in his arms.

"I'll take him to our villa to recover," Mason says to me.

"My mom will want to come as soon as she learns what happened," I tell him.

Mason nods. "She's welcome to come whenever she's ready."

Jess walks over to her husband and grabs hold of his elbow. Mason phases, and I turn my attention back to Aiden.

"Let me finish healing him, Caylin," Rafe says, politely telling me to get out of the way.

I move over and let Rafe work his healing magic.

When Aiden's eyes flutter open, Rafe stops what he's doing, and I go to Aiden.

I look down at him on the desk and caress the side of his face just giving thanks that he's still alive.

"You have *got* to stop getting hurt," I tell him. "I think I die a little bit every time you are."

"I'm fine," he reassures me, sitting up and swinging his legs over the side of the desk to face me and bring me into his arms.

"Is everyone else all right?" Aiden asks.

I start to cry again and hug him tightly around the neck. Aiden wraps his arms around me, but doesn't ask any more questions, knowing I need a moment before answering his first one.

"No," I sob, holding onto Aiden like my life depends on it, "everyone is not all right."

CHAPTER EIGHTEEN

I explain to Aiden what happened to Uncle Malcolm, and he doesn't try to sugar coat the gravity of the situation to me.

"Is there anything we can do that can completely heal him?" I ask.

"No," Aiden tells me clearly, "only Lucifer can lift the curse, and I don't see that happening without Malcolm agreeing to give up his soul."

"I was able to heal some of the damage," Rafe says. "I'm not certain how much or if it will be enough to alleviate any of the pain he'll feel, but there *is* hope. We will just have to wait until Malcolm awakens to find out the extent of the discomfort."

"How long do you think it will be until he wakes up?" I ask.

Rafe shrugs. "I have no way of knowing. I've never treated a hellhound wound before. Have you had any experience with it Aiden?"

"The people I knew who were bitten went mad from the pain almost instantly," Aiden says. "I'm not sure how Malcolm stayed sane for as long as he did as it is."

"Well, I'm afraid there isn't anything further we can do about it until he wakes up and tells us how he's feeling."

"I need to go home," I say to Aiden. "I need to tell my mother what happened."

Aiden stands from the desk and slips one of his arms around my shoulders.

"We'll go tell her together," he says.

"Tell Mason to come and get me the second Malcolm wakes up," Rafe tells us.

I nod. "I will. Thank you, Rafe."

Rafe smiles tight lipped, and I know he wishes he could have done more to help my uncle.

Aiden phases us to my home in Lakewood, and I see my parents pacing around the living room floor. As soon as they see us phase in, they both come to me. Aiden steps aside to allow my parents to take me into their arms. They don't say anything, just hug me between them. I know that the embrace is more for them than me which is why I simply stand there and try to reassure them that I'm all right, hoping the words will erase their worry.

"Where is Will?" I ask them.

"He's upstairs," my mom says. "He was pretty shaken up by what happened. I think he just needs some time alone."

Once my parents let me go, I tell them what happened at the school and about the injury Uncle Malcolm sustained.

"I need to go to him," my mom says to my dad.

He nods. "Go. I'll take care of the kids."

My mom phases to Mason and Jess' villa.

My dad looks to Aiden. "How are you doing?"

"I'm fine," Aiden replies, unconsciously rubbing at his neck. "Thanks for asking."

"So you were able to place one of the daggers into Mammon," my dad says to me. "Do you know if Jess and Mason were successful in taking down Amon before they came to the school?"

"I have no idea," I realize. "I didn't even think to ask about that with everything else that was happening."

"Aiden, would you go talk with Jess or Mason to see what happened on their mission?" My dad asks. "I would like to know."

"Yes," Aiden says. "I'll be right back."

Aiden phases and my dad brings me into his arms again.

"How are you holding up?" He asks me.

I hold my dad and rest my head on his chest.

"All those people are dead because of me, Dad," I say. "And Uncle Malcolm could lose his soul. Overall, it hasn't been a very good day."

"None of this is your fault," he says to me. "I want you to remember that. You're an innocent in all of this."

"But those kids are dead because I went to that school. Hunter is dead because he fell in love with me. How can you say none of this is my fault when I'm the common denominator in everything?"

I hear my dad sigh.

"Caylin, sometimes sacrifices have to be made for the greater good. We don't always like it, and we don't always understand why they have to be made. But nothing that has happened was caused by you. Everything that's happened, everything that *will* happen will be caused by one person, Lucifer. He has been a thorn in my father's side for eons. One day, I hope he can be stopped, but I don't think either of us will ever see that day come while we're still alive. All we can do is follow the path God leads us down and trust that He knows what's best. You need to keep your faith in Him. Trust that He knows what needs to be done in order for us to win this war."

"But Uncle Malcolm…"

My dad hugs me tighter. "Why don't we wait until he wakes up before we start worrying too much about your Uncle Malcolm? He's one of the toughest and most stubborn people I know. He won't lose his soul to Lucifer, not without a fight. You need to have some faith in him too, that he's stronger than that."

I pull away from my dad and wipe at the tears on my face.

"He is stubborn," I try to laugh. "If anyone can fight against this curse, it's him."

"And maybe there's a purpose for it that we just don't understand yet," my dad points out. "Sometimes when something bad happens, it's only later that we're able to figure out why it was allowed to happen in the first place."

I nod, knowing my dad is right.

I just wish someone would tell me the purpose now.

As I stand at the back French doors and watch Tristan play chase with Mae in the backyard, I ask my dad, “Don’t you find it the least bit disturbing that they seem so connected to one another?”

My dad comes over to me from the kitchen with a cup of freshly made coffee in his hands.

“I’ve seen stranger things happen,” my dad says as he watches them with me. “But Mae has always had that effect on people.”

“I just get this feeling that there’s something else going on here that we’re not seeing,” I say, having a hard time putting my finger on what’s truly taking place.

Mae finally sees me and stops playing. She grabs Tristan’s hand and basically drags him back up to the house. But, he seems to be a willing victim to my cute little sister’s desires.

“KK!” Mae says, letting go of Tristan’s hand and flinging herself into my arms.

I hug Mae close to me and realize one of the special gifts my sister possesses. She has the uncanny ability to lighten your heart with a single hug, even when it feels overburdened with doubt and worry.

"KK," Mae says, leaning back from me, "Puppy and me have been playing."

"I know," I tell her having a hard time not smiling because of Mae's nickname for Tristan.

"I love my Puppy," Mae tells me, like the feeling is a complete declaration from her heart.

"Why?" I ask, needing to know what on Earth this strange relationship my sister has with this werewolf is.

Mae is quiet for a moment and just stares at me like I should know the answer already.

"Why do you love him, Mae?" I ask again.

"Because he's mine," she says simply.

She leans over and kisses me on the mouth then scrambles down to go stand by Tristan and takes his hand.

I look at Tristan and he looks just as befuddled by Mae's announcement as my dad and me.

"I really don't know what's going on," Tristan says to us, obviously seeing our reaction to Mae's words on our faces. "But I promise you both, I would never do anything to harm her."

"What is it that you feel exactly?" I have to ask.

"I feel…loyal to her," he says, like he's trying to find the right words to describe his new found attachment to Mae. "I feel like I need to protect her."

"Do you love her?"

"I'm not even sure how that's supposed to feel to be honest," Tristan says. "I've never really felt it for anyone in my life. I thought I felt it for my father, but I'm not even sure about that anymore. I think I just felt blind loyalty for him."

"You're welcome to stay here," my father says, "but you *do* understand this isn't a permanent living arrangement for you, right?"

"Yes, I understand that," Tristan says. "And I don't plan to be a burden on your family for very much longer, but," Tristan looks over at me, "I have a feeling you might need some help. If there's anything I can do to repay your kindness, I would be more than willing to lend a hand."

"We'll keep that in mind," I tell him, not quite sure what we would need Tristan for exactly.

Aiden phases back to the living room from his quest to gather information from Jess and Mason for my father.

"How is Uncle Malcolm?" I immediately ask him as he walks over to where I am.

"He hasn't woken up yet," Aiden tells me.

"And were Jess and the others successful in capturing Amon earlier?" My dad asks, again voicing the question he wanted Aiden to get an answer to.

"Yes," Aiden tells us, but he doesn't look as happy as he should about the answer.

"What's wrong?" I ask.

Aiden sighs. "Jess and Mason think Amon was just a distraction to get them out of the picture for the attack at your school. They said he lead them on a wild goose chase for most of the day and they almost missed the 911 call Malcolm sent them when the attack started. They were smack dab in the middle of a fight with Amon when it came, which couldn't have been a coincidence. But, I don't think they counted on me being there today, and since I was invisible, they didn't see me until the attack began."

"So three princes came after me thinking I only had Uncle Malcolm for back up," I say.

"I think their plan was to hit you fast and hard," Aiden says. "And by doing it in such a public environment, take you by surprise. I think they knew you wouldn't just leave all those people to their mercy."

"Have they already taken Amon's body somewhere?" I ask.

"Yes, Andre was placed in charge of hiding him."

I must look as disappointed as I feel.

"Why?" Aiden asks, not missing a thing.

"I…ok this is going to sound weird, but I wanted to check his body for something."

"What?" Aiden and my dad ask at the same time, both in surprise.

"It's something I noticed on Belphagor while we were in the French Market. And then I noticed something similar on Mammon at the school."

“Noticed what exactly?” My dad asks, crossing his arms in front of him and looking concerned by this new revelation.

“It was like a raised brand,” I tell him. “Like something was burned into their skin and it scarred over.”

“Like a symbol of some sort?” My dad asks.

I nod. “Yeah. But it had archangel writing on it.”

“Were you able to understand what was written?”

“Yes, but the words just seem random to me.”

“What did they say?”

“The word on Belphagor was ‘sacrifice’ and the word on Mammon was ‘want’.”

“I’ve seen what you’re talking about,” Tristan says. “My father met with the princes a lot. I’ve seen the brands. They all have them, even Lucifer.”

“Do you remember what they look like?” I ask excitedly. “Could you draw them out?”

Tristan shakes his head. “No, I’m sorry. I was usually in wolf form during the meetings. My dad liked to parade me around in front of them because I was something they could never have. I think that might be one reason Lucifer made the hellhounds. He wanted pets too."

"Jess and Mason have had the most contact with them," I say. "Maybe we should go talk to them about it. They might already know what they mean."

"Why don't you and Aiden go speak with them," my dad suggests. "I think your brother needs some more time to deal with what happened at the school or we would all go."

"Do you think it would help if I went up and talked to him?"

My dad shakes his head. "Maybe later. I think he just needs some time alone right now."

I nod. "Ok."

Aiden touches me on the shoulder and phases us to Jess and Mason's villa.

We phase into a bedroom I haven't been in before. Uncle Malcolm is lying beneath a patchwork quilt on the bed, and my mother is sitting beside him holding one of his large hands between both of hers.

Jess and Mason are standing by a set of doors, which lead out onto a balcony.

“Hey kiddo,” Jess says when she sees me.

My mom turns to look at Aiden and me, and I can tell she’s been crying from the red puffiness surrounding her eyes. She doesn’t say anything to us, just returns her attention back to Uncle Malcolm.

“Jess,” I say in a whisper as Aiden and I go stand by them, “could we go somewhere to talk about something?”

I don’t want to say anything about the brands in front of my mother. They could mean something or they could be nothing. She has enough on her plate at the moment, and I don’t want to add to it unnecessarily.

“Sure,” Jess says.

Jess goes over to my mother and touches her on the shoulder.

“We’ll be in the kitchen if his condition changes or if you need anything, Lilly.”

My mom nods but doesn’t seem to be able to take her eyes off Uncle Malcolm. I’m worried about her. She's taking what happened to Uncle Malcolm harder than I thought she would. She looks completely devastated, like we've lost him already.

When we reach the kitchen, Mason offers us something to drink, and we all agree to have the sweet tea he already has prepared.

"Mason's gone completely native," Jess tells us as we all sit down at the kitchen table. "Ever since he started living in Cypress Hollow, he's become addicted to sweet tea."

"I like sweet things," Mason says to Jess with a smile.

"I know," she replies returning his smile.

"Jess," I say regaining her attention, "I came over to ask if you've ever noticed brands on the princes?"

"Yes," Jess says, surprised by the question. "The first one I saw was on Lucifer. Then I noticed one on Amon."

"I saw them on Belphagor and Mammon. And from what Tristan told me a little while ago, all of the princes have one. Do you know what they are?"

Jess shrugs. "I don't have a clue. I talked to Michael about it once, and he said they were probably something Lucifer did to mark them."

"Did my grandfather tell you what Lucifer and Amon's marks said?"

"Yeah, he did say it was archangel writing. Lucifer's said 'silence' and Amon's said 'conflict'. What did Belphagor's and Mammon's say?"

“’Sacrifice’ and ‘want’.”

“Sounds like some random bad words to me,” Jess says.

I see her look over my shoulder. “You have any ideas?”

I look behind me but don’t see anyone. I don’t have to ask whom Jess is speaking to. I already know she can see and speak with my grandfather whenever she wants. All of the vessels can. Their mental connection with their respective archangels allows them to communicate at any time.

“Michael’s not sure what they mean either. It’s probably just some sort of stupid evil thing Lucifer concocted to keep tabs on the other princes. My guess is that it links them in some way. I’m not sure it’s something for us to worry about right now.”

“You’re probably right,” I say. “But, I can’t shake this feeling that they’re somehow important.”

“Well, let’s just keep our eyes and ears open for any more clues,” Jess suggests. “I’m sure if these brands are significant we’ll be told why eventually. God might not be the most forthcoming about handing out information, but when it’s important, He normally gives us just enough help to figure things out on our own.”

My mother phases into the kitchen.

“Malcolm’s awake,” she says, looking at my untouched glass of sweet tea and snagging it. “And he’s thirsty.”

She phases and we all follow her back to the room.

Uncle Malcolm is still lying in bed, but he’s sitting up now with the help of some pillows behind his back. The term ‘death warmed over’ comes to my mind because that’s exactly the way Uncle Malcolm looks. He looks pale and his eyes look tired.

“Here, drink this,” my mom tells Uncle Malcolm, handing him my glass of sweet tea.

Uncle Malcolm takes the glass and drinks it slowly, but he manages to drink it all down.

“Thank you, dearest,” he says, handing the empty glass back to her.

“Do you want some more?” My mom asks.

Uncle Malcolm shakes his head.

“No, not right now,” he replies in a weak voice.

I walk over to the bed to get a better look at him.

“How do you feel?”

“A little tired,” Uncle Malcolm says. “I’ll be fine though. Don’t worry about me.”

“Any…pain?” Mason asks as if he expects Uncle Malcolm to be in a great deal of it.

“There’s some,” Uncle Malcolm admits. “But not as much as there was at first. Whatever you did seems to have alleviated the vast majority of it.”

Hmm, Uncle Malcolm isn’t exactly lying, that much I can tell. But, I don’t need my lie detector to know he’s down playing how much discomfort he’s actually in.

“What happened when Aiden and I left you in that hallway with Baal?” I ask.

“Baal and I fought,” Uncle Malcolm says. “I was pretty much able to keep his dogs at bay while we were going at it, but one of them got lucky and bit me during the fight. I killed the dogs off quickly, but after that, Baal had already run away. Then I went to find you and Leah.”

“Are you hungry?” My mother asks seeming desperate to do something for Uncle Malcolm. “You need to keep up your strength.”

“If it would make you feel better,” Uncle Malcolm says to her gently, “I will eat whatever you bring me.”

“Ok,” my mother says standing up, “I’ll be right back.”

She phases and I have to assume she's probably gone back home to get my father to cook something.

I don't think Uncle Malcolm minds my mother pampering him though if the small smile that appears on his face is any evidence.

I go over to the bed and sit where my mother did. When I lean in to give Uncle Malcolm a hug, I do something I probably shouldn't, but I have to know. I ask Jess' bracelet to tell me what Uncle Malcolm is feeling.

As soon as I touch him, I'm hit in the pit of my stomach with a searing pain so intense I almost cry out, but I just gasp instead, finding it difficult to even breathe.

Uncle Malcolm puts his lips next to my ear and whispers, "Don't tell anyone."

Tears well in my eyes, but I nod my head slightly to let him know I heard what he said.

I hold onto him even tighter. The pain he's in won't be a fleeting one. It will never heal. And I know he will have to endure his own private torture for many years to come.

CHAPTER NINETEEN

While my mother is gone, Mason brings Rafe over to examine Uncle Malcolm.

"And the pain," Rafe says to Uncle Malcolm, "on a scale between 1 and 10, how would you rate it?"

"Three," Uncle Malcolm lies.

He looks at Mason and me because he knows of anyone in the room, we will know he just lied.

"It's bearable," he says for our benefit.

"I wish there was more I could do for you, my friend," Rafe tells Uncle Malcolm.

"You did what you could, Rafe. And I appreciate that."

Desmond phases to the villa to speak with Aiden while Mason takes Rafe back to his clinic.

I'm not quite sure what all is said, but I have a sneaking suspicion it concerns me considering the way Desmond keeps glancing in my direction. After Desmond leaves, Aiden comes over to me.

"I need to go somewhere for a little while," he tells me. "But I won't be gone for long."

"Where are you going?" I ask, worried he might be heading into danger and just not telling me.

"I'm just going to my house in the Bahamas," he says. "And I'll be back in a little while to get you, ok?"

"Is there a reason I can't come with you now?"

"How would I be able to surprise you with anything if you came with me?"

"What kind of surprise?" I ask, completely intrigued.

"No more questions," he says gently, leaning down and kissing me chastely on the lips. "I'll be back in a little bit."

"Don't take too long," I request.

"I won't," he promises before phasing.

When my mother comes back, she's carrying a basket full of food. It looks like enough food to feed a family of four for a week.

Uncle Malcolm looks inside the basket and says, "Dearest, I don't think I'll be able to eat all that."

"I wasn't sure what you would be in the mood for," my mother says looking slightly flustered. "So I just brought everything

I thought you might want. You don't have to eat it all…I just… I just didn't know what you were hungry for so I …"

My mother's voice trails off, and I see her eyes begin to tear up again.

Uncle Malcolm puts a comforting hand on top of my mother's, which is holding the basket.

"Lilly," Uncle Malcolm says, "I'm alive. Yes, I'm in some pain, but don't let that upset you so much. It's nothing I can't handle."

"But, for how long?" My mother asks, openly crying.

It's then I know she realizes Uncle Malcolm is downplaying the pain he's in for her benefit.

"I'll never make a deal with him," Uncle Malcolm says. "I make that promise to you, and I will never break a promise I make to you, Lilly."

"I would rather see you die than lose your soul to him," my mother says vehemently. "I need you to make another promise to me. Promise me that if the pain becomes more than you can bear, you'll come to me first."

"I will," Uncle Malcolm says, one of the few times I've seen him completely serious. "I promise, Lilly."

This seems to make my mother feel a little better, and she wipes away the tears from her eyes.

I don't have to ask what she's talking about. I know.

We can kill angels. All of us kids can do it, but I'm hoping we never have to use that particular inherited trait from my grandfather. Too bad we can't kill archangels though. That sure would come in handy right about now.

I hope if the pain becomes more than he can bear my Uncle Malcolm will come to me instead of my mother. Killing him would definitely hurt me, but it would absolutely break my mother. I would rather have the guilt on my soul than have her live with it. But, I have a feeling neither of us will ever have to face that gruesome task.

According to God, Uncle Malcolm will live a long time. Long enough to help my descendant defeat the princes and take back what they stole from Heaven. I wish I knew what it was they stole so I could get it back myself. I don't see why it has to be Anna who does it. What will be different about her? What power am I lacking that she will ultimately come to have?

About thirty minutes after he left, Aiden comes back. Unfortunately, he's changed out of the tight fitting black leather outfit JoJo made him. He's in more relaxed clothing now consisting of a pair of jeans, black t-shirt, and flip-flops.

"Lilly," Aiden says to my mother as she's spoon-feeding Uncle Malcolm some chicken soup, "I'm taking Caylin to my home in the Bahamas now like we discussed earlier."

"Ok," my mom says, "just have her back home by eleven."

I almost ask why I get the extra hour but realize the answer before I ask it.

I don't have a school to go back to the next day. I'm not really sure what will happen now that it's been burnt to the ground by Leah's Heavenly fire.

"Are you ready?" Aiden asks, holding his hand out to me.

"I guess," I say a little uncertain. "What exactly are we doing?"

Aiden smiles. "Boy, you sure are hard to give a surprise to. Stop asking so many questions, beautiful, and just trust me."

I place my hand in Aiden's.

"I do trust you," I tell him. "And I always will."

Aiden tightens his grip on my hand and phases us to his house.

We end up in a bathroom I've never been in before. White candles are lit everywhere and a large, round bathtub in the middle of the marble floor is almost overflowing with bubbles. The faint scent of vanilla fills the air. I feel calm in this space, which is what I have to assume Aiden was going for.

"I thought you might like a relaxing bath," Aiden says, turning to me and slipping my school blazer down off my shoulders. He folds it and sets it on a nearby glass top table by a black velvet and steel chair.

He turns back to me and pulls the tie around my neck off then lays it on top of the blazer.

"Sit down," he says, indicating the chair with a nod of his head.

I sit down and Aiden kneels down in front of me.

He unzips one boot and tugs it off my foot. Then does the same with the second. He then runs his hands down one calf and pulls the knee high sock off before taking the other one off too.

Before I even have a chance to wonder what else he'll help me take off, Aiden stands.

"I've put some fresh clothes in the connecting bedroom. Your mother picked it out of your closet for me to bring."

"My mom?"

"She was home getting Malcolm's food when I phased over there. I wanted to make sure it was all right for me to bring you back here. I didn't think you would want to stay in the clothes you're in."

No, I most certainly did not. After all the smoke from Leah's fire then the subsequent water from the sprinkler system cementing the smell in, my clothes definitely needed to be changed.

"I left a towel by the bathtub for you," Aiden says. "Come downstairs when you're ready. But, there's no rush. We're still making your supper."

"We?" I ask.

"Me and some of the guys," Aiden says. "Andre is the best cook out of the seven of us so he and Brutus were put in charge of preparing the meal."

"And the others?"

“Jered and Slade are back outside in their spots to watch over the house while you’re here. And Desmond and Daniel have a special surprise for you.”

“A good surprise I hope?”

“Well,” Aiden says with a smile, “I guess you’ll have to be the judge of that, beautiful. So, take your time. You’ve had a bad day. We just want to make sure it ends on a good note.”

“Will you stay with me while I bathe?” I ask.

“I don’t think that would be a good idea,” Aiden says. “You’re enough of a temptation fully clothed much less completely naked, Caylin.”

“You could keep your eyes closed,” I suggest.

Aiden chuckles.

“Angel,” he reminds me. “Not saint. I don’t think I would be able to keep myself from sneaking a peek. So, thank you for your offer, but I will have to respectfully decline for the time being. But one day in the near future, you may not be able to keep me out of any tub you’re frolicking naked in.”

This time it’s my turn to blush.

"Well, I guess I'll just have to wait for that day to come," I say.

Aiden leans down and gives me a quick kiss.

"Come down stairs when you're ready," he says as he pulls away. "We'll be waiting."

Aiden leaves through the door that connects to the bedroom. I wait until I hear him exit through the bedroom door before I begin to strip off the rest of my clothes.

I don't linger in the tub. I don't really want to be alone. I stay just long enough to wash my body and hair. When I get out of the bath, I wrap the fluffy white towel Aiden left for me to dry off with around my body and go about the room to blow out all the candles. All I need is another fire being set that day.

I find my clothes laid out for me on the bed in the next room and smile when I see the underwear set separately away from the clothes. It makes me wonder how Aiden felt handling my intimate apparel. Did it make him uncomfortable? Did it turn him on?

I'm hoping for the latter.

I dress quickly in the jeans and white peasant style blouse my mom sent. I slip on the flip-flops sitting by the bed and make my way downstairs. Aiden's laughter fills the house as I walk towards the back where the kitchen is, and I can't help but smile at the sound of it.

I hear a lot of rattling of cookware when I enter the kitchen and have to stifle a laugh of my own when I see Andre and Brutus. They're both wearing white aprons and tall white chef hats on their heads. Why? I have no idea. I don't see how the hats could possibly help them cook better. But, maybe they're wearing them to make me laugh.

Brutus is sautéing something that kicks up a flame on the gas stove while Andre is checking on something cooking in the oven.

Aiden is lighting two candles on the rectangular glass dining table in the room. The table is arranged with two place settings of china and crystal goblets with a small red rose bouquet between them. When he sees me enter the room, he lays the lighter in his hand on the table and comes to me.

"Do you feel better?" He asks, taking me into his arms and making me feel more relaxed than any bath could.

"I do now," I tell him, wrapping my arms around him and resting one of my cheeks against his chest.

He kisses the top of my head and just holds me for a little while, letting me decompress from the day's events.

I hear music come from somewhere behind me and know it's live, not recorded. I pull away from Aiden to look over my shoulder and see Desmond playing a violin and Daniel strumming the strings of an acoustic guitar. It's then I realize this must be the 'special surprise' from them that Aiden mentioned.

I don't recognize the song they're playing, but I don't need to. It's a beautiful tune played with skilled hands and filled with emotion. The song is a haunting melody, but it helps unravel the knots my nerves have been twisted in since the start of the princes' attack.

When their song ends, I go up to them both and give them hugs.

"Thank you," I tell them. "It was beautiful."

"We were hoping it might help a little," Desmond tells me, an almost shy look on his face from my praise. "Considering the day you had we all thought you might like a stress free night."

"It's exactly what I need," I tell them.

"And we hope you're hungry," Brutus bellows from the kitchen.

It's only with the mention of food that I realize I'm starving.

"I'm very hungry," I tell him.

And that's really all I had to say to be treated like I was royalty by the Watchers around me. Aiden walks me to the table and holds out my chair for me. Brutus and Andre bring over our plates filled with roasted to perfection Cornish hens and stir fried vegetables. A platter of sliced French bread is placed in front of us with an olive oil and basil-parmesan dipping sauce.

After the four Watchers fix their own plates, they begin to leave the room, presumably to give Aiden and me time alone.

"Wait!" I call out.

They all turn to look at me.

"Aren't you going to join us?" I ask them.

"We thought you might want to be alone together," Desmond says, looking a little confused by my question.

"I would really like it if you joined us," I tell them and look over at Aiden. "If that's ok with you?"

"Of course it is," Aiden says.

He waves the others back to the table and we're soon a group of six instead of two.

No one talks about anything serious because that's not what I need. They talk about their lives in their respective parts of the world, and what they've been doing since the Tear closed.

I learn Desmond is getting ready to step down as the head of the UK headquarters to concentrate on a book of poems he's been writing.

"Haven't you been writing that book for the past century?" Aiden teases.

"Only fifty years," Desmond says like the time is just a drop in the bucket. "That's hardly a century. Plus, I think I've finally found my muse."

Desmond looks at me and smiles rather roguishly.

"Me?" I ask, not seeing how I could possibly inspire one poem much less a book of them.

Desmond shrugs. "More the situation we find ourselves in because of the love you and Aiden share. Very few people get to find their soul mate. Most go through life knowing that one special person is out there somewhere but never get to meet them. They live their lives with substitutes thinking that's all love has to offer. But to find your true mate is rare. I guess you could say it's that ideal love, more than anything, that's inspired me."

"When did you become so ...*soft*?" Brutus asks.

"I'm not soft," Desmond responds sounding slightly offended. "I've just grown to accept my sensitive side."

"Well, Mister Sensitive Side," Daniel says, picking up his guitar, "feel like playing another song for your fair muse over there?"

Desmond stands from his seat at the table and walks over to the kitchen counter to retrieve his violin.

When he comes back to sit down, Daniel starts to pluck the strings of his guitar, and Desmond falls into the tune like they've done this many times before. Andre begins to sing the words to the song in Italian. I reach under the table until I find Aiden's hand, and we hold onto each other while his friends serenade us. The boys play and sing a few more songs with Brutus joining in at one point.

I begin to feel so relaxed my eyelids start to droop at one point.

Aiden must notice because he leans over and asks, “Do you want to go home to rest?”

I shake my head. “No, I don’t want to go yet, especially not without a proper goodnight from you.”

Aiden grins and stands from his chair.

The men at the table don’t act like they see us slip out of the room together. I’m sure they notice, but they don’t stop what they’re doing just because we leave.

Aiden takes me upstairs to the sitting room there. After he opens the doors facing the back where the waterfall is, he takes me into his arms and looks down at me.

“How are you feeling now?” He asks, concern in his voice over my welfare.

“A lot better,” I tell him, even though everything that happened that day is still vividly replaying in my mind. “Kiss me. Erase the things I’ve seen today.”

“I don’t think I can erase those images permanently,” he says with regret. “But maybe I can dim them a little bit and give you something better to think about.”

Aiden pulls me into him and gently presses his lips to mine. The kiss is tender and sweet. It's a kiss only a man who truly loves and cherishes you can give. It demands nothing and gives everything.

I slip my hands underneath Aiden's shirt to rest them against his sides.

His muscles tense slightly beneath my touch, but I don't take any offense to the reaction. I slide my hands around to the middle of his back and feel Aiden moan against my mouth. Before he can protest, I dip my hands down to grab the bottom of his shirt and break our kiss to move away a little bit so I can lift his shirt up across his abdomen and chest, finally pulling it over his head forcing him to raise his arms to allow me to undress him.

I let his shirt fall to the floor and just look at him for a moment.

"Have I ever told you how beautiful you are?" I ask, lifting a hand and gently running it over the hard muscles of his chest and down the ribbed planes of his stomach.

"You're absolute perfection," I tell him.

“Physically, maybe,” he concedes. “But I’m far from perfect in other ways, Caylin.”

“Ok, then,” I tell him. “You’re perfect for me.”

I meet his eyes.

“And that’s all that matters, Aiden.”

Aiden comes at me.

Before I know it, we’re kissing again and he has me lifted up against him with his hands underneath my thighs and my legs wrapped around his hips. I soon find myself falling back on something soft and know Aiden has phased us to the bed in the bedroom on this floor.

He cradles the back of my head with one hand while his other glides over my right breast, down over my stomach only stopping when he reaches the hem of my shirt. He slides his hand underneath it and rests his hand against my waist squeezing lightly.

When he breaks our kiss, I almost ask why until he rubs his face down the length of my torso, and I feel the hand he has inside my shirt lift it partially off my stomach giving Aiden’s lips free access to the tender, sensitive flesh being exposed just above the top of my jeans. The first touch of his mouth there makes me gasp, but he doesn't stop. He kisses the area around my belly button, leaving a wet trail as evidence of his claim to my body on my skin.

I feel a rising need to feel more of him, which he must sense. He lifts his head back up to mine and continues to kiss me while his hand pulls my shirt back down to where it belongs.

I groan in complete frustration.

I feel Aiden smile against my lips as if he's pleased by my reaction.

And, I remember our bargain. No sex until marriage. Apparently, I'm in for a year of frustrating make out sessions that both excites me and makes me wonder how long I'll be able to keep my sanity if Aiden continues to tease my body like this.

After a long while of kissing and touching, I finally pull away and say, "Mercy."

Aiden peers down at me and can't seem to stop a smile of triumph from spreading his lips.

"See, told you I could make you say it."

"Was that your master plan for this evening?" I ask. "Torture me with your lips and hands until you made me say that word."

"Pleasant torture, I hope."

"Too pleasant," I say, pulling his head back down to mine. "But don't stop just yet. I think I can suffer through a little more."

Aiden chuckles softly but fulfills my request…for a little while longer…

CHAPTER TWENTY

Aiden escorts me home and we find my dad sleeping on the couch in the living room with Mae. Tristan, now in his wolf form, is lying on the floor in front of them curled up and sleeping peacefully. He doesn't even stir when we phase in.

Still holding Aiden's hand, I phase us to my bedroom.

"Was there something else you wanted before I left, beautiful?" Aiden asks in a knowing, pleased voice.

I wrap my arms around his neck.

"Why yes, Aiden, there was one more thing I wanted from you before you left me," I tell him, raising up on my toes to tease his lips with mine in one last, lingering kiss.

When I finally decide to end the kiss, I tighten my arms around his neck and whisper in his ear, "I love you."

"I love you too, Caylin."

"Would you do me a favor?" I ask as I pull away from him.

He looks at me with such tenderness I know I could ask him for the world, and he would get it for me.

"Anything you want," he tells me.

"Would you go watch over my mom? I have a feeling she won't leave Uncle Malcolm's side tonight. I don't want her to run herself ragged and not get any sleep at all."

"I'll go over there now," Aiden promises. "And you should know there are five Watchers outside watching over your house. If there's any trouble at all, they'll notify us immediately."

"Thanks for telling me."

Aiden leans down and kisses me one more time.

"I'll be back in the morning. You try to get some sleep."

I nod. "Ok. I'll try."

Aiden kisses my forehead and then phases.

I get ready for bed quickly and then bury myself underneath the safety of my covers.

My body feels tired, but my mind just won't shut off. I keep thinking about everything, the good and the bad, that happened that day. I consider taking a sleeping pill but squash that thought out as quickly as it emerges. If something unexpected happens, I need to have full control of all my faculties to deal with it.

After a lot of tossing and turning, I look at the clock on my nightstand and see that it's three o'clock in the morning. Seeing that

I'm not going to get any sleep, I decide to get up and go to my studio to see if I can get my mind off things with a new project. It should be safe enough. Aiden said there were five Watchers outside my home making sure we weren't attacked.

I slip on my pink fuzzy house shoes and phase down to my studio. When I flip the light switch on, I freeze. I stand completely still for a good minute as my mind tries to comprehend what it's seeing.

Every drawing…every painting in the room has either been smeared with red paint or ripped to shreds or both. The ceiling, the floor and every wall has been splashed in a mad, random pattern with blood red paint giving the room the appearance of a slaughterhouse. The family portrait I made for my mother's birthday present has been strategically placed on top of my worktable as if it in particular was left on display just for me to see.

It's completely shredded and all of our faces have been marked out with red X's.

I feel my body begin to shake uncontrollably. I feel violated. I feel like someone has just ripped out my soul and trampled all over it, only to leave it out in a cold rain shower to rot.

I immediately slam the door of the boathouse open to let some fresh air in because I'm finding it almost impossible to breathe.

"Caylin."

I look up and see Jered standing in front of me.

"What's wrong?" He asks in alarm.

I move away from the doorway to stand out on the dock. Jered walks into what was once my studio, my sanctuary away from the madness of the world.

When he walks in, he surveys the damage, taking in the savagery of what's been done.

"When was the last time you were in here?" Jered finally asks me.

I stand there silently for a minute, having to think back.

"Right before I chose you and the others," I say, just then realizing how long it's been since I was last in my studio.

"So this could have happened anytime within the past few days?" Jered asks.

I nod. "Yes. It wasn't recent because the paint is dry."

Jered sighs heavily, and he walks out of the room to stand beside me.

"Why don't you go back inside?" Jered suggest. "We'll clean this up for you."

"Why would they bother to do such a petty thing?" I ask.

"To throw you off your game," Jered replies. "They want to put as much turmoil as they can in your life and destroy the things you count on the most. If they do that, it might make you less focused on them."

I shake my head. "Then they don't know me very well. If anything, this makes me more determined to defeat them."

"Good," Jered says. "Stay that way. Use this to make you even more resolute in your mission against them. We only have four more princes to take down. It won't be long before this is all over and you can go on with your life."

I look back at my studio.

"I'll go get some cleaning supplies," I tell Jered.

"Caylin, we can clean it up," Jered says to me again. "Let us do that for you."

I shake my head. "No, I want to help. It's mine."

"What's wrong?" A familiar voice says.

Andre is standing with us now. He drapes his coat over my shoulders before I can even make a protest. His eyes are immediately drawn to the interior of the boathouse.

"Oh, Caylin," Andre says sympathetically, surveying the damage, "I am so sorry. I promise you that whoever did this will be made to pay."

I feel like I'm about to breakdown, and I don't want either of them to witness it.

"I'll go get some stuff so we can start cleaning," I tell them both as I phase into the house.

I phase directly into the laundry room where we keep most of our cleaning supplies. I take the coat Andre gave me off and lay it on top of the washing machine. I grab a bucket from the supply closet, some bleach, a couple of spray bottles of cleaning solution and a stack of old rags. I look down at it all and realize it's not going to be enough. The red paint completely covers every wall, even the floor and ceiling. There's no way it can be removed no matter how much scrubbing we do.

Years of work are gone in what probably only took minutes to destroy. But it wasn't just the fact that it was all gone that was bothering me. It was the thought of someone going into what had been my safe zone and maliciously destroying what I held dear. The history of my family had been stored in those paintings and drawings. Now, it was gone. I could never replace what had been taken from me.

I feel the tears come and am helpless to stop them. I detest the fact that I'm letting whomever did this to me win even this small victory.

I feel a gentle hand rest on my shoulder and know whom it is without needing to turn around.

"They destroyed everything, Aiden," I say, closing my eyes and lowering my head, feeling the warm tears I shed land on my hands propped on top of the counter.

Aiden squeezes my shoulder in sympathy.

"I know. I'm so sorry."

I take in a deep breath and turn towards Aiden. He brings me into the shelter of his embrace providing me a safe place to unburden my sorrow. I let the anguish over my loss consume me and relinquish the physical evidence of my grief all over the front of Aiden's shirt. He doesn't seem to mind though.

At one point, he picks me up into his arms as I continue to cry. I faintly feel him sit down and hold me against him as he rocks me back and forth in his arms. He begins to hum a tune, presumably to help calm my nerves. But, his humming has a strange effect on me. It makes me giggle.

I raise my head from his shoulder and notice we're in my room now sitting in a rocking chair I recognize, but I'm not sure how it got here.

I look at Aiden and he stops humming.

"What?" he asks as I just stare at him.

"You were right," I tell him. "You aren't perfect. Are you tone deaf or something?"

Aiden smiles, looking a little embarrassed.

"That could very well be the problem," Aiden admits. "I don't think I was built to sing, just fight."

I look at the white rocking chair we're sitting in.

"I've seen this chair before," I tell him. "When I was in the vessels' inner realm, I saw myself rocking our baby girl in it. Where did it come from?"

"The nursery."

"Nursery?"

"In the home I built us in Colorado, there's a nursery," Aiden says, gently smoothing the wet strands of my hair away from my tear stained face. "I assumed we would need one at some point."

"Yes," I agree, finding a reason to smile, "we will."

I rest my head back on Aiden's shoulder, and he continues to rock me but thankfully refrains from trying to hum anymore.

At some point, my physical and emotional exhaustion catches up with me, and I fall into a dreamless sleep in Aiden's arms.

When I wake up, the sun is shining through my bedroom window, and I'm lying in my bed safely tucked underneath my covers. I have to assume Aiden put me in bed after I fell asleep on him. I notice a folded piece of white paper sitting on top of my phone with "*Open Me*" written on the front.

I pick the note up and read what's written on the inside.

Good morning, Beautiful,

I hope you slept well and had sweet dreams. Text me when you are up and dressed for the day. We have something to show you.

Love,

Aiden

I've concluded after yesterday that whenever Aiden mentions 'we' he's referring to himself and my chosen. I get out of bed and shower quickly to get ready for my day. I silently pray it's a better day than the day before.

Once I'm dressed, I text Aiden. He immediately texts me back and asks me to come down to my studio.

But come to the door and knock on it when you're here.

I assume Aiden and the others probably worked through the night to repair the damage that was done by my intruder. I phase down and knock on the door of the boathouse.

I hear someone, who sounds like Brutus, say "She's here!"

There's the faint sound of other voices in the room until finally the door is opened by Aiden. He's still wearing the same clothes from the night before, black t-shirt and jeans, but they're smeared with spots of purple and green paint. He steps out of the building quickly like he doesn't want me to see what's inside yet.

He smiles and I feel like the Heavens themselves have opened up to bestow the light of pure joy on me.

"Good morning, beautiful," he says, leaning his head down to give me a kiss. He pulls back and asks, "Are you ready for a surprise this morning?"

"Depends," I say apprehensively. "Is it a good one? Because I don't think I can take another bad one after yesterday."

Aiden's grin widens. "I think so. But, I guess you'll have to be the judge of that for yourself. Close your eyes and give me one of your hands. And no peeking until I tell you to open your eyes."

It seems like an odd request, but I trust Aiden.

I close my eyes and hold out my right hand for him to take.

I feel him take my hand into one of his and hear him open the door to the boathouse.

He leads me into the building, and I instantly smell the scent of fresh paint.

We don't walk into the room too far, just a couple of steps, before Aiden tells me to stop.

"Ok, open your eyes," he tells me.

As soon as I open my eyes, my heart becomes overwhelmed with emotion by what I see. I feel like I'm having a moment of sensory overload and decide to concentrate on one thing at a time. I look at the floor first.

It's painted as a 3D image of a field of lavender that stretches on and on in an illusion that it goes on forever.

"I did that," Aiden tells me. "But I'm going to have to wait for the paint to dry before I can finish it."

It's then I notice we are standing on the only patch of floor that isn't painted.

I look around the room and notice almost all of my chosen Watchers are standing on plank wood platforms about a foot off the floor and twice as wide in front of their respective walls. Presumably, this gave Aiden free reign to paint the floor beneath them.

To the left of me stands Brutus. The wall behind him is painted with a vivid depiction of the blue-green Mediterranean Sea where his home is. The water meets a rocky shoreline in a layer of white sea foam.

On the long wall opposite me is Daniel's mural of a river flowing through an array of lush, green rolling hills with steep cliffs. A fisherman wearing a pointed bamboo hat sits on a wooden platform where he's fishing with trained cormorant birds.

On the short wall to the right of Daniel is Desmond. His painting is of a loch in between twin mountain ranges covered by vibrant green trees. A mysterious white mist weaves its way between the two peaks like a serpent.

I have to strain to see Andre's painting which is on the same wall as the door. It's a painting of a Venetian canal replete with gondolas and having the same depth of field as the rest of the paintings in the room making me feel like I could actually step inside any of them and get lost within the terrain being depicted.

I see Jered standing beside Andre on the same platform. He points up towards the ceiling and smiles. I look up and smile too.

On the ceiling is a mural of puffy clouds on a bright sunny day. It's one of those days where everything seems right and perfect in the world even if it isn't. And just like real clouds, you can just make out shapes from some of them. Two in particular catch my attention. If you look really hard, you can see me and Aiden kissing.

I lift a shaky hand to my lips and feel the threat of tears as I take in all of their hard work.

"There wasn't any way we could get rid of the red paint completely," Aiden tells me. "So we decided to cover it up with something from each of us so you wouldn't be reminded of what they did."

I pull myself together enough to ask, "Where's Slade?"

Aiden lets out a half laugh. "His contribution was the priming."

"Slade couldn't paint a stick man straight if his life depended on it," Desmond tells me. "Feel lucky he knows his limitations."

"I don't know what to say," I tell them all. "This is…so much more than I ever would have expected you to do for me. Thank you so much for making this a happy place again. I will treasure this gift for as long as I live."

"And we plan to make sure that's a long time," Andre tells me.

"Yes," Aiden agrees, wrapping his arms around me from behind and resting his chin on my shoulder to whisper in my ear, "a very long *long* time, beautiful."

I sigh, feeling content and happy again.

I pray that the feeling lasts…

CHAPTER TWENTY-ONE

I invite everyone into the house for breakfast. I feel sure my dad won't mind the extra company. Slade must see us going in because he phases over right before we reach the back door.

"Is it eating time?" Slade asks. "I'm starving."

"Are Lavern and Shirley hungry?" Desmond asks.

"Lavern and Shirley?" I ask in return, completely clueless to who Desmond is talking about.

Slade raises his arms and pops up his biceps.

"Lavern," he says kissing the right bicep, "and Shirley," he finishes, kissing the left one.

"Not conceited at all," Daniel says with a roll of his eyes at Slade.

When we walk inside the house, I get one extra Watcher for breakfast that I wasn't expecting.

Uncle Malcolm is sitting at the dining table holding Mae in his lap as she feeds him a forkful of omelet.

"Well, look what the cat drug in," Desmond says good-naturedly to Uncle Malcolm.

"I didn't want you boys to think I was down for the count," Uncle Malcolm tells them.

"We never thought that, Malcolm," Andre says, walking up to Uncle Malcolm and shaking his hand. "We're just glad to see you back on your feet."

"How are you even walking and talking?" Slade asks, for once truly amazed by someone other than himself. "Isn't the pain driving you crazy?"

"It's manageable," Uncle Malcolm answers, glancing in my direction because he knows I'm the only one who truly understands the pain he's suffering.

He's not lying though. To him the pain *is* 'manageable', but to a lesser person it would be unbearable.

I let go of Aiden's hand to go to him. I hug him around the back of the neck and kiss his cheek.

"It's good to have you here," I tell him.

He pats my overlapped hands on his chest.

"Stop worrying about me," he says. "I'll be fine."

I kiss him on the cheek one more time, which earns me a smile.

My mom walks down the stairs. Her hair is still wet from a shower and she has no make-up on, but somehow she still manages to be the most beautiful woman I know.

"I think trying to take care of you has become a full time job for the women in this family," my mom tells Uncle Malcolm as Mae tries to feed him another forkful of omelet from his plate.

"Well, I could think of worse ways to live out the remaining days of my life," Uncle Malcolm replies before opening his mouth to accept Mae's offering of food.

My mother and I exchange brief glances because we both know Uncle Malcolm's life will be far longer than he knows.

My mother comes to me and hugs me.

"I heard what happened," she says as she pulls away. "Are you ok?"

I nod. "Yes." I look at my Watchers and smile. "I'm a lot better now."

"Good," my dad says from the kitchen as he flips an omelet in the frying pan on the stove. "Then you and Aiden can come in here and cut up some more vegetables for the rest of the omelets."

Aiden and I do as my father requests, and eventually we get everyone a plate filled with food in front of them.

I notice Will missing from breakfast and ask my dad about it.

"I think yesterday is the first day he's had to deal with being different from everyone else," my dad says.

"Yeah," I say, "I guess everyone knows we're not your typical family now."

"No," Uncle Malcolm says from the table, "they don't."

"What do you mean?" I ask. "A lot of them saw us phase and fight at the school."

"Apparently, you haven't seen the latest news on the tragedy," Uncle Malcolm says.

"What do you mean?"

"There was a methane gas leak at the school, at least that's what the media is reporting. It caused some of the students to hallucinate and see things that didn't actually happen," my Uncle

Malcolm says. "It even caused some of them to run into a burning building instead of out of it."

"But what about the girls from Leah's swim team that I phased to Mama Lynn's house?"

"Oh, Chandler took care of those lovelies," Desmond informs me.

"Took care of them?" I ask apprehensively. "How?"

"He played them a sweet tune that made them forget the last 24 hours of their lives," Daniel tells me. "We took them home and now they just think the memory loss is a by-product of methane poisoning."

"So, no one knows about us?" I ask in amazement.

"No," Uncle Malcolm assures me. "No one knows anything. And any evidence …student cellphones, surveillance cameras…was wiped clean by Joshua."

I'm relieved that our true identities haven't been revealed to the general population, but I still feel a sense of guilt over the lives that were lost.

"I'm going to go talk to Will," I tell everyone.

"Do you want me to come with you?" Aiden asks.

I shake my head. “No. I think he needs his big sister right now.”

I phase up to Will’s room and knock on his door.

“Come in,” I hear him say.

When I go into his room, I find Will sitting on his bed with his phone in his hands just staring down at it. I close his door behind me and go sit on the bed with him.

“What’s up, little bro? Why have you been cooped up in your room since yesterday?”

“I think she’s dead.”

It takes me a minute, but I soon realize whom Will is talking about.

“Katie Ann? Why do you think that?”

Will holds up his phone. “Because she hasn’t replied to any of the texts I’ve sent her. She would have replied back by now if she was alive, KK.”

I shake my head. “That’s not proof, Will. Have you tried to call her?”

“I’ve called her number, but I just get sent straight to her voice mail.”

"Have you tried to call her parents?"

"I don't know their number."

"I'll be right back," I tell him before I phase to my room to grab the student directory from the desk. When I phase back to Will's room, I've already found Katie Ann's mom's phone number.

"Here, hand me your phone," I tell him.

Will hands it to me, and I call Katie Ann's mom.

After a few rings, she finally answers.

"Hi, Mrs. Parish. This is Caylin Cole. I'm Will Cole's sister…"

I go on to ask about Katie Ann's welfare and learn that she is alive and has been in the hospital under observation all night. Apparently, she was knocked unconscious in a fall during the student mass exodus from the school, but someone found her and brought her to the hospital.

I quickly tell Will this information, and he falls back on his bed breathing a sigh of relief.

"Please tell Katie Ann that she's in our prayers, Mrs. Parish," I say. "And if she can, I think my brother would appreciate a call from her when she's well enough."

Mrs. Parish assures me that either Katie Ann or she will give my brother a call to let him know when she's well enough to have visitors.

After I end the call, Will does something he almost never does. He gives me a hug.

"Thank you, KK," Will says squeezing me tightly. "Thank you for calling."

I hug him back because I don't know when I'll ever get the chance to again.

"You're welcome."

Will lets me go and sits back to look at me.

"Can I ask you for one more favor?"

"What?" I ask hesitantly.

"Could you drive me into town today? I still need to get mom's birthday present."

I suddenly realize I need to get mom something too. My gift was unceremoniously destroyed.

"Sure, I can do that. But why don't we go down to breakfast first? Then I'll take you. Did you want to go somewhere in particular?"

"Yeah, *Clive Jewelers*."

"Just how much money did you win the other night?" I ask, knowing anything at *Clive's* will be expensive.

"Enough," Will says vaguely as he stands from the bed. "Come on. Let's go eat. I haven't had any food since lunch yesterday."

As Will and I are heading out of his room, we see Tristan sitting at the head of the stairs. He seems to be listening to the others talking as they have breakfast but doesn't seem to have any plans to join them.

"Coming for breakfast?" I ask Tristan.

"I wasn't sure how welcomed I would be down there," Tristan replies.

"As welcomed as anyone else," I tell him.

I hold my hand out to him.

Tristan looks at it for a split second as if he's trying to decide whether or not I'm just helping him up out of politeness or extending the hand as a sign of friendship. To be honest, I'm not even sure why I'm doing it. But, I know Tristan doesn't mean us any harm. I actually kind of feel sorry for him to tell the truth. He sacrificed his bond to his family to protect a member of mine. Not that his life with his father sounded all that great, but family was family. It's a bond that's hard to break. Yet, Tristan broke his to his father to protect Mae. That was worth something. It was worth me trusting him until he did something to destroy that trust.

No one seems surprised when Tristan comes down with us. My mother even gives up her seat at the table so Tristan can take it. He refuses at first, of course, but no one denies my mother for very long.

I see Uncle Malcolm eyeing our resident werewolf suspiciously, but, to me at least, it simply means he's becoming accustomed to his new circumstances and acting like his old, over-protective self again.

Things were finally starting to get, at least a little bit, back to normal.

After breakfast, I tell Aiden I'm going to take Will into town.

"I'm coming with you," he automatically says.

"Well, that's fine but my car only holds two people."

"Then we'll just phase there together," he says.

"I want to drive my car there like a normal person," I inform him. "And, I'll be safe in it. None of the princes have been inside my car. Plus, you can't exactly phase into a moving vehicle anyway."

Aiden sighs because he knows I'm right.

"All right," he relents, "tell me where you're going and a few of us will be there to meet you. And, Caylin, please drive carefully. I can't take anything happening to you."

"I'm just going shopping, Aiden, not off to war."

"But we are in a war," he tells me, like I shouldn't take the circumstances we find ourselves in lightly. "We're fighting to keep our family safe. I don't think it gets any more serious than that."

"I'm sorry. I didn't mean to sound flippant about it," I tell him. "I know it's serious. But, I need to do something that's completely normal for once. And going shopping to get my mother a birthday present is that something for me right now."

Aiden takes both my hands into his.

"I understand that," he says. "And I won't argue about you taking your car. But I will have to insist that some of us come along with you."

"I don't have a problem with that," I tell him with a smile.

He smiles back and brings me in closer, loosely wrapping his arms around me.

“Good,” he murmurs. “And you should know that I don’t plan to spend much of my life without being near you.”

“That actually works for me because I don’t want to spend much of my life without you in it either. Three years of that was enough for me.”

“Would you guys like kiss or something already so we can go to town?” Will says to us slightly exasperated.

Aiden chuckles. “Avert your eyes then, Will, because I am indeed about to kiss your sister.”

Will covers his eyes with both his hands.

“Let me know when it’s over,” he tells us in total disgust.

Aiden raises his hands and cups my face between them before bringing his lips to mine. I feel sure he only meant for the kiss to be a brief meeting of our lips, but I don’t let him go that easily. I wrap my arms around his neck and deepen the kiss, which makes Aiden involuntarily moan in pleasure.

“I don’t need sound effects!” Will complains.

I break the kiss because I can't keep myself from laughing at what my little brother said.

"I rather enjoy the sound effects," I whisper to Aiden.

Aiden smiles shyly and just shakes his head at my statement like he can't believe I just said it.

"Where should we meet you?" He asks.

I tell him what store we're going to first.

"Ok. Jered, Slade and I will meet you at the jewelry store," he tells me, leaning down to give me one more kiss. "Drive safely."

Will and I hop into my car and drive into town.

It's kind of weird knowing I have the freedom to go 65mph on the highway. Yet, I still find myself driving 55mph. Old habits die hard, I guess.

"I heard about your studio," Will tells me on the drive into town. "Sorry, KK. I know how much your art means to you."

"It's ok," I tell him. "But I don't have a clue what I'm going to get mom for her birthday now. They completely destroyed the painting I did for her. And there just isn't enough time to do another one."

"Well, why don't we make what I'm planning to buy from the both of us?" Will suggests. "I'll pay for it but you can help me pick out the charms."

"Charms?"

"Yeah, I'm going to buy her one of those bracelets that has the special charms that slide on it. I have enough money to get a few, but you would probably know what she'd like on it more than I would. Sound like a deal to you?"

"Who are you?" I ask, briefly taking my eyes off the road to glance at Will. "And what did you do with my brother?"

Will rolls his eyes at me. "Geesh, I can be nice, you know. I just don't do it that often."

I laugh and Will smiles.

When we reach the jewelry store, my three Watchers are already in front of it waiting on us. We all go inside the store together, and Will and I pick out my mother's birthday present. We end up buying eight charms and a sterling silver chain bracelet to slide them all on.

When Will pulls out his wad of cash to pay for it all, I hear Slade chuckle.

"Well, at least it's all going to a good cause," Slade says, not seeming to mind being hustled out of his money now that he knows what it's being used for.

Will and I decide to make one more stop and go to a baby store in the same shopping center as *Clive's*. We pick out a double stroller for the twins. It's something my mother doesn't have since we kids were all born a few years apart. And, it's something we know she'll definitely use.

While Will is paying for the stroller with the last of his money, I go to the ladies room and Aiden stands outside the door to wait on me.

While I'm in one of the stalls, the lady in the one beside me says, "Excuse me. Would you mind giving me some toilet paper? There's like none in here."

"Sure," I say, taking one of the spare rolls in my stall and handing it to her underneath the metal wall separating us.

"Thank you," the lady says, relief in her voice. "You're an absolute life saver."

"You're welcome."

The lady exits her stall before I do, and I hear her turn the water on to wash her hands. By the time I'm finished, the water is still running and my bracelet begins to grow warm. It's only after I open the door to leave my stall that I see the reason why.

Asmodeus is standing by the sink with one of his arms around the woman's neck. As if he were simply waiting on me to bear witness, he snaps her neck and places his right index finger over his pursed lips telling me to be quiet.

"Unless you want me to kill every human in this store," he whispers to me, "I would advise you not to phase or scream out for help."

Asmodeus gently lays the woman down on the tiled floor of the bathroom.

"Now, give me the keys to your car," he tells me.

My promise to Uncle Malcolm not to let anyone but me drive my car flits through my mind. But, I don't have much choice. I know Asmodeus will do what he says and kill every human being in the baby store, many of them pregnant. Even with my three Watchers present, he will have time to kill at least one person in the store, and that's one person too many in my book.

I look down at the woman who just had her life ended in pure terror for a cause she knew nothing about. She had mistakenly called me a 'life saver' a moment ago when, in fact, it was because of me her life had just been ended.

I refuse to be the cause of any more deaths.

I reach into the right front pocket of my jeans and pull out the keys to my Corvette.

Asmodeus grabs my hand with the keys in it and phases us inside my car. He's sitting in the driver's seat, and I'm in the passenger seat.

It's something he shouldn't have been able to do. He's never been inside my car before, at least not to my knowledge.

He snatches the keys from my hand and starts the car.

He drives out of the parking lot with a squeal of tires against the pavement. Just as we're merging onto the highway, I see Aiden phase to the curb of the sidewalk and helplessly watch me being driven away.

He can't come after me, at least not until we stop somewhere because you can't phase into a moving target.

"What's to keep me from just phasing?" I ask Asmodeus.

"Well, you could. Then what's to stop me from phasing back to the store and doing just what I threatened? Plus," he says pulling out something he shouldn't even be able to touch from an inside pocket of his black wool coat, "I have this."

Before I can even blink, much less think of a way to stop him, Asmodeus buries one of the silver daggers into the middle of my stomach.

I gasp for air. The pain from the stab wound seems to radiate out from its epicenter reaching every nerve cell in my body. I try to phase because I know if I stay, I'm as good as dead.

But, I can't phase.

The dagger, Zack's dagger, is preventing it. His gift to negate all angelic powers is encased within the dagger, and I can't escape.

I try to move Asmodeus' hand, but he keeps it firmly in place and simply buries the dagger even deeper into my gut. I'm not sure, but I think I feel the tip of it scrape against the bone in my spinal column.

"Just sit still," Asmodeus says to me. "We're almost there."

Asmodeus phases us, car and all, to an old wooden bridge I've only seen once before in my life.

My mother brought me to this bridge a long time ago and told me the story of how her best friend Will saved her from drowning when she was eight years old. It was the same night the real Will died and the rebellion angel who Lucifer sent to watch over my mother took his body over to save her life.

Asmodeus must press the gas pedal to the floorboard because the car guns forward quickly reaching its top speed. There's one unique feature about this bridge that sticks out in my mind. It's only half a bridge. The other half collapsed into the lake years ago when my mother was a kid.

"Ironic you should die where your mother should have perished years ago," Asmodeus says. To add insult to injury, he twists the knife in my gut causing me to involuntarily scream out in pain. I hear him laugh like the more pain he can inflict on me the more joy he gains from it.

"Have a fun trip to the bottom of the lake!" He yells at me.

There's a moment of near silence as the tires leave the planks of the bridge and the car flies off its edge, soaring in mid-air for a few seconds before heading nose first into the dark abyss of the lake.

I look over at Asmodeus and see him phase just as the car hits the surface of the water causing my whole body to hit the dashboard and disorienting me even further. I'm faintly aware of the lake water beginning to surround me and welcome the cold numbness it brings with it.

Right before I'm about to completely lose consciousness, I feel someone grab my left arm.

"It's not your time," I hear a man say just as my tether to the real world is broken.

CHAPTER TWENTY-TWO

I feel something warm and comforting press against my belly. Like a spiral of heat, it radiates out to every muscle, every blood vessel, every nerve and square inch of skin on my body. It reminds me of laying out underneath the sun on a bright, clear summer day. Sweet air that tastes a lot like cotton candy slides down my throat and fills my collapsed lungs to almost bursting. I gasp like I'm taking my first full breath of life.

Slowly, I open my eyes and see a man knelt down beside me who looks as soaking wet as I feel. His dirty blonde hair is matted to his head, and his blue eyes look at me in worry, like he wasn't quite sure I would return to the land of the living. As I stare up at him, I realize he isn't a stranger, not exactly.

I've been surrounded by his pictures all my life. My mother never let his memory fade just because he was no longer a member of the land of the living.

His name passes over my lips naturally because it's one I say every day.

"Will?"

My mother's Will smiles as he looks down at me.

"Hi, Caylin."

I don't quite understand why I'm seeing my mother's dead friend unless…

"Am I dead?" I ask.

Will shakes his head.

"No, not if I did my job right."

"Your job?" I ask.

Will's eyes shift away from me, and he looks reluctant to say more.

"Here," he says instead, "let me help you sit up."

Will places one of his arms behind my back and easily lifts me up to a sitting position. The glare of the sun off the lake water is blinding, and I have to shield my eyes against the bright reflection. When I look back at Will, he's glowing to my eyes. At first, I think it's just a halo effect from the glaring sun, but I soon realize it's not a glare at all. This glow is more like the one I saw surrounding my chosen Watchers. But, what did that mean?

"If I'm not dead," I say, "how are you here?"

Will lowers his head slightly and looks almost embarrassed to say his next words.

He runs a hand through his wet hair nervously before saying, "I guess you could say I did my job of keeping your mother alive a little too well. God's sort of put me in charge of keeping all you girls alive until Anna is born."

"So you're like…what? A guardian angel or something?"

"Or something," Will agrees, smiling at me.

"Will you always be watching us?" I ask, not exactly liking the idea of someone constantly watching me too closely.

"No," Will assures me, "I won't be watching every little move you make, if that's what you're worried about. But, if you are in mortal danger, I'll feel it. It's only then that I'll be allowed to breach the divide between Heaven and Earth. And when I do, I'm only permitted give you the breath of life and heal your wounds."

I place a hand where the dagger wound should have been on my stomach and feel that it's completely healed now. I look down and lift my shirt up slightly but see no sign of a wound ever being there.

"Where's the dagger?" I ask.

Will looks down beside me, and I see it lying next to me. I pick it up and notice the enchanted leather JoJo wrapped around the hilt is no longer there. Someone must have taken it off. That's why Asmodeus was able to hold it. But who would do such a thing and who would give the dagger to one of the princes?

As I stare at the dagger in my hand, I say, "We have a traitor, don't we?"

"I can't answer that for certain," Will says. "But from what I *do* know, I would say your assumption is the correct one."

"But who?"

"I guess you should start with the people who have access to the daggers."

I look over at Will again.

"My mother still thinks about you," I tell him. "She even named my little brother after you."

Will smiles. "Yes, I knew that."

"How long can you stay?"

"I have to go soon. I'm not allowed to stay here for very long."

"So you don't have time to go see her?"

Will shakes his head. “No. Not this trip. Like I said, I’m only allowed to come when one of you or one of your descendants are in mortal danger. My guardianship, if that’s what you want to call it, is tied to you, Caylin, and making sure your line survives until Anna is born.”

“Do you know when she will be born?”

“No, I don’t know how long Malcolm will have to remain here,” he says, knowing the real reason for the question.

I smile. “I guess you do know us pretty well.”

“I wish I had more answers for you, but I just don’t. I’m only granted permission to help keep you alive. I’m not allowed to join in your fight. That’s not how this works.”

“I understand,” I say. “But, my mom will be disappointed that she wasn’t able to see you again.”

Will smiles. “Tell Lilly…hello. And that she’s often in my thoughts.”

I tilt my head as I look into Will’s eyes.

“Even after all this time you’re still in love with her?” I ask in surprise, seeing his feelings for my mother plainly written on his face.

"Death doesn't mean you stop caring for the ones you leave behind," he tells me. "It only means you can't see them as often as you'd like."

I look down at the dagger in my hand and sigh, resigned to the fact that I have to figure out who the traitor is. We're all in danger until I do.

I look back at Will.

"You're glowing," I tell him. "You're glowing like the other Watchers I chose to watch over my family and take care of the princes."

"It means that I'm devoted to you," Will tells me. "As devoted as the ones you chose to help you."

"Could one of my chosen be the traitor?" I ask, not liking the idea but seeing it as a real possibility.

"I wouldn't rule anyone out," Will says. "You're smart though. I'm sure you'll find whoever did this."

Will stands up and holds a hand out for me to take. I grasp it with my free hand, and he pulls me up onto my feet.

"I need to leave now," Will tells me. "But before I do, God wanted me to deliver a message to you."

“What?”

“He doesn't want any of the vessels except for Jess to be involved in the battle to come. Apparently, she's the only one who can handle Lucifer.”

“Why can't they help us?”

“He said they have their own battle to face soon and they need to save their strength for what they will have to face. You and the Watchers can handle this one on your own.”

“Will I ever see you again?”

Will smiles. “Don’t take this the wrong way, but I sincerely hope not.”

I let out a small, half laugh. “Right. I would have to be almost dead for you to be allowed to come back, right?”

Will nods. “Yes. So, although I would love to get to know you better, I’m afraid that would only happen if you were in a continual flux between life and death. I don’t think either of us want that.”

“I would have to agree with you on that.”

I walk the few steps to Will and give him a hug around the neck.

"Thank you," I tell him. "Thank you for saving me."

Will hugs me back. "You're welcome. Now, go find your traitor before he can do any more harm. And show Lucifer that the women from the line of Lillith should never be messed with."

I pull back from Will and promise, "I will."

He nods to me as if to say he has faith that I'll get the job done.

Will phases and I'm left alone standing on the lakeshore.

I look at the dagger in my hand and tighten my hold around the naked hilt.

I feel an anger build up inside me and brace myself for the first thing on my list.

Finding our traitor and making him pay.

I phase to my home and find Aiden frantically pacing back and forth in the living room.

He has me in his arms before I even have a chance to take a breath much less get a word out.

"What happened?" He asks worriedly. "Where did he take you? What did he want with you?"

I hug Aiden tightly around the waist before gently pushing him away from me.

"Aiden, I love you more than life itself, but you need to let me go. We have work to do."

"Caylin," Uncle Malcolm says to me, "what did Asmodeus want? And why are you all wet and holding one of the daggers?"

My mother grabs the black wool blanket off the back of the couch in the living room and wraps me in it, rubbing my shoulders to help warm me up.

"Did he hurt you?" My mother asks, and I can see her eyes go into mama bear mode.

I know as soon as I tell her what Asmodeus did she's going to want to go for his jugular. It's what I'm counting on…

I tell them about Asmodeus killing the lady in the bathroom of the baby store and being able to phase into my car. I tell them about him driving the Corvette off the old wood bridge near where my mom grew up and Will bringing me back to life.

"Will?" My mom asks. "My Will?"

I nod. "Yes. He told me that he would be watching over my descendants and me until the girl is born. He wasn't able to stay long though, or I think he would have come to see you. He did tell me to tell you hello and that he thinks of you often."

I see my mother's eyes tear up, but she doesn't break down. "God chose a good protector for your family then."

"When the hell was Asmodeus allowed inside your car?" My dad asks, anger in his voice over the breach.

"Good question," I say, holding up the dagger in my hand. "Which brings us to this. How many people have access to these?"

"Only a handful," Andre says. "The Watchers you chose, Malcolm, Mason, and Jess."

I know it's not Uncle Malcolm, Mason or Jess which only leaves the six Watchers I've chosen.

Apparently, Uncle Malcolm comes to the same conclusion…

Before I know it, he has Jered pinned up against a wall with his hand clamped tightly around the other man's throat.

"Was it you?" Uncle Malcolm demands harshly. "Did you let that son of a bitch get into her car when you drove it back here from the school last night? Did you do that to her studio?"

Uncle Malcolm slams Jered's head against the wall so hard it shakes the house.

Jered could phase but he doesn't. He just looks at Uncle Malcolm like he's patiently waiting for my uncle to let his throat go so he can defend himself.

"Uncle Malcolm," I say, going up to him and touching him on the arm. "Let me talk to him."

I'm not quite sure Uncle Malcolm hears me until he releases his hold on Jered's throat and takes a step back.

I take hold of Jered's arm and ask Jess' bracelet what Jered feels in that moment.

I feel an overwhelming sorrow and unworthiness. He doesn't feel worthy enough to be one of my chosen. It's something that I've known for a long time without the benefit of Jess' bracelet. He feels sorrow for the loss of a child he once had, and there is a need to right the wrongs of his past. Not only for himself though. I sense he wants to help someone else as well.

Tristan.

He wants to help him find his way. He feels like he might have been given a second chance with Tristan. To provide him the guidance he never gave his own son.

"Jered, did you help Asmodeus?" I ask directly.

"No," Jered is quick to reply.

"He's telling the truth," I tell Uncle Malcolm.

"You're sure?" Uncle Malcolm asks me.

"Yes. Positive."

I turn to face the others in the room and notice someone missing.

"Where is Slade?"

Everyone looks around because no one else noticed Slade phase out either.

"He must have left when we were watching Malcolm attack Jered," Desmond says.

I look around for his phase trail and see it towards the back of the kitchen.

"Where does his trail lead?" I ask those in the room because all I see is a pitch black void.

"Hell," Jered says, like maybe he's been there before. "The one place none of us will follow him to."

"But when did he turn traitor?" Brutus asks. "He's always been egotistical, but I never would have pegged Slade as a turncoat."

"I guess we'll have to ask him," Uncle Malcolm says, "if he ever has the nerve to show his face to us again."

"It doesn't make any sense," I say. "I never felt any danger from him. Jess' bracelet never tried to warn me that he meant me any harm."

"Maybe he didn't," my dad says. "Maybe harming you wasn't his primary motivation."

"But he did have the means and the opportunity to grant Asmodeus access to your car," Uncle Malcolm says. "I wondered why he wanted to sit inside it when I was taking the governor off the other day."

"And he could have destroyed the studio at any time within the last few days," Daniel points out.

"But why did he glow to me during the choosing?"

"We glowed?" Desmond asks in surprise. "I don't remember you telling us that."

"I told Jered," I admit, "but no I didn't tell the rest of you. God told me you glowed to me because you were the ones who desired to help me the most."

"'Desired to help you the most'," Uncle Malcolm repeats. "That could have been true for Slade even though he desired it for the wrong reasons. My guess is he's been working with Lucifer for a while now. Maybe Lucifer has a hold over him that we don't know about."

"Well, it doesn't matter now," Aiden says. "We know he's the traitor. And he'll pay for what he did one way or the other."

"I need this to end," I say to everyone in the room, hearing the weariness in my own voice. "And I need it to end soon. I'm tired of having to look over my shoulder and wait for them to attack us. I'm sick of the dread I feel in the pit of my stomach because I never know what bad thing is going to happen next. Too many innocent people have given their lives for a war they know nothing about. We need to do something, and we need to do it now!"

The room grows completely silent after my outburst. Everyone looks a little startled.

"All right then," Uncle Malcolm finally says to break the tension, "I guess we need to come up with a plan."

"Maybe I can help with that."

We all look to see Tristan walk into the room holding hands with Mae.

"What are you thinking?" Jered asks.

"Let me help you set a trap," Tristan says. "I can go back to my father and tell him whatever it is you want the others to know."

"Tristan," I say, recognizing the sacrifice he's about to make, "you don't have to do that."

"Yes," he says, "I do. You don't know the things I've done in my life, Caylin. I need to start earning my own forgiveness, and this sounds like the perfect opportunity for me to start doing that. Let me help you." Tristan looks down at Mae. "Let me help all of you be safe from them."

Uncle Malcolm calls Jess and Mason to come over so we can come up with a strategy to end this fight with the princes once and for all. I tell Jess God's rule about the other vessels not being involved in the fight. She doesn't look surprised.

"He's always throwing in one obscure rule or another," she quips.

As our plan evolves, it turns out Tristan's sacrifice is the key to everything.

I just hope it works.

Once our plan is set, I go up to my room to take a quick shower. When I make it back downstairs, Aiden is in the kitchen being tutored by my dad in another cooking lesson. I see Jess and Mason speaking with Uncle Malcolm and my mom at the dining table.

"I don't understand why you want me to come along on this little expedition of yours," Uncle Malcolm says to them. "From the message God sent through Will, it sounds like you and the vessels are the ones who need to go handle this."

"I just think you're meant to go there with us," Jess tells him. "I keep seeing you in the dream."

"What dream, Jess?" I ask, coming to sit with them at the table.

Jess sighs. "For the past year, I keep having the same dream every night," she tells me. "Mason and I, along with the other vessels, are standing in the middle of New York City on the alternate Earth we went to after Faison went through the Tear. But, something bad has happened because a lot of the buildings are damaged, like there was an earthquake or something. I'm standing on a tall pile of rubble and looking up into the sky. The moon is blood red and it's giving everything around us a red cast. I've always seen Malcolm standing with us, but I just assumed it was alt Earth's version of him. Only, I could never understand why he was always holding a cane. After what's happened, I think I was actually seeing our Malcolm, not theirs. I've always thought the dream was telling me to go back there and now with the message you got from Will I'm certain of it. I think they need our help."

"So you think they're in trouble?" I ask.

Jess nods. "Yes. And I don't think I'll stop having this dream until I go back."

"How are you going to go back?" My mom asks. "The Tear is sealed."

"It's actually an idea Caylin came up with," Mason says, looking at me. "We're going to try to use the vessels inner realm to connect to their reality. We haven't actually tried it yet to see if it will work, but I have no reason to believe it won't. Obviously, we're meant to go back there. I'm just not sure why."

"When are you going?" I ask.

"We thought we would wait for Leah to get out for spring break," Jess says.

"You're taking Leah back there? I don't think she's going to want to go back to that place, Jess."

"We'll give her the option of not doing it," Jess tells me. "But, there are people there she still cares about. I think if she knows they're in trouble, she might want to go back to help them."

I know Jess is right. Leah will go back to alt Earth if she thinks those people need help. She's just too good of a person to say no.

"Excuse me," Aiden says coming to stand by my chair. "Would you all mind if I borrowed Caylin for a moment?'

"As long as you bring her back," Uncle Malcolm quips.

I stand from my chair and Aiden takes one of my hands into his, lacing our fingers together.

"I will," Aiden promises before phasing us to my studio.

The paint in the room is dry now and we're able to stand on the floor without having to worry about damaging Aiden's field of lavender.

He takes me into his arms as he leans his back against the worktable and buries his head against the right side of my neck.

Aiden sighs heavily, and I can tell it's a worried sigh.

"Don't take any unnecessary risks tomorrow," he tells me.

"I died and came back to life today, Aiden. I don't think God's going to let anything happen to me."

Aiden lifts his head and looks down at me.

"And don't let that give you a false confidence," he warns. "You might be safe, but others around you don't have an angel at the ready to bring them back to life."

"I know," I say, fully realizing that fact. "I won't take any unnecessary chances if you promise me the same thing."

"I won't do anything that I don't have to do," he promises.

I think of something and smile.

"What's making you smile like that, beautiful?" Aiden asks, having a hard time suppressing a smile of his own as he looks at me.

"I just realized that after tomorrow, it'll all be over. We can start to live our life together without having to worry about something bad happening to someone we love."

"I will do everything in my power to make sure the rest of your life is a happy one."

"Of course I'll be happy. I'll have you."

Apparently, these words earn me a kiss… or two…. or three….

When we go back inside the house, Tristan is kneeling in front of Mae with Jered standing a short distance behind him.

"I need to leave for a while, Mae."

"No." Mae says. "You stay with me, Puppy."

Tristan grins. "Puppy needs to leave for a little while. But, I promise I'll see you again one day."

Mae throws herself at Tristan, giving him no other choice but to hold her and give her one last hug.

"Don't leave," she begs.

I can see Tristan is having a hard time not getting emotional, but he pulls it together before he leans back from Mae enough to look into her tear-streaked face.

"I'll come back one day. I promise."

My dad goes over to them and picks Mae up into his arms as she begins to cry.

"Good luck," my dad says to Tristan. "And thank you."

Tristan nods and reaches out to touch Mae's back one last time, but he seems to think better of it and lets his hand drop back down to his side. He turns to Jered and nods.

Jered rests a hand on his shoulder and phases them away.

"What do you think his father will do to him for his disobedience and leaving with Mae?" I ask.

"You don't want to know."

I look at Aiden.

"Why? What's going to happen? Do we need to bring him back?"

"He made his own decision, Caylin. He knows what waits for him, and he's willing to suffer through it."

"But I didn't know he would be made to suffer," I say, realizing I should have known. Maybe I just didn't want to think about it because I was so desperate to have everything behind us.

"They may be more lenient on him than they normally would be for being insubordinate. Especially if they believe he just came here to gather intel on us. I just hope he's a good enough actor to make them believe what he says. But, maybe what Jered has to do will be enough to sell the story."

"What Jered has to do?" I ask, not having heard this part of the plan before now either. "What do you mean by that? I thought he was just going to take Tristan home."

"If Tristan shows up on his father's doorstep without any signs of being harmed, he'll know something's wrong."

"What is Jered going to do?"

"He'll make it look like he was beat up."

"How?"

"By beating him up," Aiden says, know I wouldn't like his answer.

"We should have found another way."

"There is no other way. This is our best shot to have them all attack at once. There's no going back now, Caylin. We have to go through with the plan. The first step has already been taken."

I shiver slightly at the thought of what will happen to Tristan.

I look over at Mae and see her heart wrenching tears spill freely from her eyes as she holds onto my father's neck and cries over the loss of her 'puppy'. With the full extent of Tristan's sacrifice known to me now, I fully realize how much he must truly care for Mae.

And I vow to make sure his sacrifice isn't one made in vain.

CHAPTER TWENTY-THREE

"Now, why do I feel like the sacrificial lamb being led to slaughter?" My Aunt Tara complains.

"Uh, because we are?" Will asks.

I slap Will playfully on the side of the head.

"No one is being sacrificed here," I say, handing Aunt Tara a cardboard box from the dining table filled with party supplies.

"You two are just for show."

"And you won't be alone," Aiden tells Aunt Tara, walking up to me and placing an arm around my shoulders. "None of you will."

"So let me get this straight," Aunt Tara says. "We're going to the house in Colorado and acting like we're decorating it for Lilly's party. Is that about right?"

"Yes," I say. "It's something we do every year so they won't consider it odd or out of the ordinary. If Tristan was allowed to deliver his message last night, they'll know when we're supposed to be there, and that I will be there alone with the two of you."

"Won't they know it's a set up though? They can't be that stupid," Aunt Tara says.

"We're counting on them to know it's a set up," I say. "And we're counting on them to bring everyone to the fight just like we are. That's the whole point. We want to get this over and done with tonight."

"Once it starts," Aiden tells Aunt Tara, "Will will phase you to Jess and Mason's villa where you can wait out the fight with everyone else."

"Baby," Aunt Tara says to me, "is there no other way?"

"No." I tell her. "This has to end, Aunt Tara, or none of us will be safe. This is the best way to finish it once and for all."

Aunt Tara sighs and nods. She's been in our world long enough to know that sometimes you have to fight to ensure the safety of the ones you love.

My dad and Mae have already gone to the villa. Everyone else is set into place except for the four of us. We're the trigger for the fight and the last to the party, as it were.

I look at Aiden and can't help but admire the outfit he's wearing. It's quickly become my favorite of his wardrobe.

"Remind me to thank JoJo later for making you that outfit," I whisper to him as I pick up the white cake box.

"I'll be sure to do that," Aiden whispers back just before turning invisible.

I'm not completely sure he turns invisible because he needs to be that way before he phases with us or if my constant leering of his person has made him shy. Either way, I sigh in disappointment.

"Ok," I tell Will and Aunt Tara, "let's go."

Will phases Aunt Tara and I phase myself.

When we get there, I make sure to open up the curtains in the living room so that anyone who is outside can look in and see that we're there.

"So what do we do?" Aunt Tara asks me.

"We do what we would normally do," I tell her. "Let's decorate."

We go through the motions of decorating the living room with balloons and streamers like we intend to have my mother's birthday party.

Almost thirty minutes later, I finally hear and feel what we've been waiting for.

It's the sound of a strange weight shifting the wood on the front porch and making it creak. Jess' bracelet grows almost red hot around my wrist indicating someone definitely means to harm me.

"They're here," I whisper, knowing Aiden is nearby.

I turn to Aunt Tara and Will.

"Time for us to get the cake out," I say, using the code phrase we picked earlier to signal their departure.

Aunt Tara makes to come hug me, but I discretely shake my head stopping her. If they see her doing it, they might try to attack before she has a chance to leave. She stops in mid-stride and winks at me instead.

"It's in the kitchen," Will says. "Can you help me get it Aunt Tara?"

"Sure thing, hon," Aunt Tara says.

I watch them walk towards the kitchen together. Will lightly touches Aunt Tara's arm and they phase.

I take a deep breath.

This is it.

I'm nervous and excited all at the same time.

"Are you ready?" Aiden asks, caressing my cheek gently with the tips of his fingers.

I close my eyes and let his invisible touch calm my nerves.

"Yes," I whisper.

"Then open the door."

I walk over to the front door and rest my hand on the knob.

As soon as I open it, I know all hell is going to break loose.

"We will win this fight," Aiden whispers in my ear.

I nod letting him know I heard him.

I take in a deep breath and open the door.

To be honest, I expected to be attacked immediately. But, there's no one at the door, not even a soul in the front yard. I step out onto the porch and look around.

Nothing.

Maybe we over-estimated the princes want to see me dead.

I turn to go back inside the house when I feel them come.

Phasing causing a disturbance in the air around the one phasing. Most of the time you don't notice it. The only time you do is when a large group phases in together.

I find myself surrounded by three cloaked Watchers.

Jess materializes and slices one Watcher's head clean off in one swing of her sword. Aiden grabs another by the neck and tears it off. The third makes to phase away, but I grab one of his arms and negate his phasing by phasing him back, giving Aiden just enough time to phase behind him and rip his head from his shoulders too.

"First wave?" Jess asks Aiden, twirling her sword in front of her preparing for another attack.

"Yes," he answers. "They're testing to see what we have. It's what I would do."

Before I know it, I feel someone grab me from behind by the throat. Just as he phases me, I see two cloaked Watchers grab Jess and Aiden and phase them away. The person holding me phases us to the living room inside the house.

I reach both my hands back and grab his head as I bend forward to throw him down on the floor in front of me. It's only then that I see it's Asmodeus.

He quickly phases upright again.

"Shouldn't you be dead already?" He asks me, looking disgusted that I'm still alive. "Though, I guess I should thank you for giving me the pleasure of killing you twice."

"I can't be killed," I tell him, feeling somewhat smug in that fact.

"Everyone can be killed," Asmodeus says like I must be the most stupid person in the world.

"True," I concede, "but very few have their own personal angel to bring them back to life."

"Well, let's put this angel of yours to the test and see if he can reattach limbs and a head," Asmodeus says.

He phases over to me and grabs me by the throat with both of his hands.

I pull the dagger I had hidden in the back of my jeans out and thrust it up towards his stomach, but he sees me do it and grabs the hand with the dagger in it before I can stab him with it, twisting my wrist until it breaks. I drop the dagger to the floor with a clatter. I grasp the hand he has at my throat with my good hand and squeeze with all the strength I have.

The earth trembles beneath my feet, like we're in the middle of an earthquake.

I see Asmodeus' eyes widen in fear as he releases his hold around my throat and looks at the hand I crushed.

"What have you done?" He screams at me.

I look at his hand and read what the brand there says. It's similar in appearance to the ones I saw on Belphagor and Mammon. But this brand is cracked now and glowing red like it's burning.

Asmodeus drops to his knees and grabs the silver dagger that I dropped. He rears his hand back and stabs his other hand smack dab in the middle of the brand.

The earthquake subsides as Asmodeus falls to the floor. I phase Asmodeus' body to the small cove on the mountain for safekeeping.

I phase back to the front yard to find the others. I'm not completely ready for what I see.

Jess and Mason are in the middle of a fight with Lucifer. Instead of looking worried that he's fighting two people at one time, Lucifer looks exhilarated by it as he taunts them both.

"Is this the best the two of you can do?" Lucifer scoffs as he fights them both off with his glowing black sword, a fitting contrast to the righteousness of Jess' flaming orange one.

I look to the right and see Aiden in a fight with Baal. I see the flash of the dagger in Aiden's hand and pray that he finds a way to bury into the prince's body at some point. I don't know how to help him because of the way he fights by phasing. I'm having a hard enough time just recognizing that it's him.

It's to the left that I see my only opportunity to be of help.

The large group of our Watchers that we brought with us, being led by Uncle Malcolm, are fighting a mixture of changelings, hellhounds, cloaked Watchers and their werewolf children. I see one of our Watchers about to attack a werewolf with a head that looks like it's been battered almost to a pulp already. There's only one wolf I know who would have been beaten up before the fight.

I phase over to it.

"Stop," I tell the Watcher about to attack it, "this one is mine."

"Whatever you say, Caylin," the Watcher says, turning his attention to another target.

"Tristan?" I ask the wolf.

It turns to look at me and gives a small whine in answer.

I place my hand on its shoulder and phase it to the little cove on the side of the mountain across the lake from my house.

"Stay here," I tell him, "and keep hidden."

He whines again, and I take that as him understanding my orders.

I phase back to the fight and know one faction of it I can control.

I phase on top of the picnic table and yell, “Kneel!”

The wolves in the mayhem all look at me like they’re of one mind. They walk through the fighting Watchers and hellhounds to kneel on the ground by the picnic table, bowing their heads in my direction. Unfortunately, no one else pays as much attention to me.

Except for one person standing off to the side of the fight like a spectator.

Slade.

I phase behind Slade and push him to the ground. Slowly, he rolls over and looks up at me. I expect to see anger or even hatred on his face for me. But, instead I see emotions I wasn’t prepared to see, sadness and shame.

“Why did you betray us?” I demand. “We trusted you. I brought you into my family. How can you live with yourself after what you’ve done?”

“I can’t,” Slade says. “I’d rather be dead.”

He rises up and kneels before me.

“Please, Caylin, end my life. I can’t go on living like this.”

My hands burst into blue flames, and I wrap the fingers of my good hand around the front of Slade’s neck.

“Tell me why you betrayed us!” I demand.

“I’ve been Lucifer’s spy for years,” Slade confesses. “I was bit by one of his hellhounds here,” he says, grasping his left arm where the tattoo is, “and ended up trading in my soul to him for an end to the pain. I was weak. I hoped that by helping you, I could reclaim at least a little bit of my soul and be free of him, but it didn't work out that way. He owns me body and soul. Kill me, Caylin. Put an end to my torment.”

I loosen my hold on Slade’s neck realizing he is living out a life Uncle Malcolm might choose one day. Would I be able to kill Uncle Malcolm so easily?

Slade grabs my loosened hand and presses it hard against his neck.

“Please, Caylin,” he begs, “end me! End this nightmare I'm living in once and for all!”

I yank my hand out of his grasp.

"No," I tell him. "You made your choice and now you have to live with it."

"Then I'll make you do it," Slade says, filled with a new determination.

He stands and barrels into my midsection with his shoulder, pinning me up against a large oak in the yard. I feel my breath being knocked out as more than a couple of my ribs are broken by the impact.

I bring my right leg up swiftly and knee Slade in the chest as hard as I can. I hear bone break and feel him completely relinquish his hold on me as he staggers back.

I try to take in a deep breath, but the pain from just trying to breathe normally is torturous enough.

With a growl, Slade comes at me again, but is stopped before he can even take a step forward.

The pack of werewolves I left kneeling by the picnic table descend on Slade like rabid dogs. I hear Slade scream out in pain and wonder why he doesn't just phase away.

"Stop!" I yell to the wolves, paying the price for my command with lancing pain from my broken ribs.

The wolves immediately stop attacking Slade but continue to surround him, snapping their jaws at his prone body lying helplessly on the ground.

I walk over and the wolves in my path part to allow me entry into their circle.

I see what's left of Slade's body on the ground. His limbs have been pulled from his torso and half the flesh from his face is gone. His bare chest and abdomen are covered with deep lacerations.

"Caylin," he begs, "end me…"

I kneel down beside him.

"You can heal from this," I tell him.

"It doesn't matter," he tells me, his breath wheezing. "My soul is lost. Destroy me before I take more innocent lives. Stop me before I kill someone you love. Lucifer will have me do it just to torture me even more than I already am. Put an end to me now, Caylin. I'm begging you…"

Slade's last words come out as a desperate plea from a desperate man. He wants to die. But was death truly the answer?

"But if I kill you," I say to him, "your soul will be lost forever."

“It’s already lost,” he says. “Send me to Hell with fewer deaths on my conscience. Give me at least that much peace. Please…end my pain…”

I place my good hand on Slade’s chest. It burst into blue flames.

“Thank you…” Slade says to me and closes his eyes, welcoming the end of his life.

With one thought, I kill Slade, reducing him to a pile of black ash.

I weep over his loss, and I cry over the possibility that his fate will be Uncle Malcolm’s one day.

I quickly pull myself together because I know this fight is far from over.

I phase back onto the picnic table to see what else I can do to help.

I arrive just in time to see Aiden finally gain an advantage over Baal and stab the prince in the gut with one of the silver daggers. Baal falls to the ground and Aiden phases him away to a safe place before phasing back to the same spot.

I see Aiden scan the yard and find me. The triumph of his defeat of Baal fades when he catches his first glimpse of my condition. He phases to me.

"Caylin," he says, anguish over my injuries clear in his voice, "we need to get you to Rafe."

"No," I tell him, watching the fight that's still raging between Lucifer, Jess, and Mason.

As Aiden tears his eyes away from me to look at the fight, Mason phases to the back of Lucifer seeming to hope to surprise the last prince standing from behind. Lucifer raises one leg and kicks Mason in the stomach with so much force it propels Mason completely across the lake to somewhcre on the other side.

Jess uses an ability granted to her from my grandfather and flies above Lucifer, spinning in the air until she lands on the other side of him. As Lucifer turns to face her, someone I knew was waiting in the wings, watching for an opening phases into the fight.

My mother stands behind Lucifer with one of the silver daggers in her hand and stabs him in the back of his shoulder.

Lucifer drops his sword to the ground and falls to his knees.

But, he doesn't go into stasis.

He reaches back for the dagger in his shoulder and pulls it out. He sits down on the ground and stares at it for a second before he begins to laugh.

"After all your efforts to get me here," Lucifer says to Jess, "it's now we learn this thing is useless against me."

Lucifer continues to laugh like it's the funniest thing he's ever encountered in his whole life.

Before any of us can react, Lucifer throws the dagger straight at Jess' chest, presumably aiming for her heart.

But the dagger never reaches her.

God phases in front of Jess and the dagger disintegrates into sand at His feet.

"Enough, Lucifer."

Lucifer stands to face his father.

"Why are you interfering?" Lucifer questions harshly.

"Jess' life isn't meant to end here and certainly not by your hand," God tells him.

"You've always cared about these monkeys more than us," Lucifer accuses. "I don't know why I should be surprised that you would choose her over me."

"Why must you see things so black and white?" God asks. "I have never chosen one over the other. That has always been your assumption, not fact. I love you, Lucifer. I still have hope for you."

"Hope that I'll come groveling at your feet and beg for your forgiveness?" Lucifer says as if the mere idea of such a thing happening is ludicrous. "As the monkeys say, it'll be a cold day in Hell before that happens, father. So I would advise you not to hold your breath for that day to come."

"I will remain hopeful," God says.

"Then it's a fool's hope," Lucifer replies. "You're wasting your time."

"I suppose it's a good thing I have plenty of it to spare. Now," God says surveying the carnage in the front yard, "it's time for you and your men to leave. Enough blood has been shed over this."

Lucifer stands and picks up his sword from the ground.

"Too bad your little dagger trick didn't work on me," Lucifer taunts.

"It was never meant to work on you," God informs him. "Only your brothers."

“I still have Levi,” Lucifer points out.

“I’m fully aware of that fact,” God replies. “And if I were you, I would keep him in Hell for a long time to come. Otherwise, you will lose him too.”

“I don’t see what the point of all this is,” Lucifer says in disgust.

“No,” God replies, a resigned sigh in His voice, “I don’t suppose you would.”

“This isn’t over,” Lucifer says to God.

“No,” God replies, “it isn’t.”

Lucifer phases and I finally allow myself to collapse into unconsciousness.

“Is she awake?” I hear Rafe say nearby.

“She’s coming around, I think,” Aiden replies, even closer to me.

When I open my eyes, I see Aiden lying beside me in my bed holding me.

"Am I dreaming?" I ask him.

"No," he replies, kissing me on the forehead, "you're finally awake."

"Finally?" I ask. "How long have I been out?"

"A few hours."

I sit up straight and look around my room. Only Rafe and Aiden are present.

"Glad to see you awake," Rafe says to me. "How are you feeling?"

I take a mental inventory of my body and can't seem to find anything wrong.

"I feel fine," I tell him. "Nothing hurts."

"Good. I'll go down and let the others know you're up."

I look at Aiden. "Did we all make it?"

"Yes, we didn't lose anyone," Aiden tells me. "Everyone is downstairs waiting for you to wake up."

I lay back down and snuggle against Aiden.

"Then let's stay like this for as long as they let us," I tell him, finding comfort in his warmth.

"I can do that," he says, hugging me closer.

But, we're not left alone for long. My parents are soon in my room fawning all over me and insisting that I come downstairs to eat something.

"Everyone is waiting to see you too," my mom says. "We've all been worried about you, sweetie."

"Ok," I tell her, even though all I want to do is lay in bed with Aiden. "I'll be down in just a minute."

After my parents leave, I snuggle back up with Aiden. I feel more than hear him chuckle.

"I thought you said you were going down?" He teases, not seeming to mind me holding onto him for a little while longer.

"I am," I tell him closing my eyes and just enjoying the feel of him beneath me. "Can't you see I'm moving very slowly out of bed?"

"Uh, no. I can't."

"It's very... very... very... slow."

Aiden kisses the top of my head and stands up from the bed. He holds one of his hands out to me.

"Come on, beautiful. Your family wants to see you."

I sigh. I know he's right.

"I want more cuddling later," I inform him.

"As you wish," he tells me, taking the hand I offer him and pulling me out of bed.

When I get out of bed, I see that my whole family is indeed downstairs, even the newest members.

"And she finally emerges," Desmond says to the others as he sees us walk down the stairs.

All of my chosen Watchers are present except Jered…and Slade, of course.

"Where's Jered?" I ask Desmond.

"He's helping Tristan," he tells me. "But he'll be back afterwards."

Aunt Tara comes and gives me a hug.

"I swear to the good Lord above," she say squeezing me tightly to her, "you and your mother are gonna be the death of me. No more fights with Lucifer, ya hear?"

I nod. "No more fights."

"I second that motion," Uncle Malcolm says, picking up the hug when Aunt Tara finally lets me go.

I notice he's holding a cane in his right hand. It's made of black metal with a wolf head at the top.

"Nice cane," I say as Uncle Malcolm lets me go.

"Brutus' handiwork," he tells me with a sly smile, "so it has a surprise on the inside. Speaking of surprises…"

Uncle Malcolm reaches into a front pocket of his khaki pants, pulls out a set of keys and hands them to me.

"I'm giving you my Bugatti."

"Why?" I ask in complete shock. Uncle Malcolm's car was one of his prized possessions.

"Well, your car is at the bottom of a lake, and I can't exactly drive mine with this leg anymore. You can put it to better use. I'll have something custom made for me to drive."

"Wow, thanks, Uncle Malcolm," I say, giving him another hug.

"You did the right thing, you know," he says to me.

I pull back and look at him, not quite certain what he means.

"Killing Slade," he tells me. "It was the right thing to do. Don't feel any guilt over it. If I had been in his position, I would have asked for the same thing."

"I would hope you would come to me before making a deal with the devil," I whisper to him.

Uncle Malcolm smiles. "You don't have to worry about me. I'm stronger than some people give me credit for."

"I've always known how strong you are," I tell him. "And I know you will always do the right thing."

Jess and Mason come up to me next, each giving me a hug.

"I need to tell you guys something," I say.

I go on to tell them about what happened when Asmodeus attacked me and him stabbing himself in the hand with the dagger.

"We felt the earth shake," Jess tells me. "The whole world did in fact."

I feel sure I misheard her and have to ask, "Did you say the whole world?"

Jess nods. "Yes. And we think we've figured out why."

I follow Jess to the dining table where a piece of paper lies.

Five words are written on the paper:

Conflict

Want

Sacrifice

Torment

Silence

"We couldn't read the one on Asmodeus' hand because of the dagger," Jess tells me. "Did you happen to see what it said before he stuck the dagger through it?"

"Yes, it said 'cataclysm'."

Jess adds the word to the list.

"Six of seven," she says, more to herself than the rest of us. "We don't know what Levi's said, but I think we can assume it isn't anything good."

"You said you thought you figured out why the earth shook when I crushed Asmodeus' hand," I say, reminding her that she needs to fill in this piece of information for me.

Jess nods. "We think the brands are what the princes stole from Heaven."

"The brands?"

"They're not just brands," Mason tells me. "Considering what happened when Asmodeus' seal was damaged, we think they might be the seven seals."

I try to figure out what they're talking about on my own. I've read a lot of things in my short life, but the only reference I can think of which concerns seven seals of any significance are…

"Are you talking about the seven seals in the *Book of Revelations*? The ones that are supposed to bring about the end of the world?"

"Yes," Jess and Mason say at the same time.

"And if they were opened here in the Origin, it would be the end of all worlds" Mason says.

"So that's what my descendant is meant to stop?" I ask, thinking this an impossible task for little Anna. "But how? How will she be able to take the seals away from them?"

Jess shakes her head. "We have no idea. But it's the only thing that makes sense. And," Jess looks over at Mason, "since we know Lucifer and the other princes stole the seals in this reality, we have to assume it happened in other realities too."

It doesn't take me long to see where she's going with this.

"Then you can't go there," I say adamantly. "You can't go back to the alternate Earth if the seals are being broken open. You might not make it back!"

"I don't think that decision is up to me, kiddo," Jess says with a wan smile. "I have to do what God wants. And like he told Lucifer, I have more to do."

"Don't worry so much," Uncle Malcolm tells me. "They're taking me too. What can possibly go wrong?"

"Not exactly encouraging words, Malcolm," Jess teases.

"Ok, who's ready for presents?"

The discussion is effectively broken for the time being by Will's question.

I turn to see my little brother wheeling in the double stroller we bought for my mom into the living room.

My mom laughs.

"I suppose that particular present is meant for me," she says.

"Good guess!" Will tells her, taking out a pink gift bag from one of the seats.

"This is from me and KK," Will tells my mom. "I didn't want to give it to you until she woke up."

Mae grabs at the bag giggling. "Pink!"

"Let mom have her gift first," Will tells our little sister. "Then you can have the bag."

My mom sits down on the couch, and I sit down beside her with Will sitting on the other side and Mae kneeling before her. Our father comes to stand behind us to see what we got her.

My mom opens the bag and pulls out the silver cardboard box.

She opens it and sees the bracelet.

"We thought the charms helped tell the story of our family," I tell her.

My mom pulls the bracelet out of the box and looks at the charms.

"The book represents how you and dad met at college," I tell her. "The frog prince charm is dad."

"Thanks," my dad says, but he's smiling.

"The one with wings is meant to represent all of your guardian angels," I say looking at my dad and Uncle Malcolm, but never forgetting her first guardian, Will. "The bride and groom charm is for when you got married. The baby carriage represents me, your first born. Then we have a birthstone charm for all three of us kids. We can add two more in when the twins are born. The next one is meant to represent inner strength because you're the strongest person we know. And the last one is pretty self-explanatory."

My mother reads it aloud, "'Family Forever'."

My mother takes in a deep breath, and I can tell she's trying not to cry.

"Thank you," she tells us. "I'll always treasure it."

My mom slips the bracelet on and wraps her arms around both me and Will.

"Group hug!" Mae says, propelling herself at us.

I look up and see Aiden smiling at me.

I smile back at him and hope he can read my mind.

Today is the first day we'll have without having to worry about the boogie man trying to tear down our door.

Today is the first day of our life together. And nothing under Heaven or on Earth will ever separate Aiden and me because from our union will be born a little girl named Anna.

And she will save the world…

Epilogue

The noise of cars and people from the street below is faint since I'm on the sixth floor, but the sound is still strange to my ears nonetheless. As I peer out the window of my new apartment, I see a multitude of college students scrambling to get box after box of their possessions into the building as they move into their own apartments. I turn around to look at my new place, which is all neatly decorated with items I moved from the house Aiden built us in Colorado and my parent's home in Lakewood. Being able to phase all my stuff to my new dwelling sure did come in handy.

Aiden phases in with the last item of furniture he said we needed, the white chaise lounge from his home in the Bahamas.

I giggle when I see the chair and even more so at what the love of my life is wearing.

As soon as we arrived at Yale, Aiden bought a sweatshirt. The same sweatshirt I saw him wearing in the vision of our future that I saw while in the vessels' inner realm.

"And just what do we need that for?" I ask him, crossing my arms in front of me.

With a devilish grin, Aiden phases over to me and phases us onto the chair with me beneath him. He looks down at me with such happiness it makes me want to cry. I love seeing his eyes filled with so much joy that anyone looking at him can see how blissful his life has become.

"What do you think we need it for?" He asks huskily.

"I really don't have a clue," I tell him playfully. "You're gonna need to be a little more transparent about your intentions, Aiden."

Aiden grins. "I guess the best way to tell you is to show you," he says, lowering his head towards mine.

My phone vibrates in my back pocket.

I place my index finger against Aiden's pursed lips and say, "Hold that thought."

I phase out from beneath him and grab my phone.

When I look at the display, I see that it's my mom calling.

"Hey, Mom!" I answer.

"Hey, sweetie. We just wanted to make sure you were doing all right on your first day in your new apartment."

I know why she's really calling. She already misses me, even though I haven't been gone for even a full day.

"I'm doing great," I tell her. "Aiden just brought over the last of what I needed here."

"How is his apartment shaping up?"

"We'll be working on bringing his stuff over tomorrow."

"I'm glad he was able to get an apartment right next to yours," my mother says. "Otherwise, I might be more worried about you."

She's still worried. I can hear it in her voice.

"Hey, I've got an idea," I tell her. "Why don't you guys come over tomorrow night for dinner? We can make it a housewarming party for me and Aiden."

"Are you sure?" My mom asks, even though I can hear that it's exactly what she needs.

"Yes, I'm sure. Aiden will do the cooking."

"I will?" Aiden says in surprise from the chaise lounge where he's still laying.

I wink at him, silently telling him he'll do great. He's been tutored all summer long in the culinary arts by my dad after all. Time to put my father's hard work to the test.

"Ok," my mom says, "we'll be there."

"Ask Aunt Tara and them to come too. I'll call Uncle Malcolm personally and get him to contact the other guys."

"Do you want us to bring something over?"

"No, I think we can handle it."

"Ok, sweetie." My mom is silent for a while. I can tell she doesn't want to get off the phone but doesn't know what else to say either.

"You know," I tell her, "we're not exactly like other families, Mom. You and I are only a phase away from each other."

"I know," she says. "But, I don't want to intrude into your new life all the time either."

"Mom, I love you. I would never think you were intruding. You're welcome here anytime."

"Thanks, sweetie," my mom says, and I hear a smile in her voice. "Ok, well, I better let you and Aiden finish moving stuff. You let us know if you need anything."

"I will, Mom."

"See you both tomorrow night and give Aiden my love."

"Ok, I will. Bye, Mom."

When I get off the phone, I phase back over to Aiden with me on top this time and him beneath me.

"Now," I say, "where were we?"

"Exactly where we should be, beautiful. Together."

I smile.

Aiden smiles.

And I know we will live happily forever after…

Author's Note

Thank you so much for reading Caylin's Story. If you would like more information about my current and projects, please visit my website (www.sjwest.com) or my Facebook page (https://www.facebook.com/pages/Cursed-The-Watchers-Trilogy/493117270724860).

In November or December of 2014, I will publish Aiden's Story. It is one of my 'bonus' books that I intend to write. It is NOT a book that progresses the main storyline. If you wish to continue the main storyline of the Watcher series, please read *The Redemption Series,* which centers around Malcolm and Anna.

My 'bonus' books are simply that, bonus material. Aiden's Story, The Alternate Earth Series, and Mae and Tristan's Story are all simply stories I thought would be interesting to read. They also allow me to continue the story of certain characters that I love.

Thanks again for reading my stories!

S.J. West

41358891R00259

Made in the USA
Lexington, KY
10 May 2015